Sitting behind the wheel ~~only when absolutely nec~~ Cafferty Road turnoff. With little traffic on the roads at this time of night, it shouldn't take her more than twenty minutes to reach the Branzinis' farmhouse in Erwinna.

At last she saw the sign for Cafferty Road and followed it. In the pale moonlight the house, with its slanted red roof, looked forlorn. The fields that had once yielded rich crops of corn, beans and sweet potatoes were now thick with overgrowth.

Trusting that Dot Branzini still kept the key in the birdhouse that hung from the old oak tree, Syd started to head toward the backyard, then stopped abruptly when the front door was thrown open and someone dressed in black ran out.

Frozen in place, she made out the shape of a tall man with broad shoulders and closely cropped hair. Arms hanging by his sides, he looked around him, his head moving slowly, left to right, right to left. Her heart hammering in her chest, she took her cell phone from her handbag and found the three numbers she needed: 9-1-1.

"This is assistant district attorney Sydney Cooper," she whispered when a dispatcher answered. "I'm at the—"

In the moonlight she caught the sudden glint of metal. Too late she realized the intruder had a gun. And it was aimed at her.

"Hello? Miss Cooper? Sydney?" The dispatcher's voice remained calm. "What is your location? Are you hurt?"

Syd heard the sound of a gunshot. Almost simultaneously she felt a searing pain just below one of her left ribs.

For the second time in less than forty-eight hours, she passed out.

Also by CHRISTIANE HEGGAN

SCENT OF A KILLER
DEADLY INTENT
MOMENT OF TRUTH
BLIND FAITH
ENEMY WITHIN
TRUST NO ONE
SUSPICION
DECEPTION

Watch for the latest novel of romantic suspense by
CHRISTIANE HEGGAN

NOW YOU DIE

Available November 2005

CHRISTIANE HEGGAN

THE SEARCH

MIRA

ISBN 0-7783-2126-6

THE SEARCH

Copyright © 2005 by Christiane Heggan.

www.MIRABooks.com

Printed in U.S.A.

To Mimi and Monique
For their enduring friendship
Here's to the next twenty-five years

One

Assistant District Attorney Sydney Cooper waited until the handcuffed defendant had been escorted out of the courtroom before heaving a sigh of relief. Thanks to a guilty verdict brought in only two hours after deliberations had begun, there would be one less sexual predator roaming the streets of Philadelphia tonight.

That's what this job is all about, she thought, tucking her notes into her briefcase—punishing the guilty and protecting the innocent. No matter how sappy or self-righteous that statement sounded, that's what she had always believed. Even now, after four years in the district attorney's office, she was still as enthusiastic about what she did for a living as she had been when she'd first applied for the job.

Pleased with herself, Syd snapped her briefcase shut and rose from behind the prosecution's table.

Unfortunately, the quick exit she had hoped for wasn't meant to be. In the gallery behind her, more than a dozen law students, all of whom had followed the three-day trial intently, waited, their pens poised over their notepads, their eyes bright with expectation.

A blonde with California good-looks spoke first, oozing with admiration. "Gosh, Ms. Cooper, you were awesome. The way you trapped Simon Burke was unreal. Where did you find the courage to pull that kind of stunt? And in Judge Claiborne's courtroom no less. He's a bear when it comes to theatrics."

Remembering her days as a law student and how eager she had been to absorb every bit of information practicing attorneys were willing to give her, Syd faced her admiring crowd. "I'm afraid I acted more out of sheer desperation than courage. And you're right about Judge Claiborne. The trick was not to look at him or I would have lost my nerve."

A handsome young man Syd had seen before in the courtroom spoke next. "How did you know that dangling that black thong under the defendant's nose would send him over the edge?" he asked.

"Well, Chad—it is Chad, isn't it?" She saw him blush as he bobbed his head. "I had heard of a similar case in Ohio a couple of years ago. Although that defendant was not accused of sexual assault, he became highly stimulated whenever he saw black, lacy underwear, pursuing women ardently and begging for sexual favors. Those of you who heard Jane Hunnicut's testimony on Monday will recall that Simon Burke had asked her if she was wearing a black thong. All I had to do was provide an avenue for his fantasy."

"Is the thong yours?" That slightly brazen question had come from another courtroom regular, a student known for his dry humor and clever repartees. His eyes shone with youthful mischief as he waited for Syd's answer.

Miss California gave him a hard nudge in the ribs. "I swear, Thomas, you're such a pig." Then, before Syd could say that she had bought the panties at Victoria's Secret for the sole purpose of using them in court, the girl asked, "Did you get in trouble with Judge Claiborne?"

Syd hooked the strap of her leather purse around her shoulder. "He gave me a lecture on grandstanding, then proceeded by congratulating me on a job well done."

The crowd was growing and now included a couple of reporters Syd knew. One snapped her picture. Before the informal talk could turn into a news conference she had no intention of giving, she slipped into her black wool coat. "I'd love to stay and chat," she said. "But as of this moment, I'm officially on vacation, and out of here."

"Where are you going?" one of the reporters asked.

"Cancún." She waved at the students as she made her way toward the exit. "Good luck on your finals."

Outside the courthouse, the Philadelphia skies had turned an ominous pewter-gray and a biting March wind blew in from the Delaware River, forcing pedestrians to walk with their heads lowered.

Cancún is beginning to look better with each passing second, Syd thought as she pulled her coat collar around her neck. The Mexican resort hadn't been part of her vacation plans—not on her salary. In fact, she had intended to repaint her apartment, something she had been putting off for months. She had actually been looking forward to the task, hoping that the hard work would help her get over the shock of finding her fiancé, criminal attorney Greg Underwood, in bed with another woman.

"It didn't mean anything," he had told her when she had thrown her engagement ring in his face. "You and I had an argument. I went to a bar to cool off and…she was there."

She was a six-foot Amazon with bleached-blond hair, vacant blue eyes and massive breasts. The argument he had referred to was one of many they'd had in the past several months. No matter how many times she explained to him that she loved her job, he couldn't understand why she chose to work in the district attorney's office when his father had asked her repeatedly to join his very old, very prestigious law firm. At twice the salary.

Two weeks ago, after one more plea on Greg's part to join Underwood and Sullivan, Syd had lost her temper and told him to leave her alone. That same evening, calmed down and convinced she had been too hard on him, she had gone to his apartment to apologize. But instead of finding him sulking in front of the TV, she had walked in on a scene right out of a porn flick.

Heartbroken at first, she had quickly realized that she was better off finding out about Greg's weaknesses now than after the wedding. She had no doubt that she had loved her fiancé, although not as passionately as she should have or she might have been more forgiving. The truth was, they had disagreed on so many issues, it was a wonder their relationship had lasted as long as it had.

Her plans to paint her apartment were happily derailed when her aunt Frederica had called to say that she had bought two tickets for Cancún and wanted Syd to join her at the very plush resort La Playa. The thought of spending a week in the scorching sun, while Philadelphia—and Greg—prepared for another blizzard, had done wonders for her lousy mood.

Anxious to get home and start packing, Syd bowed her head against the icy wind and hurried down Sixth Street toward Washington Square where she lived. At the intersection of Sixth and Chestnut, she took out her cell phone to check her messages. The first of three was from her aunt, saying she would be at the Cancún airport to pick her up at one-thirty tomorrow afternoon. The second was from her boss, District Attorney Ron Devlin, congratulating her on her courtroom win and wishing her a good time on her vacation.

The third call was from her best friend, Lilly Gilmore.

As always, Lilly sounded as if she had just run the New York Marathon. "Syd, it's me. I know you were planning on spending the evening packing, but could you take a couple of hours off and meet me at the Elwood Diner in South Jersey at eight o'clock tonight? It's terribly important. Elwood is off the Atlantic City Expressway, Exit 28. It shouldn't take you more than an hour to get there. I'll explain everything when I see you. Bye."

Syd let out an irritated sight. How typical of Lilly to have a last-minute emergency—or whatever it was that had her so fired up—and expect Syd to drop everything and drive all the way to South Jersey, no less. But then again, depending on each other was something both women had learned to do from the moment they met in second grade. No matter which one was in trouble, or how sticky the situation, the other could always be counted on to come to the rescue. Twenty-eight years later, nothing had changed. They were still as protective of one another as any sisters could be.

The light on Chestnut turned green and Syd crossed the street, punching the speed dial for Lilly's number. Maybe the matter wasn't so urgent after all. Or if it was, she could pack first and meet Lilly later, somewhere closer.

But instead of Lilly's breathless "hello," it was her friend's cheery voice mail that greeted her. "Hi, this is Lilly. Sorry I missed you. Leave a message and I'll call you right back."

Syd kept trying to reach her and only gave up when the winter-bare trees of Washington Square came into view. She glanced at her watch. Six-thirty. As much as she hated putting off her packing, she hated letting her friend down even more. The garage where she kept her Ford Focus was another five minutes away. If she hurried, she should be in Elwood in time to meet Lilly.

It took Syd less than an hour to reach Exit 28 and another ten minutes or so to locate the diner on Weymouth-Elwood Road. On any warm summer night, the place would have been mobbed with vacationers on their way to the Jersey shore. But in early March, and with a snowstorm on the way, only a handful of cars occupied the parking lot.

Spotting Lilly's black Pathfinder, Syd flicked her lights. Lilly responded by opening the driver's door. She had just stepped out of the car when a van tore into the parking lot and lurched to a stop beside the Pathfinder, catching Lilly's startled expression in its headlights.

Her sixth sense immediately on high alert, Syd yelled a warning and started running. Before she could reach either vehicle, two men jumped out of the van.

"Hey, you!" Syd shouted. "What do you think you're doing?"

Neither man bothered to look her way. Their intentions quite clear, they grabbed Lilly and shoved her into the truck.

"Oh, my God, Lilly!" Running alongside the van, Syd grabbed hold of the back door handle and tried desperately to yank it open. "Let her go! Do you hear me, you maniac? Let her go!"

A window slid down and Syd was viciously shoved out of the way. Stumbling back, she tried to catch her balance but couldn't stop the momentum. She was aware of a dull thud as the back of her head hit the pavement, then the diner's bright light dimmed and darkness swallowed her.

Two

The voices around her began to get louder.

"My stars!" a woman exclaimed. "What happened? Did someone get hit by a car?"

"Looks like it, Ethel." A man knelt by Syd's side. "Miss? Miss? Are you all right? Are you hurt? Can you talk?"

Syd's eyes fluttered open as she tried to focus her gaze on the people assembled around her. She counted three—one man and two women.

"She's coming to," the same female voice said.

"You're crowding her, Ethel. Move back. Give her some air." The man crouched down beside Syd.

"I'm not crowding her, you old goat. I'm trying to see if she's bleeding."

"She's not." Concerned eyes peered down at her. "Can you move, young lady?"

Syd flexed one foot, then the other. "I think so."

"She shouldn't move, Vern," the same reproachful female voice said. "I learned that in first-aid class."

The second woman, the one who had stayed back, asked, "Did someone call the paramedics?"

"I did," Ethel replied. "And I called Seth, too. He'll know what to do."

"I'm all right," Syd said firmly. She didn't need paramedics, or unnecessary questions. She needed the police. Now.

But the man who answered to the name of Vern wasn't about to let her go anywhere. Looking serious, he stuck two fingers in front of her nose. "How many fingers do you see?"

"Two."

"Who is the president of the United States?"

Ethel, apparently used to being in charge, slapped him on the arm. "Oh, for God's sake, Vern, will you cut it out? This isn't *E.R.* You're scaring that poor girl half to death."

"Do I need to remind you that I was an emergency squad volunteer for thirty years?" He sounded ticked off. "Contrary to what you may think, I know what to do in case of an emergency."

Syd braced her elbows against the asphalt surface and tried to put an end to the bickering by sitting up.

"Take it easy, young lady." Vern held her elbow. "One move at a time, okay?"

She nodded and took her first good look at the kind-looking man bending over her. He appeared to be in his seventies, with gentle eyes and wispy gray hair. One of the women wore a pink waitress uniform. A name tag in the shape of a large white rose confirmed that her name was Ethel. The other woman was petite, black-haired, and seemed content to let Vern and Ethel do all the talking. All three had rushed out of the diner without their coats.

With the man's help, Syd stood up and tested her legs. They felt steady enough.

"What happened?" the waitress asked.

"My girlfriend was just kidnapped. By two men." Syd spoke rapidly, not taking time to breathe. "I tried to stop them but they pushed me away before I could do anything." She rubbed the back of her head, where a bump was beginning to form. "I have to call the police. You *do* have a police department in Elwood, don't you?"

"Kidnapped!' The quieter woman clasped both hands on her chest. All three exchanged stunned glances, as though nothing like that had ever happened in Elwood. It probably hadn't.

"Yes, kidnapped. That's why I have to call the police." They didn't seem to be grasping the seriousness of the situation. Or its urgency. "I can give them a description of the van and of the two people who abducted her."

"Seth is our chief of police," Ethel said with a wise nod of her head. "He'll find your friend, honey. Don't you worry your pretty head."

"In the meantime, we should get you inside where

it's warm." Vern put an arm around her waist and turned her gently toward the diner. "Can you walk okay?"

"Yes." She wanted to run into the diner, grab a phone and dial 9-1-1, but she didn't think that the mighty trio would let her take another step without their assistance. She pointed at her car. "I'll need my purse. And Lilly's," she added. "Hers should be in the Pathfinder."

"Mary, you get the purses," Ethel instructed. "Vern and I will take the girl inside and get her something hot to drink."

Within moments, Syd was sitting in a booth with Vern across from her, trying to make some sense out of what had just happened. The scene that kept replaying in her head seemed to come right out of a TV thriller. Although she had prosecuted all kinds of cases and regularly crossed paths with the worst types of criminals, Syd had certainly never witnessed a kidnapping before.

"Here's some hot chocolate, honey." Ethel placed a steaming mug in front of her. "Drink some before Mary comes back and accuses me of being a slowpoke."

As if on cue, the door opened and Mary walked in, carrying the two purses. Behind her was a stocky man in his late fifties with thick gray hair and dark, watchful eyes. Mary pointed at the booth and he walked toward Syd, unbuttoning a navy parka as he went. A gold shield bearing the words Mullica Township Police was clipped to his breast pocket.

"This here is our chief of police," Vern told Syd. "You're in good hands, dear. Just tell him—"

The newcomer took off his Phillies baseball hat. "I think I can take it from here," he said quietly. When Vern made no move to leave, he added, "If you don't mind, Vern. I'd like to talk to the lady alone."

"Oh." Looking slightly miffed, Vern slid across the seat, and walked over to the counter where Mary had already climbed on a stool. Ethel was back behind the counter, refilling their coffee cups.

"Now then." The policeman sat down across from Syd. "My name is Seth Yates." He took out a small, spiraled notebook and opened it. "What's yours, young lady?"

"Sydney Cooper. Please, call me Syd. My friend, Lilly Gilmore, was kidnapped." She took a calming breath, aware that trying to speed up the process was as pointless as banging her head against a brick wall. "We need to put out an all-points-bulletin right away, before the kidnappers have a chance to—"

"How do you know your friend was kidnapped?"

"I saw it happen!" The three people at the counter glanced in her direction and she dropped her voice down a notch before continuing. "She asked me to meet her here. I had just pulled into the parking lot when a dark van drove in at high speed. Two men jumped out, grabbed Lilly, pushed her into the van and drove off."

"Ethel told me she and her friends found you laying on the ground."

None of that matters, she wanted to scream. But once again, she restrained herself. "I ran after the truck and tried to open the door. One of the men stuck his hand out the window and pushed me out of the way."

"Did the van have New Jersey plates?"

"Yes, but I didn't have time to read them. It was one of those vanity plates with a lighthouse on it and the slogan 'Shore to Please.' And there was a soccer ball decal on the rear bumper."

The chief kept writing.

She waited until he was finished before continuing. "Lilly Gilmore—that's G-I-L-M-O-R-E—is five foot seven, weighs one hundred and nineteen pounds and has blond hair and blue eyes. I don't know what she was wearing. Both men were tall, broad-shouldered and dressed in dark clothing."

"Facial features? Hair?"

Syd shook her head. "That's a blur. I'm sorry."

"Don't be. You've done pretty well so far."

"I'm trained to be observant."

"Really." Chief Yates looked up from his notes. "What do you do?"

"I'm a Philadelphia assistant district attorney."

"Ah." He leaned back against the tan vinyl seat and looked at her thoughtfully. Then he took out a cell phone from his inside pocket and punched a number. "Henry, this is Seth. We need to put out an APB for a young woman, a dark van and two kidnappers. Yes, right here in Elwood. Outside the diner actually."

He repeated what Syd had told him, without bothering to look at his notes. He sounded crisp and efficient as he gave instructions on how to proceed. Maybe she had been a little too hasty in her judgment of Chief Yates, Syd thought. He seemed a lot more competent than she had given him credit for.

When he was finished, he hung up and picked up his pen again. "Why don't you give me some basic information about your friend, such as family, job, hobbies. Let's start with her status. Is she married?"

"Divorced. Her ex-husband is a police detective with the Philadelphia narcotics division. He's also the son of a former police commissioner."

The chief seemed unimpressed. She liked him already. "Are he and Lilly on friendly terms?"

Syd let out a short laugh. "Not by a long stretch. Mike is a bossy, arrogant S.O.B. who made her life miserable. He carries a grudge because the judge awarded custody of their six-year-old daughter to Lilly. Lately, he's been pressuring her to change those arrangements."

"How so?"

"By showing up on Lilly's doorstep uninvited and demanding to have Prudence for the day. By accusing her of going away on assignments and neglecting her child, which isn't true. Lilly is an investigative reporter with the *Philadelphia Sun,* and yes, she is busy, but she is a wonderful mother. When she is away, which is rarely, her mother takes care of Prudence."

"I take it you don't like Mike Gilmore."

"That's putting it mildly."

"Has he ever been violent? With Lilly or with the child?"

"Not to my knowledge." Syd paused, only too aware that being a victim of physical abuse was something Lilly would never admit, even to her best friend. "But he could be. He's that type. What he wants, he gets."

"But he didn't get custody of his daughter."

"No."

"Why do you think that is?"

Yes, she definitely liked Chief Yates and the quick way he had of assessing a situation. "If you're asking if Lilly had some sort of hold on him, that was my first thought, although I have no idea what that could be. Lilly can be very private when it comes to family matters. Especially if they involve her child."

"You said you were meeting your friend here at the diner?"

"Yes. She called me earlier, while I was in court, and left a message on my voice mail."

"Is she also from Philadelphia?"

"Yes." She gave him Lilly's address.

"Why did she want to meet you so far from home?"

"I don't know. I wondered about that myself."

The chief gave another of his nods. "You said Lilly is an investigative reporter. Do you happen to know what she was working on at the moment?"

"This past week was a busy one for both of us. We didn't have a chance to talk much. But I'll find out."

He nodded. "Any boyfriend in the picture?"

"No. She hasn't been in a relationship since she left her husband a year ago."

"Does she have any family beside her little girl and her mother?"

"An aunt, an uncle and a cousin. They all live in Philadelphia." She gave him their names and addresses.

"Where is the little girl now?"

"With her grandmother, Dorothy Branzini, I imagine." Syd put her mug down and expelled a long breath. "I'll have to tell her what happened."

"Do you want me to come with you?"

She shook her head. "If you don't mind, I'd rather do it alone."

"That's fine with me, although I'll have to talk to Mrs. Branzini in the morning. In the meantime, I'll need to take a look at Lilly's home. Can you arrange to get me a key?"

Familiar with all the procedures necessary to conduct a criminal investigation, Syd nodded. "I have one. Why don't I meet you at Lilly's house after I've talked to her mother? We can check the place together."

If the chief picked up on her not-so-subtle attempt to be part of the investigation, he didn't show it.

"In that case, I'll go back to the station to see if there is anything on that APB." He glanced at his watch. "I'll meet you at your friend's house at about eleven? Will that give you enough time with Mrs. Branzini?"

Syd nodded.

The chief took his baseball cap from the seat and put it on. "I'll walk you to your car."

"Thank you, Chief."

Three

It was a little after 10:00 p.m. when Syd brought the Ford to a stop in front of Dorothy Branzini's town house on Waverly Street. She had thought of calling her first, then had dismissed the idea, preferring to deliver the news in person. Since the tragic death of Syd's parents eleven years ago, Dot had been like a mother to her—loving her, worrying about her and dispensing the same kind of advice she gave out so freely to her daughter. They would handle this crisis together.

A few seconds after Syd rang the bell, a light went on upstairs, then a curtain was pulled aside as Dot's face peered down at her. Looking surprised but not alarmed, she mouthed Syd's name, then quickly let go of the curtain.

Moments later, the door opened. Only four foot eleven and no heavier than ninety pounds, Dot was nonetheless a force to be reckoned with, and those around her knew it. Her only two weaknesses were her daughter, whom she adored, and Prudence, who, at her tender age, knew how to wrap her Nanna around her little finger.

Dot's hair was in curlers and she wore the navy fleece robe Lilly had given her last Christmas. "Syd! Good Heaven. What are you doing here at this time of—" Then, as though she suddenly understood that only bad news could have brought Syd to her doorstep at this hour, her face paled. "Lilly?" She spoke her daughter's name in a half whisper. "Something happened to Lilly."

Syd walked into the small foyer and closed the door. "She's missing, Dot." Better to ease into the truth one step at a time.

"Missing?" Dot's deeply veined hand went to her throat. "What does that mean?"

"Let's go in there." Nodding toward the tidy living room, with its familiar early American furniture and cream carpet, she led her to the sofa. "Sit down, Dot."

"I don't want to sit down." Dot's voice rose slightly. "I want to know where my daughter is!"

"She's been kidnapped." It was harsh. It was shocking. But there was just no other way to say it.

A gasp escaped from Dot's throat and her eyes filled with a mixture of disbelief and fear. "Kidnapped? My baby has been kidnapped? When? Why? Who would do such a thing?"

"We don't have a lot of details yet." Holding Dorothy's trembling hands in hers, Syd recounted the events of the past two hours, omitting nothing but choosing her words carefully. "We'll find her," she said, trying to work up the right amount of conviction in her voice.

Dot yanked her hands away. "No, you won't. You said yourself you have no idea who those two men are, where they took her or why. How can you say you'll find her?"

"There is an all-points-bulletin out for her, for the van and for the two men."

But Dot was no longer listening. She started walking up and down the living room, her hands waving toward the heavens. "I knew something like this would happen someday. That job of hers. So dangerous."

"Dot—"

"I'll never see her again, will I? Tell me the truth."

"Of course, you will. In fact, you can help. Would you like that?"

Dot squared her shoulders. "What do you want me to do?" She looked ready to form a posse.

"Just answer a few questions. Did Lilly say anything recently about an unusual assignment?"

"She never tells me anything. She knows I get upset." She clasped her hands again. "But I knew something was up when she took Prudence away."

Syd glanced toward the staircase. "Prudence is not with you?"

"No. Lilly made arrangements for her to stay with…an old friend of mine."

"Who?"

Dot looked uncomfortable. "Lilly made me swear I wouldn't breathe a word."

"Dot, I'm sure she didn't mean me."

"Of course not. I'm sorry." She rubbed her brow. "This is too much for me to take. I'm a little confused." Then, in a lower voice, as though admitting it was an act of weakness, she added, "And I'm scared, Syd. So very scared."

"I know." Gently, Syd pulled her down onto the sofa. "Where is Prudence?"

"With Sister Madeline. My friend Sandra," she added when Syd gave a puzzled shake of her head.

Syd vaguely remembered the name. The two women had gone to school together and continued to stay close after Sandra joined the church. "I thought she ran a retreat somewhere in Delaware."

"She left that order to come here about a year ago. Very few people know she's back in this area, including Mike."

"Is that who Lilly was afraid of?"

"She wouldn't tell me. All I know is that ever since Mike started dating that rich girl, he's been driving Lilly crazy."

Syd nodded, remembering her last conversation with Lilly. "Is he still asking for shared custody of Prudence?"

"More so than ever. And you know why?"

"Lilly didn't tell me. I don't think she knew."

"She does now. Mike stopped by her house the other day and told her. It seems that his new girlfriend, a spoiled bitch if you ask me, can't have children, but she's *developed a liking for Prudence*. Those were his exact words," she added sarcastically. "*Developed a liking for Prudence*. As if they were talking about a dog they were thinking of adopting." She gave a disapproving shake of her head. "After the wedding, Miss Money Bags wants Prudence to come and live with them six months out of the year."

"What did Lilly say?"

"She laughed in his face, and he got angry. He accused Lilly of being selfish and of trying to ruin his new relationship with Vanessa."

"If they want a child so badly, why don't they adopt?"

"Vanessa won't hear of adopting. And now she's set her sights on Prudence and won't let go of that ridiculous idea. She's even told Mike that if she can't have Prudence, there won't be a wedding. How mature is that?"

"I should have known that Mike's renewed interest in his daughter was motivated by more than fatherly love."

"I don't trust him, Syd. That man is capable of anything."

"As much as I agree with you, I doubt he would resort to kidnapping to get his way."

Unless he wanted to get his hands on whatever Lilly had on him. With incriminating evidence out of the way, Lilly would no longer have leverage and he could live in happy, and rich, bliss forever after.

Syd stayed until Dot's sister, Luciana, arrived. Once again, she repeated what she had witnessed, offered words of encouragement, then left the two sisters to go and meet Chief Yates.

As Syd headed for Lilly's house, she thought of her friend and her annoying habit of always thinking she could handle any situation on her own, without help from anyone. Yet, it was that same fierce independence that had drawn Syd to the spunky seven-year-old in the first place.

The friendship had surprised both families. Lilly was a daredevil, always pushing the envelope and getting herself in trouble as a result. Syd was more grounded. She was the peacekeeper, the mediator who kept disasters out of Lilly's life. Most of the time.

Lilly's family and friends believed that it was her destiny to become an investigative reporter. As a child, she'd had a talent for snooping that many around her found irritating. In time, that talent had paid off. Twenty-seven years and one Pulitzer later, Lilly was one of the best journalists in the Delaware Valley.

At first, her marriage to Detective Mike Gilmore seven years ago had seemed like a match made in heaven. Both were good-looking, popular and ambitious. Then, a year ago, on the eve of little Prudence's fifth birthday, Lilly had announced she was filing for divorce.

"Mike's been paying less and less attention to Prudence and me," she had told Syd. "And he's obsessed with the fact that he's not, and will never be, the cop his father was. I've grown tired of his whining night after night."

To Syd's surprise, Mike had not contested the divorce, nor Lilly's decision to seek custody of their daughter. According to Lilly, he was as disillusioned with their marriage as she was, and anxious to end it all amicably. Syd hadn't bought it. Mike's huge ego and need to control wouldn't have allowed him to give in so easily. He would have fought, if not for his marriage, at least for partial custody of his daughter.

Distrustful by nature, Syd had suspected Lilly of having something on her husband—an ace card she had kept carefully hidden. The possibilities were endless. Infidelity, abuse, drugs, not to mention the proverbial kickbacks.

Looking back, Syd wished she hadn't been so preoccupied with her own work these past few weeks and had paid more attention to Lilly. And Mike.

As she turned onto Lombard Street, she spotted the chief's car, with the Mullica township logo on the side, and pulled up behind it.

Maybe Lilly's town house would provide the clue they so desperately needed.

Four

The gray clouds that had hung over Baton Rouge all day had become heavier, threatening to burst at any moment, and bring with them the torrential downpours for which southern Louisiana was so famous.

Sitting behind the wheel of his old but dependable GMC truck, Jake Sloan left Interstate 10 and headed north on College Drive, glad that his shift on the Jupiter oil rig was over. After working sixteen hours a day for an entire month, he was looking forward to two weeks of R&R. Maybe he'd drive down to Galveston for some serious fishing. Or farther south, toward the Mexican coast where the marlins liked to migrate at this time of year.

Technically, he should have been entitled to three weeks off instead of two, but recent cutbacks had made it necessary for the remaining crews to work longer hours. Jake didn't mind. He liked hard work. And with no wife and no children to answer to, he was free to work and play as hard as he pleased.

Ten years from now, when and if he ever got tired of drilling, he'd buy himself the boat he had always wanted and start a deep-sea fishing business. But that dream was still a long way off. The money was there; he just didn't want to make any final decisions until he was absolutely sure he'd be happy.

The streets of Baton Rouge were quiet at this time of night and the parking spaces full, except for one half a block away from his apartment building on Seven Oaks Avenue. He slid the GMC into it, cut the engine and reached in the back seat for his duffel bag.

"Mr. Sloan?"

At the sound of his name, Jake glanced over his shoulder. The man standing behind him was about his age, tall, solidly built, with neatly trimmed black hair and a steady gaze. He wore a dark suit, which meant he was either from out-of-town or he had just come from a funeral. In his hand was a black briefcase.

Jake jumped out of the truck and slammed the door shut. "Yeah, I'm Jake Sloan."

The stranger took a small leather case from his pocket and flipped it open. "I'm Agent Paul Ramirez, FBI. Could we go somewhere and talk?"

In the glow of the streetlight, Jake read his credentials, which confirmed that Paul Ramirez was an FBI agent attached to the Philadelphia division.

Unfazed, he swung his duffel bag over his shoulder. "It depends. What do you want to talk to me about?"

"Someone I'm sure will interest you." Then, before Jake could tell him that the only thing that could hold his interest at the moment was a cold beer, the agent added, "Victor van Heusen."

Jake went still as the face of his former commanding officer slowly, reluctantly, came into focus. "What about him?" he asked.

The agent looked up and down the street as if to make sure no one was eavesdropping. "I'd rather not discuss the matter here. Maybe your apartment?"

All right, Jake admitted to himself, the man had his attention. So why not give him a few minutes? Nodding toward his building, he led the way through the downstairs door and up to his first-floor apartment.

The place, which he had been renting for the past six years, was sparsely furnished with comfortable dark green furniture, functional appliances in the galley-size kitchen and a bed and dresser in the single bedroom. With his bank account, he could have afforded much more, including his own home, but he didn't like the idea of putting down roots. Until he made up his mind about what he really wanted to do with his life, what he had here suited him just fine.

He dropped his duffel bag on a chair. "How about a beer?"

"Just water, please."

A minute later, Jake returned from the kitchen, one glass of iced water in one hand, a bottle of Budweiser in the other. "So," he said, after taking a long sip. "How did you know I'd be interested in Victor van Heusen?"

"I do my homework."

"What exactly do *you* know?"

"Well, let's see." Ramirez leaned back in his chair. "You are two months shy of your forty-second birthday. You were born and raised in Philadelphia and attended Drexel University, where you graduated with a degree in engineering. Following your graduation, you married your high school sweetheart and turned down a lucrative job with Lockheed Martin to enlist in the army. After earning your commission, you signed up for flight school and were eventually sent to Germany for a three-year tour. While in Germany, you were one of a few men selected to train for the Special Forces—DELTA, to be specific. Unfortunately, your marriage did not survive your lengthy absences from home. Your wife filed for divorce in 1991, shortly before you were deployed to Iraq to fight in Desert Storm. Need I go on?"

"No." Jake had no doubt that Agent Ramirez knew every detail of what had happened in Iraq afterwards. And since he had no desire to hear how his military career had come to a crashing, humiliating halt, he waved him off. "Why don't you just tell me why you're here?"

"Very well." Ramirez kept his gaze on Jake. "Are

you aware that after being discharged from the army, Colonel van Heusen, who now calls himself *General* van Heusen, moved to your home state?"

Jake brought his beer bottle down. "Victor is in Pennsylvania?"

"Lancaster County, to be exact."

"What is he doing there?"

"He put together a militia and made himself commander in chief. Camp Freedom is not only his brainchild, it has become a very successful operation with more than twelve thousand members nationwide. Nine hundred are from Pennsylvania and neighboring states alone. They meet in Lancaster every other weekend. The rest of the membership keeps properly motivated through van Heusen's Web site, which averages more than a thousand hits a day, and his shortwave radio show, 'Being a True American,' which he hosts.

"Only fifteen men, all carefully selected, live at the camp. A handful of them serve on some kind of committee headed by van Heusen. They could be privy to highly classified information."

Although Jake was taken aback at the news, he wasn't entirely surprised. A graduate of West Point, his former commander came from a long line of military men, and soldiering was in his blood. "I don't know what I would do without a uniform on my back," he had once told Jake.

It was possible that his disappointment with the army had triggered his decision to form a militia. His qualifications as a battlefield commander were indisputable. He possessed excellent leadership qualities, although he had proven, at least once, that when the occasion demanded it, he didn't mind coloring outside the lines.

"All right, so van Heusen is a militia activist," Jake said at last. "What does that have to do with me?"

"The man has been on our radar screen for some time now, and not because of his antigovernment stand. Two years ago, acting on a tip, we set up a surveillance team to observe the going-ons inside the camp. Unfortunately, we came up empty."

"What is he supposed to have done?"

"We suspect him of brokering the sales of illegal weapons to terrorist countries."

Jake slowly sat up. "You're kidding."

Ramirez rattled the ice in his glass. "Our source told the bureau that van Heusen supplies weapons to Sierra Leone, Somalia, Indonesia and the Middle East. Because of his vast connections throughout the military, it is believed he can broker anything from AK-47's to rocket launchers and even Blackhawk helicopters. The problem is, we can't prove it."

"With all the resources at the bureau's disposal, you haven't found a way to catch van Heusen at his game?" Jake had difficulty keeping the surprise from his voice.

"It's not for lack of trying, believe me. In the past two years, we have conducted a number of sting operations, going as far as infiltrating the camp. Van Heusen must conduct extensive background checks on all volunteers, because three days later the agents' applications to join were turned down. No explanation was given."

Jake smiled. No one had ever accused van Heusen of being dumb. "You guys must be slipping."

Ramirez kept twirling the ice in his glass. "That's when we thought of you."

Jake was beginning to see where Agent Ramirez was heading, but he asked anyway. "Why me?"

"Because you know him better than anyone else. You know what makes him tick, what he is capable of, how far he'll go to get what he wants."

Jake leaned forward. "Are you saying that if I agree to help you—and I haven't—I would have to go to Lancaster County?" Snowdrifts and subzero temperatures were not exactly what he'd had in mind for his vacation.

"No, that would be too obvious. We would like you to go to Philadelphia."

"For how long?"

"That's up to you. The faster you bring us proof that van Heusen is an illegal arms' dealer, the faster you'll be able to return home. Naturally, all your expenses would be paid."

"You're aware that I have a job."

"And the next two weeks off. Yes, I'm aware of it."

He *had* done his homework. "Can you guarantee I'll finish the mission in two weeks?"

"No, but you wouldn't lose your job at Jupiter Oil. We would make sure of that."

Jake took a long pull on the bottle. How many times in the past fourteen years had he wished he could get even with his former CO? Ruin the man's life the way van Heusen had ruined his.

Well, now is your chance, Jacky boy.

So why did the thought of trapping a man he despised and handing him over to the feds leave him with such a bad taste in his mouth?

When his gaze returned to Ramirez, the agent had drained his glass and was leafing through a *Sports Illustrated* magazine Jake had left on the coffee table.

He put the magazine back. "Shall we go over the details of your assignment?"

"That won't be necessary." Jake stood up. "The answer is no."

Five

Ramirez's expression didn't change. In fact, he looked as though he had expected Jake to turn him down. Calmly, he asked, "May I show you something?"

Before Jake could reply, the agent took a manila envelope from his briefcase and emptied the contents on the coffee table. A dozen pictures spilled out. Ramírez fanned them out to allow Jake to see them all. It wasn't pretty. Men and women lay on the floor of what appeared to be a hotel lobby, their bodies riddled with bullets, their faces bloodied. A child, no more than six or seven, was among the victims.

"Those pictures were taken two weeks ago," Ramirez said, "shortly after rebels in Singapore stormed a hotel filled with Americans. There was no reason for the carnage, no provocation of any kind. Six heavily armed men rushed into the hotel and started firing. Nine Americans and two Indonesians died. According to several of the survivors, the killers were armed with AK-47's and M-16 assault rifles, the kind of weapons Victor van Heusen is suspected of selling."

"Do you have proof that they're his weapons?"

"If we did, I wouldn't be here, Mr. Sloan." Ramirez's voice had sharpened slightly. Jake understood why. It was difficult to look at those pictures and not feel angry and frustrated. "I showed you these pictures because I wanted you to see, firsthand, what happens when illegal arms are placed into the hands of irresponsible fanatics. What you see here is only a fraction of what takes place every day in various parts of the world. Most of the time, rebels kill each other, or they'll attack a defenseless village where they kill everyone in sight. Lately, their target of choice seems to be locations where Americans gather."

Jake couldn't take his eyes off the picture of the child, a little boy, he realized, who had died clutching an action hero figure.

"I don't know if van Heusen is responsible for that particular attack," Ramirez went on. "He may not be. But this is the kind of business he is in. A ruthless, dirty business he and dozens of other international arms' dealers conduct every day for only one reason—money. We can't stop every criminal, but we have a good chance to stop this one, with your help. If not, he'll go on providing arms to anyone who can afford his fee without ever giving a second thought to the innocent people he is killing, or the grieving relatives who are left behind."

The picture of that little boy vivid in his mind, Jake walked over to the window. One floor below, the street was quiet and peaceful. It was a scene he and millions of Americans enjoyed every day—a scene he took for granted, even now post-September 11th. But no matter how desperately Americans wanted to believe that life had returned to normal, nothing would ever be the same again. Nineteen al-Qaeda terrorists and a man named Osama Bin Laden had made sure of that.

He took another few seconds before turning around. Ramirez had put the photographs away and was observing him quietly.

"What exactly is your plan?"

"We want you to renew contact with van Heusen and get him to open up to you. Once he trusts you, the other fifteen men living at the compound will, too. Find out all you can about them."

"Haven't you already done that?"

"To some extent. One person in particular caught our attention. His name is Philip Jenkins. He is as much of a fanatic as van Heusen. He's definitely a man who bears watching."

"What's his background?"

"He was a paratrooper in the 101st Airborne before receiving a dishonorable discharge for brutally attacking another soldier. As a civilian, he did time for disorderly conduct, assault and vandalism. He is an expert marksman but is more comfortable with a knife in his hand. He is presently working as van Heusen's aide, although I suspect he is much more than that."

"So what you're saying is that I'm supposed to reappear in Victor's life, after fourteen years of silence, claim to want to be his buddy and he'll fall for it?" Jake shook his head. "I'm telling you right now, that will never happen."

"It will if you play your cards right."

Jake walked back to the sofa and sat down again. "I'm listening."

Ramirez looked briefly at his hands. "Before I discuss the scenario we have in mind, I need to ask you a question."

One corner of Jake's mouth pulled up in a half smile. "You mean there is actually something about me you don't know?"

Ramirez didn't return the smile. "When was the last time you spoke to your father?"

Jake's expression sobered quickly. "On his birthday three months ago."

"Not since then?"

"My father and I don't have what you'd call a typical father and son relationship."

"I'm sorry."

Jake couldn't tell if Ramirez knew more than he let on. "Why are we talking about my father?"

"He's sick. I thought you might know that."

Something in Jake's gut twisted. "I didn't. What's wrong with him?"

"Lung cancer. He was diagnosed about four months ago and given nine-to-twelve months to live."

Closing his eyes, Jake took a raspy breath, then another. The old man hadn't said a word. He knew his days were counted and he hadn't thought enough of his son to share that devastating news with him during their brief conversation.

"I'm sorry, Jake." Apparently the somber situation called for being on a first-name basis. "I wish I hadn't had to tell you, but…" Ramirez licked his lips. "It was necessary."

"Why?"

"Because your father's illness will be your reason for returning to Philadelphia."

At that, Jake had difficulty controlling his anger. "You cold son of a bitch—"

Ramirez put up his hands, palms out. "Now, don't go ballistic on me. I know what you're thinking and I don't blame you. But if we're going to fool van Heusen, we've got to use our heads. You said it yourself, he won't fall for anything that isn't completely on the up and up."

"That's before I knew you were going to use my father."

"Only indirectly. He's not part of the actual plan. He's only a means to get you back to Philadelphia. You want to see him, don't you? Now that you know he's sick?"

"You know I do."

"Good. Now, are you willing to listen to what I have to say? Without snapping my head off?"

Jake leaned back in his chair. "I'll try."

Ramirez remained his serious self. "You go to Philadelphia and handle the reunion with your father any way you see fit. By then, we will have leaked the news of your return home to the right people."

"You're going to tell me who?"

"Another old pal of yours, Ralph Gordon."

Jake laughed. "The nerd of Richfield High?"

"That nerd, as you well know, became a reporter for the *Daily Globe*."

"He also hates my guts. He thinks I stole his girl."

"I'm aware of that. Just as I'm aware that he didn't cut you any slack when you were discharged from the army fourteen years ago."

"And that makes him the perfect mark?"

"I couldn't think of a better one. He'll jump at the chance to embarrass you one more time. A refresher on your military history should fit his bill. And when van Heusen reads his article—and he will, because he's an avid newspaper reader—we're hoping he'll contact you."

"Why should he?"

"Because he won't be able to resist. He's proud of what he's accomplished and he'll want to brag a little."

"Why me? I despise him and he knows it."

"But that wasn't always the case. In fact, the two

of you were more than army buddies once. You were soul brothers. There was nothing you wouldn't have done for him and he for you. Am I right?"

"A lot has happened since then, and anyway, if he had wanted to contact me, he would have done so long ago. I'm not hard to find."

"Let's just assume he *does* contact you. You want to hear the rest?"

Jake nodded.

"Okay." A trace of excitement could be heard in the agent's voice. "He makes contact. How and where will be up to him. When he does, you play it cool. Very cool. Don't hide the fact that you're pissed at him."

"Go on."

"Let him do all the talking. If he wants to know how you feel toward the army, tell him that's all in the past now."

"That's the truth."

"Good. The truth is almost always more believable."

Jake wasn't convinced. "I don't know. I'm no actor. He'll see right through me."

"Do your best, Jake. I'm hoping that the relationship you two had and what you did for him back in Iraq are two factors that will play in your favor. He might even trust you enough to invite you to visit his camp. If he does, tell him you're not interested. That should convince him you're not a plant."

"What if he takes no for an answer and I never see him again?"

"I don't think that will happen, but if it does, you get to go home early. And we go back to the drawing board." Ramirez watched him intently. "What do you say, Jake? Think you can handle it?"

Jake chuckled. "What is this? A challenge?"

"I think I know better than to challenge you. So let me rephrase that. Will you do it? Will you help us?"

This time Jake didn't have to think about it. His mind had been made up the moment he'd seen that dead child on the floor of the Singapore hotel. "When do I leave?"

"Eight o'clock tomorrow morning." Ramirez reached into his briefcase again. He produced another manila envelope, much thicker this time, and dropped it on the table. "In there you'll find an airline ticket to Philadelphia and five thousand dollars in cash. Holler when you need more. I'll only be a phone call away.

"I've also enclosed a copy of the *Philadelphia Inquirer,* opened at the classified section. An apartment on Washington Square has been circled in red. The place is up for sale, but until the owner finds a buyer, he's renting it on a short-term basis. Agree to whatever price he wants. We'll pay for it. We could have made the arrangements ourselves, but it's important that *you* make them, in case van Heusen checks it out."

He would. "Why Washington Square?"

"One of van Heusen's men, Doug Avery, has been

accused of beating a prostitute. Van Heusen posted his bail and the trial is scheduled for September. An assistant district attorney by the name of Sydney Cooper is handling Avery's prosecution. She lives across the hall from the apartment you'll be renting. During the course of her investigation, she visited van Heusen's camp and questioned him. She may know something useful. It's up to you to find out." He waved at the envelope. "There's a complete dossier on her. By the time your plane lands in Philadelphia, you'll know as much about Sydney Cooper as we do. Oh, and she likes to run. Every morning, rain or shine, you'll find her doing her thing around Washington Park. If you're not a runner, I suggest you become one. It could come in handy."

"How will Victor find me?"

"You'll stay at the Double Tree Hotel on your first night in Philadelphia. When you check out, leave a forwarding address. It would also be a good idea to frequent some of the bars and restaurants in the area." He closed his briefcase. "I assume you have a cell phone?"

Jake nodded.

"My number is in that envelope," he said, nodding toward the coffee table. "Use it to call me, but never from your apartment. Van Heusen may decide to bug your new home."

"What if there is an emergency and you need to talk to me?"

"I'll call and ask to speak to Nancy. If you can't

talk, say 'wrong number' and hang up. Then find a secure place and call me back."

Jake couldn't help but admire the man's thoroughness. "You seem to have thought of everything. Were you that sure I'd agree to your little proposition?"

Ramirez allowed himself a rare smile. "Let's just say that I don't like to be caught unprepared." He stretched his legs in front of him. "I'll have that beer now, if you don't mind."

Six

After Agent Ramirez left, Jake dropped the envelope on the coffee table. He was no longer tired, or thirsty, or sleepy. Those memories he had managed to suppress in his mind over the years had come back with a vengeance and there was little he could do to chase them away.

It was hard to believe that fourteen years had passed since that fateful night inside the Iraqi border. Or that it had happened at all. Not that he hadn't found himself in a difficult situation before. For the members of DELTA Force, difficulties were a daily occurrence, a challenge the men in that particular branch of the special forces were well trained to handle. Even failure was an accepted part of the job.

He could still feel the excitement, the eagerness he had experienced when General Randolph Sanders, the DELTA commander in Kuwait, had outlined that particular mission. Headed by his good friend, Colonel Victor C. van Heusen, a crisis action team of eight highly trained men would attempt to rescue two American fighter pilots held prisoner inside the Iraqi border.

Jake, newly promoted to captain, was second in command. Between the two of them, he and van Heusen had successfully carried out more than a dozen training operations similar to that one. Assigned to Iraq at the same time and alike in so many ways, the two men had hit it off immediately in spite of their age difference. Van Heusen had been forty-two, Jake twenty-seven.

The mission was fairly routine. At 0200 hours, three all-terrain Fast Attack Vehicles had taken the eight-man team across several miles of Kuwaiti desert and four miles behind enemy lines. Collaborators previously screened by U.S. intelligence officers had given them the all-clear signal to cross the border into Iraqi territory.

That's when all hell had broken loose. Betrayed by their so-called collaborators, the DELTA team had come under attack. As the staccato of machine guns ripped into the night, van Heusen and his men returned fire.

Then, over the radio, the order from central command had been issued, loud and clear.

"Cease fire and return home! Repeat, cease fire and return home!"

But instead of ordering his troops to retreat, van Heusen had instructed them to move forward.

"The camp where those American pilots are being held is less than one kilometer away," he had told Jake. "I'm not going back without them."

Jake tried to reason with him, explaining that central command probably knew something he and van Heusen didn't know. Maybe more Iraqi soldiers were waiting for them, ready to ambush the team. Van Heusen paid no attention. He signaled his men to forge ahead.

It wasn't until the team came under fire again and suffered serious injuries that the colonel finally gave the order to retreat.

As van Heusen and Jake faced their superiors the following morning, the colonel sprang another surprise on Jake. Standing at attention, his gaze unwavering, he claimed he never heard the cease fire order from central command.

Unfortunately for van Heusen, one other man besides Jake had heard the order. Angry that five of his comrades had been injured, Sergeant Daniel Pratfield came forward with what he knew.

Van Heusen's fate now rested in Jake's hands. His confirmation of Pratfield's statements meant a certain court martial for Victor, along with a stiff prison sentence.

In the end, the code of honor Jake had adhered to for so many years, combined with his deep loyalty for a man he had always admired, won. Aware that his own career was on the line, he had backed van Heusen's statement and told the review board that he had not heard the cease fire order.

Jake's loyalty was poorly rewarded, or justly rewarded, depending on how you looked at it. Because a court martial would have been demoralizing for the troops, the army had recommended a "non-judicial" punishment. Both men were stripped of their ranks, given a dishonorable discharge and sent back to the United States.

Until the very last moment, Jake had hoped that van Heusen would step forward with the truth and spare his old buddy the humiliation of a dishonorable discharge. He hadn't.

The first couple of years found Jake drifting from town to town and job to job. Then, after seeing an ad for a roughneck with an oil company, he flew to Chicago for an interview and was hired on the spot.

Strong, smart and hardworking, he was quickly promoted to the position of offshore driller and had recently been interviewed for an executive position, which he wasn't sure he would accept.

At last, van Heusen's face began to fade, and Jake sat down in the chair Ramirez had vacated. Only mildly interested, he opened the folder on Sydney Cooper. Her picture took him by surprise. For some reason, he had expected a middle-aged woman with hard features, mousy brown hair and a body like a box. What he saw instead was a lovely face with wide, intelligent eyes he couldn't decide were blue, green or gray, and a mouth that was almost sinfully sexy. Chin-length hair the color of rich honey completed the picture.

Another photograph, taken outside the courthouse, proved him wrong once again. She definitely did not have a body like a box. To put it simply, the lady was a knockout.

Her background was as unexpected as her looks. After graduating from Temple University with a degree in marketing, she had joined the Philadelphia police force rather than seek employment with a large corporation. As a rookie, she had quickly proved that she was smart, resourceful and dedicated. Then, three years into the job, she and her partner had responded to a call—a robbery in progress at a Center City convenience store. Before backup could arrive, Officers Cooper and O'Hara had found themselves under fire. Gun in hand, aimed at the perp, Officer Cooper had frozen.

The indecision had cost her partner his life.

Sydney's return to duty—*desk* duty—hadn't gone well. Resentment and hostility on the part of her co-workers were a constant reminder of that tragic day. Disillusioned but still determined to serve the people in some way, she had left the force and gone to law school. Three years later she had graduated in the top five percent of her class, turned down offers from several law firms and chosen to go to work for the district attorney's office.

Her personal life was rather lonely. Her parents

had died in an avalanche while skiing in the Italian Alps some years ago, and she had recently ended a two-year engagement to one of Philadelphia's most promising criminal attorneys. All she seemed to be doing with her time was work.

There was more, but Jake was beat and he had an early morning flight. He'd catch up with the rest of Sydney Cooper's life in the plane.

Seven

By eight o'clock on Thursday morning, news of Lilly's abduction was front page news and the main subject of conversation on local talk shows. Listeners called in, offering their views and their suggestions on how to keep the streets of Philadelphia safe. A few claimed to have spotted the van Syd had described either on the New Jersey Turnpike, or on I-95. One woman even attested to having seen it parked outside her house.

Although all leads were being checked, the truck had not been recovered.

Removing the earphones of her Sony radio from around her head, Syd ran the last few steps to the six-story building that housed the district attorney's office on Arch Street, the one place where she had not counted on being on this chilly, damp morning. Parked strategically along the streets of Philadelphia, the snowplows were ready, their ominous presence reminding Philadelphians that the Nor'easter forecasters had promised was still very much on schedule.

Violet Sorrensen, who had been the senior administrative assistant in the D.A.'s office for the past seven years, was already at her post. She was a compact, attractive brunette in her mid-forties with an almost fanatical passion for tidiness, a penchant for matchmaking and a deep affection for Syd.

As Syd entered, she put her phone down. "Oh, honey, are you all right? You weren't hurt? Did you see a doctor?"

"No need to. All I have is a bruised ego."

"Any news of Lilly?"

"Not yet."

"Don't lose faith, honey. She'll be found." As her phone started ringing again, she directed the call then picked up a folder from her desk. "This is yours. A law student by the name of Chad Quinn dropped it off. He said you left it at the courthouse yesterday."

Syd took the folder, which contained her notes on the Simon Burke trial. It was useless now that the case was over, but still, she shouldn't have left it behind, no matter how eager she had been to leave.

"Thanks, Violet. I didn't realize it was missing." She slid the yellow pad in her briefcase. "I'll call Chad to thank him. Did he leave a number?"

"No. He was late for class and rushed out of here before I could ask him. I'm sure you'll see him in court. He says he tries to catch you whenever you are scheduled." She winked. "I think he's got a crush on you."

Before Syd could deny that statement, Violet added, "Great job on the Burke case, by the way." The secretary gave her a fond smile. "You made the boss happy and that's always a good thing."

"The boss" was Ron Devlin, a hands-on district attorney who believed in an open-door policy and encouraged his A.D.A.s to do the same. Demanding and sometimes critical, his fairness and genuine caring had earned him the respect and admiration of the three hundred prosecutors who worked for him.

He was sitting at his desk when Syd walked in, half-hidden behind a mountain of files and newspapers. At the sound of the door closing, he looked up, and, in a moment of rare compassion, he stood up and walked around his desk, meeting Syd halfway. He was a bear of a man, with a massive chest and a deep, commanding voice.

"Jesus, kid, I'm so sorry about your friend. I heard what happened while driving to work this morning." No hugs. Ron wasn't the hugging type, but he pulled up a chair for her, then hitched his hip on the corner of his desk. "Have you heard anything?"

"Not yet. Chief Yates is in the city, talking to various people, trying to piece the puzzle together."

"What's your take on him? And where the hell is Elwood?"

"South Jersey, about twenty miles from Atlantic City. As for Chief Yates, he may not have a lot of experience with kidnappings, or any kind of serious crimes, but he knows his job and he's been very thorough so far. I admit I was skeptical at first. He seemed a little too relaxed for me, but Lilly had just been kidnapped, right in front of my eyes, and I was frantic. He's really quite competent. I have complete faith in him."

"I'm glad to hear that." He brushed an invisible speck of lint from his immaculate gray trousers. "I take it you're ready to go back to work."

"Well, that's what I came to talk to you about." Under his hard stare, Syd felt her confidence waver. "I cancelled my trip to Cancún, but since I'm officially on vacation, I'd like to use the time to help Chief Yates look for Lilly."

"Did Chief Yates ask you to help him?"

"No, but—"

"Then you'd best let him do his job, Syd, and concentrate on the work here. God knows there's plenty of it."

"But I'm on vacation," she protested.

"And taking it now couldn't come at a worse time. Barbara went into labor at four o'clock this morning."

Syd leaned back in her chair. A senior A.D.A., Barbara Cummings had a full load. Reassigning her cases amongst the other attorneys wouldn't be easy. "She wasn't due for another two months."

"Yes, well, tell that to her baby. Anyway, she'll be on maternity leave for another six weeks and I don't have anyone to take over, except you. If I recall, you cleared your desk before you left." He didn't wait for an answer, but walked around his desk, picked up a half-dozen files and came back to set them on her lap.

"Ron—"

"I tell you what," he said as though he was making a huge concession. "If you can manage not to fall behind, we can arrange for you to work six-hour days. That will leave you a couple of hours and your evenings to do what you have to do about Lilly. How's that?"

She glanced down and counted six folders. What could she say? From the finality of Ron's tone, it was clear that he expected her to agree to what he considered a very generous offer. How many times had he stressed to his A.D.A.s that this office functioned as a team and for the good of the team, not its individual lawyers.

She sighed. She'd make it work. Somehow.

By two o'clock that afternoon, Syd had attended two bail hearings, taken statements from three witnesses and drafted one opening statement. In between tasks, she managed to connect with Chief Yates, who, after some minor coaxing, agreed to give her a brief report on his progress. There was still no news of Lilly, her abductors or the truck. His deputies were checking out a couple of chop shops they knew specialized in vans, but so far nothing had turned up.

He didn't tell her any more than that, not even when she pressed him about his meeting with Lilly's ex-husband. "That's privileged information, Syd. I'm sorry."

At three o'clock, having satisfied her six-hour commitment, Syd left the D.A.'s office and headed for the *Philadelphia Sun.* As expected, the mood there was grim. A couple of reporters Syd knew looked up from their desk as she went by, their expression hopeful. She shook her head and continued toward the editorial office at the end of the newsroom, where Stan Sherman, the editor-in-chief, was waiting for her.

In his mid-sixties, the veteran newsman showed no sign of slowing down. With his big beer belly, thick gray hair that always needed combing and trademark suspenders in a daring shade of purple, he was a commanding presence in and out of the newsroom.

He stood with his back to her, staring out the window overlooking Market Street when she entered.

"Hello, Stan."

From the moment he turned around and she met his eyes, she knew that the news of Lilly's kidnapping had hit him hard. Gruff on the surface, he was a softy inside, especially when it came to Lilly, who was high on his list of favorites. He had taken her under his wing when she was just a rookie reporter and had taught her everything he knew.

"I'm glad you came, Syd." He waved at one of the two brown leather chairs in front of his desk. "I was hoping you'd have some good news by the time you got here, but judging from the look on your face that was wishful thinking."

He walked back to his desk and sat down. "Chief Yates called, by the way. He said he'd be here at four." He made a face. "Where the hell is Elwood?"

Syd smiled. That seemed to be the question of the day. She repeated what she had told the D.A. and warned Stan not to let the chief's laid-back demeanor fool him.

Stan ran a hand through his hair, making it even more unruly. "I don't think anyone truly appreciates the risks investigative reporters face every time they take on a difficult assignment. In the past month alone, three of my reporters were threatened. *Openly* threatened, if you can believe that. One day they accuse you of being too liberal, the next too conservative. One irate reader called me on the phone yesterday and told me I was a lousy communist."

Syd sat up. "Has Lilly been threatened?"

"She's had her share of cranks. The most recent was that militia man you're prosecuting, Doug Avery. He cornered her as she left the building two nights ago. He didn't make a direct threat, but he told her to stop snooping around and harassing his friends. He was pissed off because during the course of her investigation, Lilly found out that during his high school days, he had beaten up a couple of girlfriends."

Sydney nearly jumped out of her chair. "Why wasn't I informed? Or Detective Cranston?"

"Lilly swore it was no big deal. In fact, she wasn't even going to mention it to me. The security guard who chased Avery away is the one who told me."

A construction worker with a volatile temper, Doug Avery was accused of beating a prostitute to within an inch of her life. Syd had fought hard to keep him behind bars until his trial in September but the judge had let him out on one hundred thousand dollars bail. Not surprisingly, the money had been paid by Victor van Heusen, the founder and commander of the militia Avery belonged to. Concerned that the organization was encouraging unnecessary violence, Syd had questioned van Heusen at the time of Avery's arrest. To her surprise, she had found the militia commander to be not only cooperative but deeply regretful about the incident.

"I don't know if Sergeant Avery is guilty or not," he had told Syd. "But if he is, I expect him to face up to the consequences like a true soldier."

The thought that Avery may have kidnapped Lilly and subjected her to the same fate as that prostitute, or worse, sent a chill of terror throughout her system.

Forcing herself to stay calm, she took out her cell phone and punched a number. "Detective Cranston, this is Sydney Cooper," she said when the detective answered. "Did you know that Doug Avery threatened Lilly Gilmore?"

As always when Syd talked to a member of the Philadelphia police, the reception was cool. "No, I didn't. When did that happen?"

"Monday night. I want him brought in, Detective, and I want to be there when you question him."

"Yes, ma'am."

She ignored the sarcastic tone and gave him her cell phone number, which he already had but conveniently kept losing.

"What else was Lilly working on?" she asked Stan after she hung up.

"The accident involving Senator Fairbanks and his daughter."

Syd frowned. "Wasn't that case closed after the other driver admitted she was in the wrong?"

"Apparently Lilly wasn't satisfied. You know how she gets when she smells a rat."

Syd nodded, remembering Lilly's conviction that something about that accident wasn't quite right. Two weeks ago, seventeen-year-old Lauren Fairbanks, with her father at her side, had been practicing her night driving on a deserted Pennsylvania road in preparation for her road test. As they approached an intersection, their car was hit broadside by another vehicle. Although both cars sustained damages, there were no injuries. The other driver, a middle-aged woman who had failed to stop at the stop sign, had taken full responsibility for the accident. With the determination of a hunting dog, Lilly had stayed on the story and visited the accident site. To Syd's knowledge, she had found nothing to confirm her suspicions.

"According to the calendar on her desk," Stan

continued, "Lilly was trying to schedule an appointment with Senator Fairbanks."

"Trying?"

"She couldn't get past the senator's press secretary—Muriel Hathaway."

Syd nodded. "The barracuda."

"And believe me, she's living up to her name. Now that the senator is the front runner in the presidential race, she won't let anyone near him, even though he's been dubbed the most approachable candidate since Jimmy Carter."

"Lilly couldn't have been very happy about that."

"She was grandly pissed, but she refused to give up on her hunch. She tracked down Ana Lee and was planning on questioning her."

"Who is Ana Lee?"

"The other driver. Unfortunately, Lilly was kidnapped that same day and I never had a chance to talk to her about the outcome of that interview."

Syd wrote down the name. "Do you have an address for Mrs. Lee?"

"She runs a food cart at the corner of Eleventh and Market."

Eight

Syd wasn't surprised to find reporters waiting for her outside the *Philadelphia Sun* when she left. Lilly's kidnapping had now made the national news and the media were milking it for all its worth.

"Ms. Cooper!" A bleached blonde Syd recognized as Belle Chiaro, of the *Daily Globe,* was in the front row as usual. "Is there any news of Lilly Gilmore? Have her kidnappers made any demands yet?"

A man pushed a microphone with the CBS logo in Syd's face. "Do you think Lilly's still alive?"

"What about that militia man you're prosecuting? We know Lilly was investigating him. Is he a suspect?"

"Why was Lilly investigating Senator Fairbanks?"

Accustomed to the media's rapid-fire form of questioning, Syd patiently waited until the last question had been asked before replying.

"I can't go into details," she said, ignoring the groan of disappointment that rippled through the crowd. "Partly because that duty falls on Chief Yates of the Mullica Township police, and partly because by talking to you I would be compromising the investigation. I can tell you this, however—Chief Yates and I will leave no stone unturned. Whatever needs to be done to find Lilly Gilmore will be done."

"Do you suspect a mafia connection?" That question came from a CNN reporter.

Remembering that Lilly had done an exposé on Philadelphia mob boss Joe Caputo not too long ago, Syd shook her head. "We have no reason to suspect the mafia is involved."

"Will *you* be investigating Senator Fairbanks?" Belle Chiaro pressed.

"As I said, Belle, we will leave no stone unturned." Then, with a smile that signified the end of the questioning, she made her way through the crowd and headed down Market Street.

After making sure that no overzealous reporter was following her, she dialed information, memorized the number for Senator Fairbanks's office and punched the appropriate keys. She got as far as Muriel Hathaway's secretary, a pleasant-sounding woman whose amiability vanished when Syd introduced herself.

"The senator and his staff are in Florida for the primaries," she stated crisply. "He won't be back until the end of the week."

Before Syd could ask for an appointment, the woman had hung up.

Syd closed her phone with an angry snap. She was beginning to understand Lilly's frustration.

Syd reached the corner of Eleventh and Market a few minutes before five o'clock. At her inquiry, a vendor pointed to a cart.

"That's Ana over there. You can't miss her. She's the one who's always yapping."

Several hospital workers from nearby Jefferson University Hospital were waiting in line, giving Syd ample time to observe the woman manning the cart. Petite and of Asian descent, she greeted her customers by name and chatted nonstop as she handed them their food or beverage. She smiled easily and talked rapidly, with a pleasant, musical accent. Syd heard Ana tell one of her customers that she could barely put two sentences together when she had first arrived on American soil two years ago.

"And look at me now," she said, plopping a hot dog into a bun and smothering it with sauerkraut. "I talk, talk, talk."

When her last customer was gone and only Syd was left, Ana didn't miss a beat. "Hi, Lady. What you like? Chili dog? Hot Pocket? Fruit smoothie? You name it, I have it."

Syd returned the friendly smile. "Actually, I don't want any food."

"What you mean, no food? How you going to be strong with no food?"

Syd came to stand close to the cart and took out her ID. "I'm Sydney Cooper of the district attorney's office."

Ana Lee's friendly smile faded a little, but she remained pleasant. "What you want with me?"

"I'd like to ask you a few questions regarding the accident you had two weeks ago."

"Oh, that." The woman shook her head. "I give all information to police already. Nobody say I must talk to district attorney."

"You don't. I'm not here in an official capacity."

Ana frowned. "What you mean?"

Syd had no choice but level with her, partly because she hated to deceive anyone and partly because if Ron heard she was misrepresenting his office, she'd be out of a job. "I'm investigating the kidnapping of Lilly Gilmore. She's a reporter for the *Philadelphia Sun*."

"Ah." The frown disappeared and Ana bobbed her head several times. "I hear about her." She pointed a slender finger at Syd. "And I see you on TV. You put pervert in jail." She looked pleased. "That's good."

Okay, so maybe all that unwanted publicity had done her some good after all. "Lilly Gilmore is my best friend," she explained. "She was investigating Senator Fairbanks's accident just before she was kidnapped."

"Why investigate Senator Fairbanks?" Another hospital staffer in a white coat stopped by for a soda. She served him with a smile and took his money before returning her attention to Syd. "Accident my fault. I tell that to senator. And to police."

"But for some reason, Lilly Gilmore thought differently."

Ana looked offended. "I not lie."

"I'm sure you didn't. Did Lilly talk to you?"

"No. I not know about her and kidnapping until I hear on TV."

So Lilly had not had a chance to talk to her. "Would you mind going over the accident one more time?" Syd asked.

Ana Lee's mouth pinched a little in annoyance, but she nodded. "What you want to know?"

"Tell me exactly what happened. Everything as you remember it."

Ana took a dry cloth from a shelf under the counter and started wiping the already spotless counter. "I come back from my mother's house in Allentown. She old and not well. I worry. You know how it is."

Syd nodded to show that she understood.

"Not good to worry about loved ones. You pay no attention to things." She sighed. "I see senator's car too late. I—" She made a waving motion with her small hand.

"Swerved?"

"Yes, swerved. And other car try to stop, but…" Her voice shook a little at the recollection.

"Did you recognize the senator right away?"

She bobbed her head again. "Oh, yes. I see him on TV many times."

"And you are sure *he* wasn't the one driving."

"Oh, very sure. I see his daughter behind wheel."

"Did she get out of the car?"

"Yes. Poor kid. Very upset."

"What did the senator do?"

"Call police. I tell them accident my fault."

"I understand that your car needed towing. How did you get home?"

"State trooper took me." She smiled. "Nice young man. Very polite."

"And the senator was able to drive?"

"Yes. His car not too damaged."

Syd wondered how much farther she could push Ana's patience. "Did the senator's daughter appear to have been drinking?"

Ana looked horrified. "Drinking? Liquor?" When Syd nodded, she gave a vehement shake of her head. "No! Where you hear that? I never say that."

"No, no," Syd said quickly, "I didn't mean to imply that you had. I was merely curious."

"No, no drinking. Poor girl very upset. Ran into bushes and got sick. You know." She made an upward gesture from her stomach to explain what she meant.

Syd wasn't surprised. The girl was young, only seventeen. An accident such as that one could have caused her to throw up. But then again, so could have alcohol.

"What happened the following day?" she asked.

"I go to police station, give statement and sign it."

"Were the senator and his daughter there?"

"No. Police go to Mr. Fairbanks's house."

Ah, the advantages of being a presidential candidate.

After thanking her and buying a bottle of water, Syd left, feeling a little disappointed. She had expected Ana Lee to be evasive, or inconsistent in her recount of the accident. She had been neither. The woman had told the truth—at least, as she knew it.

If there was more to that accident, as Lilly seemed to think, Syd would have to dig out the information herself.

Nine

From his fourth-floor room at the Double Tree Hotel on Broad Street, Jake watched the wide thoroughfare Philadelphians proudly called Avenue of the Arts, and took in the familiar sights. The hundred-and-fifty-year-old Academy of Music, which for years had been the uncontested grande dame of Broad Street, was still there, but now the famous landmark shared the limelight with the Kimmel Center, a soaring glass-and-concrete structure that had become home to the Philadelphia Orchestra. Less than a block away, the Wilma and Merriam theaters enjoyed a friendly competition as they featured some of Broadway's most popular shows. To the right, and straddling Broad Street, the vast monolith of City Hall stood proudly, topped by the statue of the city's founding father, William Penn.

Upon landing at Philadelphia International Airport, Jake had rented a car and called the real estate agent whose name Agent Ramirez had circled in red. The two men had made plans to meet at the apartment on Washington Square at four o'clock, which left Jake plenty of time to go see his father.

He wished he could work up a little more enthusiasm about the visit. But the truth was, after spending the entire flight thinking of nothing else, he still wasn't sure how he felt about seeing his father again. A part of him wanted to be here and offer any help his dad might need, emotional or financial. The other part dreaded the visit. The last one hadn't gone so well and if he was to believe his father's last words "—don't bother coming back—" this attempt was a waste of time.

That was, unless the illness had mellowed him, which was doubtful. Wendell Sloan was a hard man with a stubborn streak Jake was grateful he hadn't inherited. In either case, Jake was here now and he would make the best of it. Angry or not, his father would find it a lot more difficult to slam a door in his face than it was to hang up on him.

Putting the homecoming aside for the moment, Jake turned away from the window and picked up the copy of the *Philadelphia Sun* he had bought at the airport. Assistant District Attorney Sydney Cooper's highly publicized courtroom win a couple of days earlier had put her in the limelight. From what Jake gathered, an overly confident defense attorney had put his client on the stand and in doing so he had given the prosecution a clear shot at the accused.

Sydney Cooper had made the most of the opportunity, leading the defendant into a conversation about pretty women and sexy underwear, specifically black thongs, which, according to the prosecution, the defendant was particularly fond of. Under Sydney Cooper's expert cross-examination, the poor sap had become more and more nervous. As his attorney began to object to the prosecution's line of questioning, the latter had produced a black thong from her suit pocket and dangled it in front of the helpless man,

Sweating profusely and looking at Sydney as if she was the special of the day, he had thrown a volley of sexually explicit comments, driving the last nail into his own coffin.

While the defense attorney jumped to his feet, shouting his objections, and the judge repeatedly banged his gavel in an attempt to regain control of the courtroom, Sydney Cooper had quietly returned to her table.

Two hours later, the jury had returned a unanimous guilty verdict.

Jake smiled. Getting to know Ms. Cooper promised to be a lot of fun.

Wendell Sloan, a retired mailman, lived in the Frankford section of Philadelphia, on a quiet loop just off Torresdale Avenue. He and his wife had moved into their row home shortly after adopting their first son, Bill, whom everyone had called Spider because of the boy's fondness for that insect. Two years later, after having given up all hope of ever having a child of her own, Katie Sloan had become pregnant with Jake.

The two boys grew up not only as brothers, but as best friends, until Bill, at twenty-five, had quit his job as assistant manager at the Ground Round and joined the marines. Two weeks later he had died of a heat stroke suffered during a grueling training exercise.

Nothing was ever the same after that.

Jake brought his rented SUV, a sturdy Ford Explorer, to a stop in front of his father's house, but didn't get out. Although he wasn't particularly fond of the cold, he was grateful for the gusting wind and dipping temperatures. Bad weather kept nosy neighbors inside. The last thing he wanted right now was for someone to witness another debacle in his attempt to mend fences with his father.

After a couple of minutes, he turned off the engine and stepped out of the truck. Winter had turned the little patch of grass in front of the house brown. Chipped, empty flowerpots were lined up along the cracked walkway, waiting to be filled, and the siding was in desperate need of a new coat of paint. The place had a slightly neglected look, yet it was still the same old, familiar house where he had spent some of the best years of his life.

He rang the bell and after about ten seconds, he

heard footsteps, not the slow shuffling he had expected from a sick man, but a familiar strong stride.

The door opened a crack and suspicious eyes peered out from the narrow opening. It took Wendell a half second for his expression to harden. The illness had taken its toll on the old man. Although he was still tall and broad-chested, like Jake, his shoulders had rounded and there were deep lines on his weathered face. Only the eyes, a deep brown, remained clear and sharp.

"Hi, Pop." The word, so seldom spoken, half caught in Jake's throat.

Apparently untouched by the emotion in his son's voice, Wendell squared his shoulders. "What are you doing here?"

Not the best welcome in the world, but at least the door was still open. "I was in the area and I thought I'd stop over."

"It was a bad idea."

He started to close the door, but Jake splayed his hand on it and held it firmly. "You're not going to get rid of me so easily this time, Pop." He gave the door a gentle push and walked into the small foyer where the same wooden console stood against the wall.

As his father let go of the door, Jake closed it softly. "Don't you think it's time we ended this feud and talked?"

"We've already had this conversation."

"And we're going to have it again, whether you like it or not."

"What's wrong with you, boy? Who gave you the right to barge into my home and give me orders? This isn't the army. And I'm not one of your soldiers."

"I'm not here to give orders. I'm here because I'm tired of you hanging up on me every time I call. And I'm tired of thinking of all the things I could have done over the years to repair our relationship and didn't do." He wasn't quite sure how the next words came out. He hadn't meant to say them quite so soon, but they tumbled out anyway. "I love you, Pop. And I miss you."

If the words did anything to mellow Wendell's sour mood, he didn't show it. His back remained just as stiff, his expression just as hostile. "I don't know what got into you all of a sudden, but for your information, nothing has changed. I still hold you responsible for what happened to this family, the *destruction* of this family."

"And that's where you're wrong." Jake kept his voice on an even keel. "Bill's death was a tragedy, but I didn't cause it."

"You were the reason he enlisted!"

"His *anger* was the reason he enlisted. He felt betrayed, not by me, but by you and mom, the two people he trusted most. If you had told him he was adopted instead of hiding it like a dirty secret, he wouldn't have had to find out the way he did."

"And I suppose you're not responsible for that either?" His father's voice was filled with sarcasm.

Jake let out a sigh. "I never meant to blurt it out

the way I did. We were celebrating my graduation from Drexel and drinking too much. When I told him I was going into the army instead of taking the job at Lockheed Martin, he got upset and we started arguing."

Flooded with memories, Jake lowered his head, focusing his gaze on the faded brown carpet. "I'm not sure how the conversation shifted from me to him, or why I told him he was adopted. Like I said, we were drinking and…" He looked up. "I screwed up, Pop. If I could take that night back, I would. I need you to believe that."

"Your mother died as a result of what happened to Bill."

"Dammit, Pop, stop blaming me for all the wrongs that happened to this family. You and I both know that Mom died because she was severely depressed and wouldn't go for help." He almost added, "You should have made her go," but didn't. He had come here to lessen the abyss between them, not deepen it.

On impulse, he reached out and laid a hand on his father's arm. "What do you say we start over?" he asked softly. "I know you're not well and I want to be here for you. I could take some time off, do a few things around the house. I'm quite handy once I put my—"

Wendell gave Jake's hand a quick swat, as though chasing an annoying fly. "Stop with all the melodrama already. I'm fine, and I certainly don't need you to look after me." He peered through the narrow side window on the front door. "Did anyone see you?"

"What if they did?"

"What if they did? Do I need to remind you of the shame you brought to this neighborhood with what happened in Iraq? I couldn't step out of this house without someone stopping me in the street to talk about what you did."

"I'm sorry." Jake had never told his father the truth about the Iraq incident. He wouldn't have understood.

"Yeah, well, sorry don't cut it." Wendell opened the door. "Leave. Before I have to explain what you're doing here."

Jake stood rooted in place for several seconds, at a complete loss for words. He hadn't expected any miracles, but he had expected better than this.

There was nothing more to do except leave. With a nod to his father, he turned around and walked out.

He had barely reached the sidewalk when a vaguely familiar voice called out his name.

"Jake Sloan, as I live and breathe. It *is* you."

Jake looked up and found himself face-to-face with Ralph Gordon, who used to be known in their high school days as "Gordo." He was still deserving of the mocking nickname. Although not as fat as he used to be in his teens, he had remained chunky and had that same malevolent smile, as though he was always up to something. He'd had a huge crush on Jennifer Parson, but his fantasies had come to a crushing end when she had started to date Jake and then later married him. More than twenty years had passed since then, and Jennifer was now remarried and the mother of three boys, but somehow the sting of being rejected had carved a deep ridge in Ralph's ego. He had never forgiven Jake for "stealing his girl."

When Jake had returned from Iraq fourteen years ago, Ralph, a writer for one of the local tabloids by then, had made sure Philadelphians were given every dirty detail of Jake's discharge.

Agent Ramirez's decision to pick Ralph as the fall guy had struck Jake as unwise at first. He no longer felt that way. Actually, it was an excellent choice. Too dumb to realize he was being set up, Ralph would jump at the chance to stick it to Jake one more time.

Getting into the part, Jake pushed past him and headed for the SUV. "Get out of my way, Gordo."

Far from being insulted, the reporter ran to keep up with Jake's long stride. "Hey, it's a free country. Besides, you're big news around here, army man. It's not every day that Philadelphians get to greet a fallen hero." He grinned, showing crooked teeth. "When I heard you were back in Philly I couldn't believe it. I mean, why would you want to come back to a town that despises you?"

He stuck his head forward, feigning an eager expression. "Come on, Jako, tell me what brings you to the city of brotherly love. You know what they say in our business. Inquiring minds want to know."

No longer playing a part, Jake grabbed Ralph by the collar and slammed him against the SUV. "Listen to me, sleazeball. If you think for one minute that I'm going to waste my breath talking to you, you are more delusional than I remember."

He released him. "Now take your sorry ass out of here and stop hanging around my father's house."

Ralph's eyes shone with spitefulness. "Or what, army man? You'll shoot me? Or are you helpless without your big, bad gun?"

All the willpower in the world couldn't have stopped Jake at that point. His reflexes kicking in, he drew his arm back and punched the little son of a bitch in the face.

Then, as the reporter stumbled back, holding his bloody nose, Jake opened the door of the SUV. "Let that be a warning," he said, sliding behind the wheel. "Next time you get in my way, I'll really hurt you."

Ten

Sacred Heart Monastery was just off the Schuylkill Expressway and only a short distance from Center City. Set on twenty-seven acres of hilly, well-tended grounds, it overlooked the lush greenery of Fairmont Park and the Wissahickon Creek. A generous benefactor had bequeathed the property to eight devoted nuns more than ten years ago. The women had immediately turned the place into an orphanage, where they took in abandoned children, gave them food, shelter, love and an education. Although their expenses were high, they managed to keep the place going through donations and by selling the produce and the chickens they raised.

At the wrought-iron gates, Syd rang the bell. Moments later, a nun walked out of the Spanish-style building, her long, black habit billowing behind her.

She was in her mid-sixties, with attractive, classic features, a serene smile and a brisk step.

"Good morning," she said when she reached the gate.

"Good morning, Sister. I'm Syd."

"I know. I recognize you from the photo Dot showed me not too long ago. I've been expecting you." Syd watched as the nun took out a heavy key ring from beneath her habit.

"We don't normally keep our gate locked," she explained, inserting a key into the lock. "But Lilly was very emphatic about the safety issue regarding Prudence." The gate squeaked as she pulled it toward her.

"Has anyone tried to see Prudence?"

"No. As I said, we've been very careful. I'm certain that except for Dot, and now you, no one knows she's here." She locked the gate again. "Prudence will be thrilled to see you. She's talked about nothing else since I told her you were coming."

"How is she?"

They started walking down a graveled path. "A little confused. She misses her mom and doesn't understand why she had to come here rather than stay with her grandmother. I explained what Lilly had already told her, that Dot had to go on a trip herself, but..." She shrugged. "She's just a little girl." Her expression grew concerned. "Has there been any news at all?"

"Not yet, but we're all working very hard to find Lilly."

"I'm sure you are." The nun led the way toward a small, red building that resembled a barn. It seemed to have been freshly painted. "Prudence is attending classes, just like the other children we have here," the sister explained. "Lilly didn't want to keep her isolated from children her own age and she was right. She has acclimated very well and loves her classmates."

At the door, she gave a discreet knock and poked her head through the opening. Syd heard a small exclamation, the scraping of a chair being pushed back, then Prudence came running out, her blue eyes bright with expectation, her blond hair flying. She was a tiny image of her mother, right down to the twin dimples in her cheeks.

"Aunt Syd!" Forty pounds of sheer energy jumped in Syd's arms. "You came! You really came!"

Syd scooped her off the ground and twirled her around. "Of course I did. How are you, pumpkin? Give your aunt Syd a big, fat kiss."

Prudence gave Syd a loud smack. Pulling back a little, she said, "Did you bring me a surprise?"

Glad she had remembered how much Prudence loved surprises, Syd put her down. "As a matter of fact, I did." Syd reached into one of the two large shopping bags she had brought with her and pulled out a brightly wrapped package.

Prudence started to tear the red foil. "What is it?"

"I'm not saying."

The paper fell off, and when Prudence saw the

doll inside the box with her light-brown pigtails and rimless eyeglasses, her mouth formed a perfect *O* and her eyes filled with delight. "An American Girl doll! Oh, Aunt Syd, thank you! And it's Molly! That's the one I wanted."

Syd was well aware of that. Ever since the craze surrounding the line of American Girl dolls had begun, Prudence had been begging for one. Of the eight dolls made, Molly was the one she kept talking about the most, possibly because that was the name of Prudence's best friend.

"I'm glad you like it." She handed the second shopping bag to Sister Madeline. "I didn't want the other children to feel left out, so I brought them all something as well. Dot said you had six girls and three boys, ranging from ages three to eleven?"

The nun beamed as she peaked into the bag. "Oh, Syd, that's so sweet of you. I know they'll all be thrilled. I'll go put them in the playroom right away and the two of you can chat." She squeezed Syd's arm. "Do come and have milk and cookies with us afterwards. The children will want to thank you in person."

"I will. Thank you, Sister."

Alone, Syd and Prudence started walking down the path. After a while, Prudence took her eyes off her new doll long enough to look up at Syd. "Aunt Syd, where is my mommy?"

Something inside Syd's gut tightened. She sat on a nearby bench and drew Prudence onto her lap. "She had to go on a very important trip. She'll be back soon."

"But I miss her."

"I know, pumpkin. All I ask is that you be patient for a little while longer. Can you do that for your aunt Syd?"

The pout softened. "I guess so," she said a little reluctantly.

"You like it here, don't you?"

The blond head bobbed up and down. "The sisters are nice. We play a lot, but we also help with some of the chores. This morning, I made pancakes."

"How did that go?"

Prudence giggled and she pressed her cheek against the doll's head. "I tried to flip one, like Sister Mary-Catherine showed me, but it fell on the floor. Charlie ate it."

"Who is Charlie?"

"The dog. He was a stray and then the sisters adopted him. He likes me because I give him my green beans." She was suddenly serious. "I'd like to have a dog. You think Mommy will get me one when she comes back from her trip?"

"I don't know. You'll have to ask her."

Serious blue eyes held hers. "When will my mommy be back?"

"Soon." Syd had to summon every ounce of self-control she had to keep her voice from trembling.

"And Grandma? When will *she* be back from her trip?"

Poor darling, Syd thought, she must think that everyone has abandoned her. "In a few days. As soon as she does, I'll bring her over. Would you like that?"

"Yes!"

That hadn't been in the script, but Syd didn't care. She couldn't bear to see that look of longing in Prudence's eyes. She'd find a way to bring Dot to see her granddaughter without Mike finding out.

To lighten up the mood, she added, "Now, why don't you show me your room?"

Prudence jumped from Syd's lap. "Okay. And after you'll come and have milk and cookies with us?"

"I wouldn't miss it for the world, pumpkin."

Eleven

Syd jumped off the bus that had brought her back from the convent and was about to cross Seventh Street at Washington Square when she saw a tall man with a large duffel bag in one hand and a guitar case in the other enter her building. Since there was only one vacant apartment in the building and it happened to be across the hall from hers, it wasn't too difficult to figure out that she had a new neighbor. That would be what? Number three in as many months?

The apartment had been up for sale for more than a year, but the outrageous price the owner was asking kept buyers at bay. In the meantime, a real estate agency rented the apartment to drifters looking for temporary housing. The last tenant, a would-be rock star with too much time on his hands, had scared the daylights out of her. Fortunately, a gig somewhere in the Midwest had taken him away after only two weeks.

The apartment had been blissfully empty ever since. After working long days in a busy, high-pressure office, peace and quiet was what Syd craved most.

Well, so much for peace and quiet, she thought as she watched the newcomer jog back to his car, a gray SUV parked down the block. Judging from the guitar case she had glimpsed a moment ago, he must be another musician. Maybe the rental agency had a monopoly on them.

She had just retrieved her mail from her box and was waiting for the elevator when she heard running footsteps behind her. "Wait a sec, will you?"

Syd had her first good look at her new neighbor as he stepped into the lobby carrying a grocery bag. He was about six-two or three, with a broad chest and square shoulders. A tanned complexion and brown hair streaked with gold suggested he was the outdoor type. He wore snug, faded jeans, a white shirt open at the neck and a well-worn leather bomber jacket.

The deep blue eyes were steady as they met hers. "Thanks." He patted the bag. "Moving day."

His appraisal of her, much more thorough than hers of him, made Syd fidget.

To hide her nervousness, she pressed the button for the sixth floor.

The newcomer grinned. "What do you know, we're neighbors."

"Is that so." Syd made up her mind right there and then that just because the man oozed charm and sex appeal there was no reason to lose her objectivity. She had learned her lesson with Bozo, aka Greg.

The stranger's right hand shot out from under the bag. "I'm Jake Sloan, by the way."

Being rude wasn't her style, so she shook his hand. Surely there was no harm in that. "Sydney Cooper."

"Sydney Cooper, Sydney Cooper." He pursed his lips and furrowed his brows. "Wait a minute." He let go of her hand and pointed a finger at her. "You're the black thong A.D.A."

Great. A drifter *and* a pervert.

"The papers said that was one hell of a coup you pulled off in the courtroom," he continued.

"All in a day's work," she said, her eyes on the floor numbers. Was it her imagination or was the elevator particularly slow tonight?

"You're being too modest. In fact, I bet you're a terrific attorney."

"Thank you, Mr. Sloan. I try." The elevator lurched to a stop.

"Oh, come on, we're next-door neighbors. Call me Jake."

We're both attorneys. Call me Greg.

The door hissed open. Her key already in her hand, Syd gave him a goodbye nod. "Good luck with the moving."

"Thanks. Maybe if you're not busy—"

"I am." Without looking at him, Syd let herself into her apartment and closed the door behind her, making it clear that she had no intention of carrying this brief encounter any further. And unless he had amplifiers to go with that guitar and he intended to crank them up to an unbearable level, he would never hear from her again.

The moment Syd was inside her apartment, with a closed door separating her from the rest of the world, the tension of the past several hours seemed to vanish.

She loved her home, with its view of Washington Square and its convenient location. It was small, even by city standards, but she had made the most of the tiny space, filling it with all the things she loved—chintz-covered chairs, small tables crowded with old mementos, beaded lampshades, brightly colored rugs and prints of contemporary artists covering the cream walls. The look was indisputably cluttered. It was also warm, comfortable and homey. What more could a hardworking girl on a budget ask for?

She was standing in front of her refrigerator, inspecting its meager contents when the insistent ring of the doorbell made her jump. When she went to answer it, she found herself staring at Lilly's ex-husband.

The visit, although unexpected, wasn't a huge surprise. Mike Gilmore wasn't the type to worry about other people's schedules. He did what he wanted when he wanted and the hell with everyone else.

Even in casual clothes he looked like a cop—well-trimmed black hair, clean-shaven face and a powerful physique he was extremely proud of. Except for a few extra pounds, which he hid well, he was fit and handsome, if one could get past the overbearing attitude he wore like a second skin.

"What took you so long?" he asked, walking past her.

"What gives you the right to barge into my apartment? Don't you know by now that you're not welcome here?"

"I have to talk to you."

"You could have called."

"I did—twice. No one at the D.A.'s office knew where you were. Don't you have to sign out or something?"

She folded her arms across her chest. "I have no news on Lilly, if that's—"

"Where is my daughter?" he interrupted rudely. "I just talked to Dot and she says she has no idea. I know she's lying."

"If Lilly wanted you to know where Prudence was, she would have told you."

"Don't give me that shit, Sydney. My ex-wife has been kidnapped, which means that someone has to take custody of Prudence. And that someone is me. So I'm asking you again, nicely," he added with a thin, nasty smile. "Where is my daughter?"

Although Syd was mildly intimidated—Mike had that effect on people—she stood her ground. "It's not my place to tell you. All you need to know is that she is being well taken care of."

"By whom?"

"Have you gone deaf? Or are you being purposely dense?"

He started to take a step forward, then thought better of it. "I won't let strangers look after my daughter, do you hear me? What if they're perverts? Or weirdos like the Branzinis?"

"The Branzinis are good people and Prudence adores them."

"They're not *normal,* Sydney. For God's sake, Dorothy's brother is a cross-dresser, her sister talks to dead people and her niece is a felon."

"Joe is an actor, as if you didn't know. Luciana is a noted psychic who has helped the police department on several occasions, and Angie was arrested *once,* for demonstrating, and released after she produced a permit. So why don't you get your facts straight, Detective, before you bad-mouth decent people."

His expression turned mean. "Was that your idea? To hide Prudence from me?"

"You give me too much credit."

"I don't think so. You were always good at polluting Lilly's mind against me. *You* are the reason she divorced me."

At that, Syd had to laugh. "Oh, Mike, you do live in a world of make-believe, don't you? You lost Lilly all on your own, with your unrealistic expectations, your tantrums, your constant complaining. It's a wonder she stayed with you as long as she did."

"If you're trying to pick a fight, you're wasting your time. I'm here to find out where my daughter is. I'm her father, dammit. I have rights."

"The only rights you have are those awarded to you by the court, and to my knowledge, they do not include taking custody of Prudence when Lilly is away."

"She didn't go to the corner store for a loaf of bread, for God's sake! She was kidnapped! She could be dead for all we know."

It took all of Syd's willpower not to slap him. Knowing him, he'd haul her to the nearest precinct and file assault charges. With that in mind, she remained calm and pointed at the door. "Get out of my apartment."

He laughed. "Or what? You'll call the cops?"

"Or you'll have to deal with me," a voice behind them said.

Twelve

Syd looked up and saw Jake Sloan. He looked relaxed, almost amused, as though he was enjoying the moment.

Both eyebrows raised, Mike turned around. "Who the hell are you?"

"A friend of Sydney's." With his fingers tucked into the front pockets of his jeans, Jake walked slowly toward Mike. "You think you can leave on your own, or would you rather be escorted?"

Always quick on the recovery, Mike laughed. It was the same condescending laugh he reserved for people he felt were beneath him. "Do you know who you're talking to?"

Jake gave a disinterested shrug. "Makes no difference to me if you're the mayor. Sydney told you to leave, so you're leaving. And I should warn you. I'm not a patient man."

Looking supremely confident, Mike took out his shield and held it up. "You still think you can make me leave?"

Jake came to stand within inches of the detective. They stood eye to eye, both tall, both fit, both angry enough right now to start a brawl. "I'm not just going to make you leave," he said in a deceptively calm voice. "I'm going to call your superiors at Philly PD, *and* the newspapers, and tell them you've been threatening this lady here. I don't think that will go over too well at the department, do you?"

Knowing Mike's ugly temper, Syd held her breath while both men appeared to engage in a staring contest. Which one would blink first was anyone's guess. She didn't know anything about Jake Sloan, except that he didn't intimidate easily. But she knew Mike. He was mean, he was cunning and he didn't take defeat well.

After a long second, Mike let out another sarcastic laugh, although this time he didn't look quite as smug. He turned to Syd. "Nothing much has changed with you, has it, Syd? You still have lousy taste in men." Then, pointing an accusing finger at her, he added, "If anything happens to my daughter, I'll hold you personally responsible."

After one last look at Jake, who hadn't moved, Mike walked out of the apartment.

Jake waited until the door had slammed shut before turning back to Syd. "Are you all right?"

She nodded. No matter how much she valued her

privacy, she could hardly ignore the man's gallantry. "Yes. Thank you."

"I hope you don't mind that I let myself in. I could hear the two of you clear across the hall and got concerned."

She smiled. "Are you sure you didn't have your ear glued to my door?"

He pretended to be offended. "Now, do I look the type who would do something like that?"

"I don't know, are you?"

"When the need warrants it," he said with disarming honesty. Then, pointing a thumb toward the door, he asked, "Friend of yours?"

"God, no. He used to be married to my best friend."

"Would that be Lilly Gilmore? The missing investigative reporter?"

"You're pretty well informed for a newcomer."

"I'm not exactly a newcomer. I'm a Philadelphian, born and raised. Whenever I get back to town, I make a point to bring myself up to speed on what's been happening."

Realizing she still hadn't looked at her mail, Syd picked up the small stack on the credenza and flipped through it. It contained the usual bills from Verizon, Philadelphia Electric, the mortgage company, Lord & Taylor. "So, what brings you back to our city?" she asked casually.

"My father. He's not well and I'm taking advantage of a two-week vacation to be near him."

"Wouldn't it have been easier to stay in a hotel than to rent an apartment?"

"My visit could last longer than expected."

"I see." She didn't, but now was not the time to play interrogator. As she kept going through her mail, her gaze fell on a postcard. The picture side showed a covered bridge and rich fall foliage. On the other was a short note in Lilly's handwriting.

Oblivious to Jake, who was looking at her curiously, she read:

Hi, Syd.

Traveling through beautiful Bucks County made me think of the summers you and I used to spend at my parents' farmhouse in Erwinna. Made me feel nostalgic. See you soon.

Love, Lilly.

Puzzled, Syd kept looking at the postcard. Lilly wasn't the type to send little mementos of the places she visited. In fact, Syd couldn't remember the last time she had received a postcard. And what was she talking about? The two girls hadn't spent their summers at the Branzinis' farmhouse. They had spent them on Long Beach Island in South Jersey, where Syd's parents had a summer home.

A chill of awareness ran through her spine as the attorney in her took over. Lilly knew perfectly well where they had vacationed every year. Which could mean only one thing—the mistake was intentional.

She glanced at the postmark: March 6. Two days before Lilly was kidnapped.

"Sydney? Is there something wrong?"

Syd looked up. Jake. She had forgotten all about him. "No." She gave a weak shake of her head. "No, nothing is wrong." She set the mail back on the table but slid the postcard into her pants pocket. "Look, I'd ask you in for a cup of coffee, but…"

"Actually, I came to ask you out, a get-to-know-each-other kind of dinner." He rubbed his hands in anticipation. "What are you in the mood for? Chinese? Italian? Thai?"

"I'm sorry. I have to go out."

"Now?" He looked at his watch.

"Something came up."

"Then why don't you let me take you wherever it is that you need to go? We'll stop for a bite afterward."

The offer was tempting, not because she was changing her mind about this most persistent man, but because the prospect of a real dinner was a whole lot better than the corn flakes she had planned on having. However, this message from Lilly could be the clue she had been looking for all day, and she had to check it out.

"This is something I have to do alone." She took her lined Burberry from the coatrack and slipped it on.

"If you are in some kind of trouble, sometimes two heads are better—"

"Look, Mr. Sloan—"

"Jake."

"All right, Jake. I appreciate what you did. Without your intervention, I might not have been able to get rid of Mike Gilmore so quickly. But to be perfectly honest, and please don't be offended, I'm accustomed to fighting my own battles." She jiggled her keys to indicate she was anxious to leave.

"No offense taken. I'll just take a rain check." To show that he meant every word, he gave her an engaging smile, then walked out. She followed him, locking the door behind her.

Thirteen

Sitting behind the wheel of the Ford Focus she drove only when absolutely necessary, Syd watched for the Cafferty Road turnoff. She was grateful that the snowstorm the local networks had predicted with such certainty had unexpectedly veered off toward the Atlantic, bypassing Philadelphia altogether. And with little traffic on the roads at this time of night, it shouldn't take her more than twenty minutes to reach the Branzinis' farmhouse in Erwinna.

From time to time she glanced in the rearview mirror, unsettled at the thought that Mike Gilmore might be following her. She wouldn't put it past him to watch her comings and goings in the hope she'd lead him to Prudence.

At last she saw the sign for Cafferty Road and followed it. In the pale moonlight, the house, with its slanted red roof, looked forlorn. The fields that had once yielded rich crops of corn, beans and sweet potatoes were now thick with overgrowth. After Dot's husband had died two years ago, she had debated whether or not to keep the farm. Lilly had convinced her to put the property up for sale and move to a Center City town house. So far, the only prospects had been developers eager to turn the fifteen-acre property into a luxury subdivision. Dot had turned them down, preferring to sell the land to someone who would maintain the integrity and pristine beauty of the area.

"She doesn't really want to sell it," Lilly had told Syd. "And since she has enough money to live comfortably, I'm not going to pressure her."

Trusting that Dot still kept the key in the birdhouse that hung from the old oak tree, Syd started to head toward the backyard, then stopped abruptly when the front door was thrown open and someone dressed in black ran out.

Frozen in place, she made out the shape of a tall man with broad shoulders and closely cropped hair. Arms hanging by his side, he looked around him, his head moving slowly, left to right, right to left. Not sure if he had already seen her, Syd stepped behind a tree, hoping it would hide as much of her as possible. Her heart hammering in her chest, she took her cell phone from her handbag and found the three numbers she needed: 9-1-1.

"This is assistant district attorney Sydney

Cooper," she whispered when a dispatcher answered. "I'm at the—"

In the moonlight, she caught the sudden glint of metal. Too late she realized the intruder had a gun. And it was aimed at her.

"Hello? Ms. Cooper? Sydney?" The dispatcher's voice remained calm. "What is your location? Are you hurt?"

Syd heard the sound of a gunshot. Almost simultaneously, she felt a searing pain just below her left rib.

For the second time in less than forty-eight hours, she passed out.

The first person Syd saw when she opened her eyes was a bespectacled young man in a white coat with a stethoscope tucked in his pocket.

Smiling down at her, he held out his hand. "Hello there. I'm Doctor Saunders. I was on duty in the E.R. when the paramedics brought you in."

"Paramedics?" The events that had taken place at the farmhouse slowly came into focus. "I was shot." It wasn't a question, just a puzzled statement.

"Indeed you were. But I must say, you're a very lucky girl. One more inch to the left and the wound could have been fatal. As it is, the bullet only grazed your rib and exited cleanly. I gave you something for the pain. You should be out of here sometime tomorrow, although you'll have to take it easy for a couple of days."

She twisted to find a more comfortable position and winced at the pain. "How did the paramedics know where to find me?"

"A neighbor who looks after Mrs. Branzini's property saw suspicious activity and went to investigate. Lucky for you she did or whoever shot you could have decided to finish the job. By the time the paramedics arrived, you were unconscious, but fortunately, the bleeding was minimal."

"Did they catch the shooter?"

"Not yet. An Erwinna detective is outside, waiting to talk to you, but only if you're up to it."

She moved again. The pain was becoming more bearable. "I am."

Detective Peter Ramsey was on the youngish side—early-thirties. His five o'clock shadow looked familiar. It was the trademark of cops everywhere who worked long after their shift had officially ended.

"I'm glad to see that you're all right, Ms. Cooper," he said after he had introduced himself. He took out the little black book no good cop was ever without. "Mind if I ask you a few questions?"

"Fire away."

He smiled at the pun. "I see that you're also in good spirits. That's a positive sign." He pulled up a chair and sat down. "Let's start with what you were doing on Mrs. Branzini's property at nine o'clock at night."

Aware that her story was getting more complicated by the minute, Syd kept her explanation as simple as possible. Fortunately, Detective Ramsey was familiar with Lilly's kidnapping and had caught Syd's news conference outside the *Philadelphia Sun* on Thursday.

"Can you give me a description of the man who shot you?"

She felt as helpless as she had been when Chief Yates had asked her to describe Lilly's kidnappers. "Tall, strong build, dressed in black." He looked at her as if waiting for more. "That's all I can tell you. I'm sorry."

"Any resemblance to either of the two men you saw abducting your friend?"

"They were similar in shape. And wore the same type of clothing—dark."

"Did you see a car?"

"No."

"Did anyone know you were coming here tonight?"

Mike Gilmore. He had been standing by the table where she had dropped her mail. He could have seen the postcard. But as badly as she wanted to point the finger at him, she couldn't give him credit for that one. Mike had had no opportunity to go through her mail. Even if he had, he wasn't smart enough to put it all together.

"No," she said reluctantly. "Not even Dorothy Branzini. It was a spur-of-the-moment decision." Concerned about the possibility of damage to the house, or theft, she asked, "Did you tell her about the break-in?"

"I just finished talking to her. She was more concerned about you than she was about her house. She said to tell you she'd be here first thing in the morning."

"Was anything taken?"

"As far as we can tell, no. We won't know for sure until Mrs. Branzini does a walk-through. Whoever broke in did a clean search, *if* a search was the motive. We still haven't ruled out burglary."

"It wasn't a burglary."

"You sound very sure."

"He was looking for something."

"The mysterious item you think Lilly Gilmore hid?" He sounded doubtful.

"Maybe. I won't know until I search the house myself." She felt her eyelids flutter. Whatever Doctor Saunders had given her was beginning to take effect. She no longer felt any pain, just a pleasant overall sensation. And a need to sleep.

"You're tired," the detective said. "I'll let you—"

She never heard the rest of his sentence.

Syd had no idea that getting shot could make her so popular. From the moment her breakfast tray was cleared the following morning, her room saw a procession of well-wishers.

Ron Devlin, Violet and three A.D.A.s with whom she worked closely were her first visitors. Violet, ever the diligent organizer, took charge, making sure everyone had chairs, fresh coffee and didn't overly tire Syd.

Ron was...well, Ron. After telling her she looked great, he ordered her to take as much time as she needed—at least a day—before coming back to work. Dot, who arrived an hour later, looked completely frazzled, not because of the break-in but because of what she called "Syd's near-miss with death." And as always, she blamed herself for letting it happen.

"You had nothing to do with the shooting," Syd told her in as firm a tone as she could manage. "It was my idea to go there, not yours. In fact, I should have asked your permission."

"Nonsense. You're family." Dot sniffed. "And you were trying to help Lilly." She tucked the crisp white sheet around Syd's waist. "What did you think you'd find in the house?"

"I don't know. Maybe I'll have the answer to that after I conduct my own search."

"I've already been there with Detective Ramsey. Nothing was taken."

"I'd like to make sure."

"Is that such a good idea? What if that intruder is still there, hiding, waiting for you to show up?"

"I doubt he would do that with the police swarming the place. And anyway, I won't be alone. Detective Ramsey has assigned two officers to go with us. We'll be well protected."

"We?"

"I'll need you to come along, Dot, if you don't mind. You might be able to think of a hiding place."

The thought that she might be helpful seemed to lift Dot's spirits. "Then I'll be there."

One visitor Syd hadn't expected, but perhaps should have, was Jake Sloan. Her new neighbor walked in as she was sipping another cup of weak, lukewarm tea. He pointed an accusing finger at her.

"You should have let me drive you."

"So you could have taken that bullet for me? Isn't that giving the expression 'being neighborly' a whole new meaning?" She sat up, favoring her left side. "How did you find out where I was?"

"I knocked on your door this morning. When I didn't get an answer, I called the district attorney's office. A very nice lady by the name of Violet told me what happened." He pulled up a chair and sat down. "You've given everyone quite a scare. And don't tell me that getting shot is all in a day's work."

She smiled. "I'm pretty sure it's not."

"Are you comfortable? In any pain? Can I get anything for you?"

"Yes, no and no." She leaned back against the stacked pillows. "You came a long way to hear me say that. A phone call would have been easier."

"I wanted to see for myself that you were all right." He leaned forward, his gaze steady. "What was so urgent that you couldn't wait until daylight, Sydney? And more important, who would want to take a shot at you?"

From her sitting position, Syd observed him for a moment. She had always considered herself a good judge of character. Not counting Bozo, who had fooled her big time, she had an excellent track record both in and out of the courtroom. Her gut instinct told her that Jake Sloan was a man she could trust. On the other hand, she couldn't ignore the fact that she had known him less than twenty-four hours. Or that he had managed, in that short time, to infiltrate himself into her life as no other man ever had. Well intended as he may be, Lilly's safety was much too important to risk it on a hunch.

"I'm as much in the dark as you are," she said. "The police are investigating. They'll let me know if they find out anything."

"You have no idea who did this to you?" He didn't seem convinced of that.

She shook her head, and although he looked skeptical, he didn't pressure her. "The floor nurse told me you'd be getting out sometime today. Mind if I stick around and take you home?"

"Lilly's mother has already volunteered to do that. But I appreciate the offer."

"Who's taking your car back to the city?"

"Detective Ramsey."

He seemed disappointed and was about to say something when a nurse's aid walked in, pushing a cart.

"Time to take your vitals," she said to Syd.

Jake stood up. "I'll get out of your way. See you at home?"

She smiled. "Do I have a choice?"

"No."

Syd didn't miss the long, appraising look the nurse's aide gave Jake's retreating back as he left the room.

Fourteen

It was almost four in the afternoon when Dot dropped Syd in front of her apartment building. The search of the farmhouse, which had gone much faster with the help of the two officers, had produced nothing. Either Syd had completely misread Lilly's message, or her friend had hid the mysterious item too well and it would take a second visit to find it.

Right now, all Syd wanted to do was go home, make a pot of coffee and relax.

"Are you sure you don't want me to come up?" Dot asked. "I could make you something to eat. You didn't touch your breakfast at the hospital. Or your lunch."

"I'm not hungry, Dot, so stop fussing, all right? I'll be fine." She kissed her on the cheek. "Call you in the morning?"

Dot put a gentle hand on her cheek. "You're like a daughter to me, you know that, don't you?"

"Yes, Mom."

"Stop mocking me. What I'm saying is that I want you to be careful. I'm very grateful that you are taking an active part in the search for Lilly. At the same time, I would never forgive myself if something happened to you."

Syd squeezed the older woman's hand. "Nothing is going to happen to me, Dot. From now on, caution is my middle name."

"No more venturing out by yourself at night?"

She made a small sign on her chest. "Cross my heart, hope to die."

"You're doing it again. Making fun of me."

"I'm sorry. I *will* be careful. I swear."

Dot shook her finger. "I'll remember that promise. You do the same."

Syd stepped out of the car with only a twinge of pain, and gave Dot one last wave before walking into the building.

Jake's door was open when Syd came out of the elevator. From inside the apartment came the sounds of someone strumming a guitar. She recognized the style as part jazz, part soul. The effect was smoky. Sexy. Just the kind of music she enjoyed at the end of a stressful day.

Her instinct told her to go home and rest, per her doctor's orders. But something, curiosity perhaps, pulled her toward the open door.

After a light knock, which wasn't answered, she

walked in and followed the sounds. Jake sat on a tan sofa, one foot propped against the edge of the coffee table, the guitar on his lap. His long fingers moved lazily across the strings and although he seemed lost in the music, he turned his head the moment she reached the threshold.

Grinning, he stood up. "Hi, neighbor. How's the pain?"

"Bearable. The wound stings a little, but that's about it." She pointed toward the hallway. "In this town, leaving your door open is an invitation to trouble."

"I was waiting for you."

"Why?"

He leaned the guitar against the sofa. "Because I wanted to make sure you made it home safely. After what happened to you last night, I'm taking nothing for granted."

"You're starting to creep me out."

"Why? Because I care?"

"Because you've known me less than twenty-four hours. All this concern is, well, a little odd."

"Haven't you ever heard of instant karma?"

"I'm not a big believer."

"Then we'll have to change that." He patted the sofa. "Come on, Counselor. Take a load off your feet. I promise I won't bite."

Those deep cushions were so appealing, the room so warm, she was afraid that if she took his offer, she might never get up again. "Actually, I'm ready for bed."

"You can't go to bed on an empty stomach."

"What if I told you that I just finished a five-course meal, compliments of Erwinna Memorial?"

"I'd call you a liar. Nurse Pat told me you sent your trays back, practically untouched."

"Have you ever had hospital food?"

"More times than I'd care to count." Holding her by the shoulders, he sat her down, handling her as gently as if she were a china doll. "How do you take your coffee?"

That's when she smelled it, strong and fragrant. Still, something held her back, although at the moment she couldn't think what. "Black, but—"

"Take off your shoes and relax. I'll be right back."

That did it. Too tired to argue, Syd did as she was told, trying to remember when was the last time a handsome man had waited on her. Greg certainly never had. "I'm a disaster in the kitchen," he had told her early on in their relationship. "That's one area of the house I leave to women."

A few minutes later, Jake was back, carrying a tray. On it was a platter of mouthwatering sandwiches and two steaming mugs of the most aromatic coffee she had smelled in the past twenty-four hours. He set the tray down on the table and handed her one of the mugs.

She took a sip. The aroma had not deceived her. "Mmm. Good. Kenya? Medium-dark roast?"

He shrugged. "I have no idea. How can you tell?"

"Force of habit."

"Are you a coffee expert?"

She laughed. "More like a coffee addict."

"Then I'm delighted to have contributed to your addiction." He pointed at the sandwiches. "Help yourself. These are Parma ham and provolone on Italian bread, and the others are smoked salmon and cream cheese on rye."

"You're a regular Martha Stewart, aren't you?" As her stomach started growling, she reached for one of the ham sandwiches and bit into it.

Jake laughed as she closed her eyes. "Is it that good or are you just starving?"

"Both." How someone hadn't already reeled this man in and put a ring on his finger was beyond comprehension. Of course, he could also be a serial killer who trapped his unsuspecting prey with the lure of gourmet sandwiches and great coffee.

"I take it you like to cook?"

"Not particularly, but in my profession, you either learn or you eat slop."

"May I ask what you do?" she asked between bites.

"I'm an oil driller. I work on a rig off the coast of Louisiana."

She looked at him with renewed interest. "An oil driller."

"Not quite what you imagined?"

"I'm not sure what I imagined." She looked at the guitar. "I had you pegged for a rocker."

He threw his head back and laughed, a good-humored laugh that sent a tingle down her spine. Surely serial killers didn't laugh with such gusto. Or looked the way he did in jeans. "A rocker," he repeated. "I don't know whether to be flattered or insulted."

"The last tenant was a musician. A very strange fellow with long, stringy hair, dark shadows under his eyes and a dubious odor."

"Well, you've settled that," Jake teased. "I'm definitely insulted."

"Don't be. You're nothing like him. Night and day." She picked up her mug and looked at him above the rim. "Actually, I kind of like having you for a neighbor."

"Even if I'm a little too nosy?"

"You can work on that."

He reached for his own cup. "Did you hear from the Erwinna police?"

"They're still investigating. The last time I spoke with Detective Ramsey, they were combing the area in search of the bullet. But even if they find it, without the weapon, they have no way of proving where it came from."

Before he could ask another question, she asked one of her own. "Have you decided how long you'll be staying in Philly?"

"Long enough to reestablish some sort of relationship with my father."

His answer surprised her. "*Re*establish? You and your father had a falling-out?"

When he didn't answer, she gave a quick shake

of her hand. "I'm sorry. I didn't mean to pry. It's just that—"

"Actually," he said unexpectedly, "I could use an objective opinion."

He talked for a long time, about his brother's tragic death, his years in the army, and his decision fourteen years ago to end his military career and become an oil driller. His fishing adventures made her smile. But beneath the quick wit, Syd's keen sense of observation picked up something more. Jake Sloan began to emerge as a loyal, grounded man who didn't back away from a conflict. At the same time she sensed a vulnerability he kept well hidden. Her earlier resolution to remain no more than neighbors was slowly melting away. This, she decided, was a man worth knowing.

She wasn't sure at what point she started to talk about herself, her parents' devastating death, her short stint with the Philadelphia police department, her friendship with Lilly and her breakup with Greg. The words flowed out, sometimes emotional, sometimes bitter, as they revealed a side of Sydney Cooper she didn't allow too many people to know.

"Seems to me, you should have dumped Bozo long ago," Jake said, using her nickname for Greg.

She leaned back against the cushion. "Looking back, I don't know why I didn't. We disagreed on so many issues. He is a strong supporter of the NRA, I want to ban guns from every household. He likes to hunt, I couldn't hurt a fly. His favorite movies are

Natural Born Killers, Pulp Fiction and *Die Hard,* while I tend to like romantic comedies."

"Why do you think you stayed in the relationship?"

She shrugged. "I guess I felt comfortable."

"Comfortable? Nothing more?"

"I loved him, if that's what you mean. I wouldn't have accepted his engagement ring otherwise. But maybe I didn't love him enough. Or I would have given him a second chance."

"In that case, you did yourself a favor."

"That's what Lilly says."

"I'm starting to see why the two of you are so close. You seem to have a lot in common." He watched her as he took another sip of his coffee. "She's the reason you ran out of here so fast last night, isn't she?"

She studied him as she ate. He asked a lot of questions, and while that made her a little suspicious, she wanted to trust him. She wanted to have someone, besides Chief Yates, with whom she could brainstorm.

After another second of hesitation, she took Lilly's postcard from her purse and handed it to him. She waited until he had read it before she told him why she had been so sure that Lilly had sent her a coded message.

He read the short note one more time before he looked up. "What if you were focusing on the obvious?"

"I don't follow you."

"The farmhouse. Lilly talks about spending her summers with you, at the farmhouse."

"And I told you that's wrong."

"Exactly. What if she was sending you a more cryptic message, rather than the obvious."

For a moment, Syd was completely silent as the words sank in and began to make sense. "Oh, my God," she said in a stunned whisper. "My parents' beach house! *That's* where she wanted me to go." She stood up. "Jake, you're a genius! An absolute genius!" She grabbed her purse and started searching for her keys.

"Where are you going?"

"Where do you think? Surf City."

"Oh, no, you don't. At least not tonight." Jake took the keys from her hand. "The only place you're going tonight is home. Tomorrow morning, *I'll* drive you to Surf City."

"I thought you were going to work on that pushy attitude of yours."

"I never said that, you did. And just in case you're planning on sneaking out after I close my door, be warned that I intend to bunk on the landing."

Syd laughed, secretly loving all the attention. "There's no need to do that. You proved your point. And you have my word that I won't try to sneak out."

"My back thanks you." He dropped the keys into her hand. "Good night, Sydney."

"Good night, Jake." At her door, she turned. "By the way, my friends call me Syd."

Fifteen

"When I said first thing in the morning," Jake grumbled as he opened his door, "I didn't mean at the crack of dawn."

Syd had slept like a baby and awakened at five, ready to go. The pain in her side, although much more tolerable, couldn't be completely ignored, but she wasn't about to say anything to Jake, who had appointed himself her protector and would insist on postponing the trip if she gave him the slightest reason to.

"And I had no idea you were so cranky in the morning," she replied. "What kind of a soldier are you, anyway?"

"An *ex*-soldier. A sleepy one at that."

"Here. This should perk you right up." She handed him a mug filled with strong Kona coffee.

He mumbled something she couldn't understand, but took the mug from her hand.

"How's the coffee?" she asked once they were in the SUV.

"Hmm."

By the time they merged onto the Benjamin Franklin Bridge, one of the four bridges that connected Philadelphia to New Jersey, Jake's mood had improved immensely.

"My uncle used to rent a house in Harvey Cedars for two weeks every summer," he said as they went through the toll booth. "He and my dad taught me everything I know about fishing."

"What were your summers like in Harvey Cedars?"

"The best. We fished from dawn to sunset, then we'd cook our catch and sit on the roof deck until the stars came out. The following day, we would start all over again."

"You never got bored?"

He sounded shocked at the question. "There's no time to get bored when you're fishing."

"But all that waiting for the fish to bite."

"That's part of the excitement. The great challenge. A battle of wills."

"My father would have agreed with you."

"Was he a fisherman?"

"Not a good one, but he always had fun trying." After a minute of silence, she glanced at him. "Have you had a chance to go to the waterfront yet?"

"No, why?"

"There are boats there available for charter. I

know it's not the best time of the year right now to go fishing, but in a couple of weeks we should start having some decent weather."

His grin was part surprise, part delight. "You want me to take you fishing?"

"Not me, silly. Your dad."

His happy smile faded. "How do you expect me to convince my father to go on a boat with me when he can't stand having me in the same room?"

"It'd be worth a try, don't you think? The worst he can do is say no."

They remained silent until they reached the causeway that connected the main land with the island. Syd inhaled deeply, breathing in the crisp ocean air. Surf City brought back memories of hot summer afternoons spent on the beach, sailing trips in Barnegat Bay and weekly clam bakes on her parents' deck.

Only eighteen miles long, with Barnegat Bay on one side and the Atlantic Ocean on the other, Long Beach Island was a ribbon of white sandy beaches, giant water slides and summer homes that ranged from modest cottages to opulent mansions.

Thanks to Eileen Cooper's talents as a hostess, the house on Sixteenth Street had been filled with guests all summer long—neighbors, friends and relatives, some of whom Syd didn't even know existed.

"That's what happens when you have a beach house," her father used to tease. "You discover cousins you never knew you had. And all of them have this sudden, uncontrollable urge to see you."

But on this dark, chilly March morning the island looked dismal and desolate. Not even the Summer Rental signs posted up and down Long Beach Boulevard could brighten up the gloomy look of the area.

"Which one is your house?" Jake asked as he turned onto Sixteenth Street.

"The three-story beach front at the end of the block."

As expected, the street was quiet and neighboring houses were still closed for the winter. Even nosy Mrs. Carpenter, who often came during the off-season to make sure she didn't miss any island gossip, had kept away.

After Jake had pulled the SUV onto the graveled driveway, Syd got out of the truck and led the way to the downstairs door. Once inside, she flipped on the light switch.

"We might as well start here," she said, pointing toward one of the three guest bedrooms. She stopped on the threshold of a small, cheery room with twin beds covered with yellow chenille bedspreads and matching pillows. "This is where Lilly and I slept."

They spent over an hour searching through each room, including the living area and master bedroom upstairs. They came up empty.

"Well, so much for your theory." Syd looked around her, at a loss where to look next. "It was a good one, though. I had high hopes."

"What's that over there?" Jake asked. "A shed?"

She joined him at the dining room window and followed his gaze. "No. That's my dollhouse. My father built it himself, board by board. Lilly and I used to—"

She never finished her sentence. Like a demon possessed, she grabbed a flashlight from the hutch drawer and tore down the stairs, Jake behind her. "How could I have been so stupid," she said, racing across the yard. "Lilly and I used to spend hours in that dollhouse. If she had anything to hide, this would be the place she'd choose." She handed Jake the flashlight. "Here, you hold this."

The small door had warped a little but she pulled it open easily.

Except for a lingering smell of mildew, everything was as she and Lilly had left it all those years ago. A small curtained window overlooked the yard and in the center was a table and two chairs, painted a bright red, with some of the paint chipped off.

"There aren't too many hiding places in here." Jake arced the beam of the flashlight across the small space.

"Just one that I remember." Excited now, Syd pushed the table aside and went down on all four. "When Lilly turned twelve, we decided to celebrate the momentous occasion by having our first cigarette." She ran her hand along the floorboards. "One of these boards was loose. That's where Lilly hid her Marlboros.

"I think it's this one," she said, feeling the slight bulging. She tried to pry it loose but couldn't budge it.

"Here, let me." Jake knelt beside her, slid his fingers beneath the board and pulled hard.

Dry and brittle with age, the board gave way, splitting in two. "Would you like to do the honors?" he asked.

Syd stuck her hand into the opening, hoping she wouldn't make contact with some unwelcome creature. Or worse, come out empty-handed.

Her doubts came to an abrupt end when her fingers felt something smooth and cold. "Jake, I found it!"

She brought out a zippered plastic bag, the kind used to store leftovers. With the flashlight now directly on the package, Syd pulled the zipper and took out a small rolled terry-cloth towel.

"It's Lilly's," she said.

"How do you know?"

"I've seen those same towels in her bathroom at home."

Jake touched the towel. "It's not wet, mildewed or even soiled, which means it was placed here fairly recently."

Syd tried to keep her euphoria under control as she unrolled the towel. Nestled into the dark green cloth was a gold chain, at the end of which hung a large opal. The clasp was broken and bits of dirt were embedded into the chain links.

"Is that Lilly's?" Jake asked.

"No way. Lilly hates jewelry. I can never get her to wear even a simple string of pearls." She looked up. "This must be what she wanted to show me the night she called. But why did she hide it?"

"My bet is that she knew she was being followed and wanted to get rid of it before those two men caught up with her."

Syd carefully rewrapped the package.

"That necklace is evidence, Syd."

"I'm aware of that. And I intend to turn it over to Chief Yates. But before I do that, I'll need to take a picture."

"What for?"

"I have a friend in Manayunk, a jeweler. If this isn't Lilly's, and I'm almost certain it's not, he might be able to tell me where it came from." She looked up. "You wouldn't happen to have a camera handy, would you?"

"No, but I saw an all-night drugstore less than five minutes from here."

"The chief never gets in before eight," one of the deputies said when Syd asked to see his boss.

"Could you call him and ask him to come here right away, please? What I have to show him is terribly important."

"He doesn't like to be disturbed in the middle of breakfast."

Syd looked at the man's name tag. "I promise you, Deputy Brady, that he'll want to see this." She patted the bundle in her arms, endured his resigned sigh and gave him an encouraging smile as he picked up the phone.

The chief walked in ten minutes later, in a worse mood than Jake had been earlier.

Nodding at Jake as Syd made the introductions, the chief grumbled a hello. "This better be worth it, Syd. I don't pass up my wife's buttermilk pancakes unless I have a damn good reason."

After setting the bundle on his desk, Syd unzipped the plastic bag, unrolled the towel and took a step back so the chief could see the contents.

"What the hell is that?"

"A necklace. I found it hidden in my old dollhouse in Surf City. Lilly put it there. That's what she wanted to show me when she called and asked me to meet her at the Elwood Diner."

She brought him up to date, explaining her initial misinterpretation of Lilly's message and her drive to the Branzinis' farmhouse on Thursday night. At the news that she had been shot, all sign of irritability vanished from the chief's demeanor.

"You were shot?" His gaze moved up and down, taking in every inch of her. "Where? Are you all right? Why aren't you in the hospital?"

"The bullet only grazed my rib. I was discharged yesterday afternoon. They needed the bed for a sick person," she added to break up some of the tension.

He didn't smile, but looked at Jake. "And you've got her running all over South Jersey when she should be in bed?"

"A SWAT team couldn't have held her down, Chief," Jake replied. "If I hadn't brought her, she was prepared to come down on her own."

The chief let out another grunt then lowered his head over the necklace, inspecting it closely. "Looks like it spent some time outside." With the point of a pencil, he flipped the broken catch. "And it could have been ripped off the neck of the person who was wearing it." He looked up. "Do you think that whoever took a shot at you was looking for this?"

"That's my guess," Jake said.

"Mine, too," Syd concurred. "Although there's a possibility that Lilly's kidnappers don't know about this necklace. Or don't care."

"Then why kidnap her?" the chief asked.

"Because she knew something." She didn't voice her fears that if her suspicions were correct, Lilly's abductors may have already killed her. She didn't have to. Everyone in this room knew that the odds of finding her alive were getting slimmer every day.

"I'll check that stone for fingerprints," the chief said. Taking possession of the evidence, he rolled-up the package.

"And in the meantime, I'll try to find out where the necklace came from." Syd told him about her friend in Manayunk.

"No," he said gruffly. "In the meantime, you go home. You've done enough for one day."

"If you say so," she said, having no intention of taking his advice. "Let me know what you find out, Chief. And give my regards to Vern, Ethel and Marie."

Sixteen

"Syd, don't be so damned stubborn. Let me take you home. Do what the doctor ordered, and tomorrow I'll take you to Manayunk."

Jake steered the SUV onto the expressway. It was still early and the only traffic was on the eastbound lane, where a stream of cars headed toward Atlantic City for another working day in the gambling town.

"Will you stop treating me as though I am an invalid?" Syd replied. "For the umpteenth time, I'm fine. And aren't I sitting? Resting? While you're doing all the driving?"

"It's not the same thing and you know it. Your wound could reopen."

She settled comfortably into her seat. "It hasn't. Of course, if you refuse to drive me, I'll have to drive myself. Would you rather I did that?"

"Blackmail is a crime, Counselor."

"Is that a yes?"

He let a short silence elapse before a small, resigned sigh escaped from his lips. "What were those directions again?"

She spent the rest of the trip telling him about Anthony Trudel. "I met him two years ago during a case I was prosecuting. He created quite a stir in the courtroom, but his testimony was one of the most credible I had ever heard. To this day, I'm convinced that he won the case for me. A few weeks later, he invited me to the grand opening of his new shop in Manayunk and we've been friends ever since."

"The last time I was in Manayunk, the town was undergoing a sort of renaissance."

"It still is. Many of the old mills were converted into fancy condominiums, and the addition of upscale boutiques, galleries and trendy restaurants along Main Street has brought in a whole new generation of visitors."

"What's the name of Anthony's shop?"

"Gold Rush. It's over there." She pointed down Main Street. "Tucked between the bank and the River Café."

It was almost noon on a Saturday and finding a parking space wasn't easy, but Jake showed more patience than she had expected. After circling the block three times, he found a space in a side street and slid the SUV into it.

Anthony was with a client when they walked in.

As he looked up and saw them, he grinned. A bejeweled hand went up discreetly, if that was possible, to indicate he'd only be a couple of minutes more.

While Jake walked around the store, Syd observed Anthony as he handed a pair of gold earrings encrusted with aquamarines to his customer, amazed that after two years of seeing him fairly regularly, he could still draw a smile out of her. Tall, attractive and openly gay, he wore colorful clothes with the same panache a runway model exhibited when wearing the latest fashions.

Gold Rush was a perfect reflection of his flamboyant personality. Chunky turquoise necklaces in every size and shape shared the limelight with more delicate pieces made out of semiprecious stones, which he preferred to diamonds and other expensive gems.

At last, the customer settled on a three-strand gold nugget bracelet, charged it to her platinum American Express and left.

Arms outstretched, Anthony came from behind the counter. "Darling, you're out of the hospital. And looking ravishing."

"Thank you, Anthony. And thanks for the flowers. They're gorgeous."

"No more so than you." He looked her up and down. "Can I hug you?"

She laughed. "Yes, you can hug me."

He gave her a little squeeze and whispered in her ear. "Darling, who is the hunk?"

"His name is Jake Sloan and he's straight," she whispered back. "So don't waste your charm on him."

Before Anthony could make another snappy remark, she motioned to Jake and waited until he had joined them before making the introductions.

Anthony held out his hand, palm down and let it dangle, like a delicate flower. "Charmed, I'm sure."

Syd held back a laugh. She had never seen a man look as awkward as Jake did at this very moment. A good sport, he shook Anthony's hand without crushing it. "Same here."

Reluctantly, Anthony tore his gaze away and returned his attention to Syd. "Have you heard anything about Lilly?" When she shook her head, he wrapped his arm around her shoulders. "You will. I have complete faith in you. But you stay away from flying bullets, you hear? You nearly gave me a heart attack."

"Don't worry. One bullet is enough to last me a lifetime." She was already digging into her handbag for the photograph she had taken with the drugstore camera. "In the meantime, you could do something for me."

Anthony was suddenly all business. "Anything."

Syd handed him the photograph. "I was hoping you could tell me where this came from."

"Not from my shop." He sniffed his disdain. "Too predictable. Not a bad piece, though. The chain appears to be antique silver and the stone, a fire opal from the looks of it, is also set in antique silver." He lowered the photograph. "Does this have anything to do with your being shot?"

"Maybe."

He nodded. "I'll see what I can do. It may take a couple of days. Is that all right?"

"That's fine. Thank you, Anthony. Now what do you say you let me take you and Jake out to lunch? Unless you have other plans?"

"For the pleasure of your company, my sweet, I'd cancel a date with Johnny Depp."

"Interesting fellow," Jake said two hours later as they headed back toward the city. "Why didn't you tell me he was gay?"

"I didn't think of it." She let out a chuckle. "And I'm glad. It was kind of fun watching you squirm while he put the moves on you during lunch."

"Not just me. He came on to every waiter in the place."

"Anthony's an incorrigible flirt. Everyone who knows him expects him to act the way he does."

"He must like you a lot to offer to paint your apartment."

"And I would have taken him up on his offer if I hadn't just asked him for a favor. Now I'd feel guilty, which is why I turned him down."

"So why not let *me* do it?"

She gave him a puzzled look. "You?"

"Don't look so surprised. Painting is one of my

many talents. That's how I put myself through college years ago." He swung onto the left lane to pass a slow moving car. "So what do you say, neighbor?"

"I don't know. That's a lot to ask of someone you've just—"

"Met twenty-four hours ago." He nodded. "Yes, I know. But you didn't ask. I offered."

He sounded so earnest that she couldn't risk disappointing him again. "Very well. Consider yourself hired."

Seventeen

Syd's Sunday passed in a flurry of activities, most of them conducted from the confines of her home, since neither Jake nor Dot would allow her out of the house.

True to his word, her handsome neighbor had showed up on Sunday morning, wearing white overalls, a baseball hat turned backwards and a huge grin. "Your personal painter reporting for duty, ma'am."

His good mood filled the apartment and lifted her spirits. Throughout the day, Jake painted, she made coffee and they laughed. He was so disarmingly charming that she found it increasingly difficult to remain objective. And to stay away from him. She tried by keeping busy with phone calls to Detective Ramsey and to Chief Yates, neither of whom had anything new to report. But for the most part, she sat in the spare room where Jake worked, and talked to him while admiring his handiwork. He hadn't exaggerated. He was good. Not a streak in sight.

By Monday morning she felt healed, rested and ready to go back to work. As she walked up Seventh Street a little after eight-thirty, her mind was already on the arraignment scheduled for ten o'clock a.m. This was one of A.D.A. Barbara Cummings's cases and Syd had spent part of last night reviewing it.

She had almost reached the D.A.'s office when a male voice called out her name.

Turning, she immediately recognized the law student who had returned the file she had left in the courtroom last week.

"Chad Quinn," he said, blushing slightly. "I was—"

"Yes, of course. Thanks for returning my file, Chad. I'm afraid I was a little distracted that day."

"You're welcome. I heard about what happened to you. I'm…I'm glad you're all right."

"Thank you."

With his middle finger, he gave a little push to his black-rimmed glasses. As he did, the stack of books he held in his arms slipped to the ground. His face turned beet-red. "I'm sorry."

Syd had noticed his shyness before, yet his questions were always insightful, suggesting he took his studies seriously. Sensing he had come to ask her a specific question, Syd gave him a gentle push. "Did you want to see me about something, Chad?"

"Actually, yes." He shifted his weight and the bundle in his arm once again began to shift dangerously. This time, however, he managed to hang on to it. "I was wondering if…you'd allow me to work for you."

"Aren't you a full-time student?"

"Third year at Temple Law. Your alma mater," he added proudly.

"So it is." She smiled. "You must have a full schedule."

"I also have several free hours each week and I'd like to spend them learning more about criminal law, preferably from…" He blushed again. "From someone like you."

"Chad, that's very flattering, but—"

"I'm a good worker," he said as he followed her into the building. "And I'd be a great help to you, especially now that you're so busy trying to find your friend."

She joined a small group waiting for the elevator. "How do you know that?"

"I was in court on Friday and I heard one of the A.D.A.s talk. That's when I got the idea of helping you out and learning at the same time." He didn't give her time to answer. "I can do just about anything—research, run errands, field phone calls, clip articles from newspapers, arrange your schedule, type. I'm an excellent typist."

"We have people who already do that."

"For free?"

"Did someone say the word free?" Ron Devlin had joined them. He looked pleased to see her. "All ready to give it hell, Counselor?" When he glanced at Chad, she made the introductions.

"Chad, this is District Attorney Ron Devlin. Ron, this is Chad Quinn, a third-year student at Temple Law. He wants to work for me, but—"

Ron turned to Chad. "What courses are you taking, son?"

Syd saw Chad's Adam's apple go up and down. "Criminal law, constitutional law, international law and advanced trial advocacy."

The elevator had left without them. "You're enjoying law school?"

"Frankly, sir, there are times I'd rather have an ice pick stuck in my eyeball."

Syd groaned inwardly. Whatever chances he may have had to work with her, he had just shot them down.

To her surprise, Ron laughed and turned to Syd. "Kid's honest. Grab him before someone else does. You can use the help." Another elevator had just returned and he hurried to it, leaving Syd and Chad behind.

"Well." Syd turned to Chad who was beaming. "I guess you're in."

Chad hugged his books and nodded happily. "When do I start?"

"When is your first class?"

"One o'clock this afternoon."

Both entered the next elevator. "In that case, you're starting right now."

In the reception room, Violet was holding the phone and waving at Syd frantically. "Detective Cranston," she said. "It's urgent."

Syd took the phone. "Yes, Detective?"

As usual, the man's voice was a few degrees below freezing. He didn't even bother to ask how she was feeling. "I've got Doug Avery in custody."

"I'll be right there." She handed the phone back to Violet and introduced her to Chad, explaining he'd be working for her on a part-time basis and would need a pass. She pointed to a door. "That's my office," she told Chad. "Go check my desk calendar and reschedule, if possible, any of the meetings I missed on Friday."

"Yes, ma'am."

"When you're done, crank up the computer and print anything you can find about the accident involving Senator Fairbanks's daughter and a Mrs. Ana Lee earlier this month."

Chad was already scribbling on a piece of paper. "I'll get on it right away."

"You're leaving?" Violet asked as Syd breezed on by. "You have an arraignment in—"

"Forty-five minutes. I know. Don't worry. I'll be there."

Looking as though he was ready to pick a fight, Doug Avery glared at Syd as she walked into the interrogation room. With his brush cut, square jaw and muscular physique, he bore a striking resemblance to martial arts actor Jean-Claude Van Damme and knew it. He had rolled up his shirtsleeves as high as they would go, exposing his biceps.

Unimpressed, Detective Cranston was leaning against the wall, waiting for Syd. He was in his late forties, with dyed blond hair Syd suspected concealed the gray, a thin mustache and watchful eyes. Like the rest of the police force, he made no effort to disguise his dislike for Syd. To his credit, however, he never let his animosity interfere with the job.

"All right," Avery said, addressing Cranston. "She's here, so why don't you tell me why you two clowns brought me in?"

"*I'll* tell you." Syd met his insolent gaze without flinching. "We brought you in because we want to know what you were doing outside the *Philadelphia Sun* on the evening of March 6th."

Avery shifted in his chair. "I don't remember."

"Then let me refresh your memory. You were waiting for Lilly Gilmore. When she came out, you started threatening her."

"I didn't threaten her. I went to talk to her."

"About what?"

"About what she's doing to me! Snooping around, talking to people, making my life miserable."

"You have something to hide, Mr. Avery? Something we missed during our initial investigation maybe?"

"Whatever that broad told you, she made it all up."

Syd leaned over the table. "You want to know what I think? I think Lilly Gilmore found something incriminating about you, something that could change the outcome of your trial in September. You got scared, so you tried to intimidate her. When that didn't work, you kidnapped her."

"*What?* You're crazy!"

"Where is she, Avery?"

He pushed his chair back. For the first time since the interrogation had begun, he looked scared. "She's trying to pin something on me," he told Cranston. "She can't do that, can she?"

Cranston shrugged. "She's the boss. She can do anything she wants. If I were you, I'd can the attitude and answer the question."

"I didn't kidnap nobody." He continued to ignore Syd and address Cranston. In his world, women of authority simply didn't exist.

"Can you prove it?" Cranston asked.

Avery seemed to search his memory. "Yeah, I can prove it. On March 6th, I left work at five-thirty and went to Moe's Hole on Front Street."

"Anybody there that can vouch for you?"

"The bartender. And two buddies from work— Tom Osborne and Jimmy Corona. Ask them where I was. They'll tell you."

Syd wrote down the names. "We intend to." But she already knew what the outcome would be. Avery wasn't the brightest person she had ever met, but he wasn't stupid enough to make up an alibi that could so easily be verified.

Looking up, she met Cranston's gaze and realized he, too, didn't believe Avery was the kidnapper.

"What happens now?" Avery asked.

The detective looked at Syd, waiting for instructions.

"We're going to check your alibi," Syd said. "Until then you'll be our guest."

"For how long?"

"It depends on how quickly we can locate your friends."

"Am I under arrest?" His confidence had returned. "If I am, I want to call my attorney."

"Would you like Detective Cranston to arrest you, Mr. Avery? Because right now, I've got enough on you to justify having your bail revoked. So either you go to your cell quietly, or I'll schedule a hearing. Which one is it going to be?"

Avery stood up. "I'll wait until you verify my alibi."

Eighteen

Whistling, Jake stood under the steaming shower and scrubbed white paint from his fingernails, not too thoroughly, since he planned on starting on Syd's hallway today. In fact, if van Heusen didn't make a move soon, he and Ramirez would have to assume the ex-colonel hadn't taken the bait. In which case, Jake would have enough time on his hands to paint every apartment in the building.

He was thinking of Syd, a habit that was becoming increasingly frequent, when his door bell rang. Cursing under his breath, he got out of the shower, wrapped a towel around his waist and went to answer it.

He was momentarily thrown at the sight of Agent Paul Ramirez standing on the landing, holding a toolbox. The dark suit and shiny oxfords had been replaced by scuffed work boots and gray overalls with the words Tony's TV Service printed on the front. A baseball cap covered his thick black hair and a clipboard was tucked under his arm. Although amused, Jake had to admit the agent definitely looked the part of a bored TV repairman.

"What play are you auditioning for?" he asked.

"Shut up and let me in."

Jake opened the door wide, then closed it. "Is all this cloak-and-dagger necessary? I feel like a character in an Agatha Christie novel."

"One of our operatives spotted a man in the park earlier. He was inconspicuous enough, minding his own business and feeding the squirrels, but he was also watching your building, so I'm taking no chances."

He followed Jake into the living room. "In the meantime, your 'accidental' meeting with your old pal, Ralph, did exactly what it was supposed to do." There was a twinkle in his eyes. "I didn't mean for you to go quite as far as you did, but what the hell, it worked."

"How do you know?"

The agent took out a folded newspaper from his clipboard and handed it to Jake. "I take it you haven't seen this?"

"Not yet." Jake read the account of his altercation with Ralph Gordon. The reporter had depicted Jake's "brutal and unprovoked attack" with semiaccuracy while reminding the readers about Jake's fall from grace fourteen years ago.

Jake handed the paper back to Ramirez. "I should have hit him harder."

"Lucky you didn't or he may have decided to sue you. This is much better. With this article, he played right into our hands. Of course, from now on, all telephone conversations between you and me will have to take place outside your apartment."

"There's no bug. I checked."

"There will be soon. Van Heusen will not take your return to Philadelphia at face value until he's absolutely sure he can trust you. Any questions?"

"No, but I'd like to talk to you about Sydney Cooper."

"What about her?"

"I'm not going to be pumping her for information."

"Why not?"

"Because she's a nice person and she trusts me. I don't want to betray that trust, or spy on her, or get into her files, or do whatever you expect me to do."

"Are you falling for her?"

"No! Where is that coming from?"

"Call it a hunch."

"Well, I'm not," Jake said a little too defensively. "I never felt comfortable with the idea of deceiving her in the first place, and now that I've met her, I *know* I don't want to deceive her."

Jake couldn't tell if Ramirez was upset about the decision or indifferent. "How is Ms. Cooper doing, by the way?" he asked casually. "I heard she got shot."

"She's recovering. The wound was only superficial."

"I'm glad to hear it." Ramirez tucked the clipboard under his arm. "I trust you'll be discreet, with Sydney I mean. In this kind of situation, romance and business don't mix well."

"I told you, there's nothing to worry about."

"Good." He made his way toward the door. Before he opened it, he added, "Good luck with van Heusen. It won't be long now."

"Syd, quick, turn on your TV set to Channel 6!" Violet sounded excited as she burst into Syd's office. "Chief Yates is about to hold a news conference."

After finding the remote under a pile of paperwork, Syd clicked it and found the right channel. This was as big as it got in Elwood, New Jersey, and she was anxious to see how the chief handled the sudden fame and the pressure that came with it.

To her surprise, he was the picture of calm and competence as he faced a crowd of more than twenty reporters and a dozen microphones. He stood outside the Mullica Township police building, with two solemn-looking deputies behind him, one of whom Syd had met the other morning.

"Good morning," the chief nodded at the crowd, "and thank you for coming. The search for Lilly Gilmore continues and I'm happy to report that more than a hundred local volunteers have joined us. At this time, most of our efforts are concentrated on the Pinebarrens, the Jersey shore and the Mullica River. Anyone with new information on the truck—a dark van with 'Shore to Please' license plates—or the abductors is asked to call the Mullica Township police department. Every lead and tip is being carefully investigated, so don't hesitate to come forward with what you know. I'll take a couple of questions."

As the crowd erupted, he put up his hand. "One at a time, please, or I'm out of here."

Syd smiled. "Way to go, Chief."

Violet gave a nod of approval. "I see what you mean. He's laid-back but tough. Tough is what you need to be with some of those reporters."

The cameras remained on Yates as someone asked, "You mentioned searching the Mullica River. Does that mean you've lost hope of finding Lilly alive?"

"No. It means that we are not overlooking any possibility."

"How many divers do you have?"

"Three. All from neighboring communities. We've already covered several miles up and down the river. More divers will be arriving tomorrow from the Chesapeake Bay area."

A voice that belonged to the ever-present Belle Chiaro rose above the crowd. "It's been five days since Lilly Gilmore was kidnapped, Chief, and you are no closer to finding her now than you were on Wednesday night. Will you be scaling back your search?"

If the chief was ticked off at the poorly disguised insult, he did a fine job of hiding it. "Would you be scaling back after only five days? Neither are we," he said. His steely gaze never wavered, as Belle sank back into the crowd. "If anything, we are broadening our search, thanks to the volunteers I mentioned earlier."

His gaze swept over the crowd. "And speaking of volunteers, we can always use extra people, so if you have time on your hands and would like to help, call our department. Doughnuts and coffee are on us."

A hand went up. "One more question, Chief. Do you think Lilly Gilmore is still alive?"

"I'd have to be a clairvoyant to answer that. I sincerely hope she is and if she is, we will find her."

Then, with another nod, he turned around and left, followed by his two deputies.

"Well done, Chief," Syd said.

"He sure put that bitch in her place, didn't he?" Violet clicked off the TV set. "People who bad-mouth cops make my blood boil. Don't they know by now that those men and women risk their lives every day to keep the rest of us safe?"

The wife of a retired police sergeant, Violet took every critical comment directed at any police department as a personal affront.

"And speaking of good men," she said. "Mr. Wonderful called."

Syd rolled her eyes. In a very short time, Jake Sloan had managed to charm every woman he had met—Dot, Nurse Pat at Erwinna Memorial and now Violet. "What did he want?"

"To make sure you had arrived safely."

"Is that what he said?"

"No. He wanted to know where you kept the turpentine, but I know better. He was checking up on you. That's kind of sweet. And he's painting your apartment. How cool is that? Frank would rather chew glass than paint. If I want it done I either do it myself or I hire somebody."

She stood up to return to her desk. "That one is a keeper, girlfriend. Don't let him get away."

"He's just a neighbor, not a suitor."

"I don't know. Seems to me that if it talks like a duck, and walks like a duck…" She winked and walked out, making quacking sounds and wobbling like a duck.

Still laughing, Syd was about to call Jake when Violet buzzed her.

"Mrs. Branzini is here. She looks upset."

Syd stood up. "Show her in."

But Dot, looking slightly disheveled, was already at her office door.

Syd walked over to her. "Dot, what is it?"

Dot's face was creased with worry as she handed Syd a note. "I was on my way to the market and I found this on my doorstep."

Syd looked down. Someone had cut large, colored letters out of a magazine and pasted them across the page. Together, they read: Your daughter will be returned to you in exchange for the sum of five-hundred-thousand dollars. Do not call the police. Further instructions will follow.

Nineteen

Syd could feel Dot watching her as she read the note. "That's good news, right, Syd? That means Lilly is alive."

Not necessarily. The note could be a trick meant to throw the police off track. Or it could be a cruel hoax. But Syd kept those thoughts to herself. Right now, Dot needed all the encouragement she could give her.

"I would think so. Most kidnappers know that in order to collect the money, they'll need to produce the person they kidnapped, unharmed."

"I have a hundred-thousand dollars in a bond fund. And another twenty-thousand in stocks—"

"Dot, you can't possibly be thinking of giving in to extortion. That's wrong."

"I don't care how wrong it is. This is my daughter we're talking about. Do you expect me to do nothing when I have the means of getting her back?"

"I want her back too, but not like that."

"Why not?"

Syd sighed. She had to tell her. "Because that ransom note could be unrelated to the kidnapping."

"You mean…" Dot searched Syd's face. "Someone is pretending to have Lilly?"

"It's possible."

"But you're not sure."

"No."

"Then I'll have to take a chance, Syd."

"You could lose the money."

"I don't care."

Syd nodded. Dot was reacting as any mother would, with her heart instead of her head. Trying to reason with her at a time like this would be a waste of time. "In that case," she said, "I have fifteen-thousand dollars in a money market. It's yours."

Dot pinched her lips in an attempt not to cry. "Thank you."

"But that's not nearly enough. Where are you going to raise the three-hundred-and-eighty-thousand dollars you'll still need?"

"I'm selling the farmhouse. Another developer approached me last week. He was willing to pay me a million for it. I'm sure he still wants it."

"A transaction like that will take weeks."

"Not if I tell him that I need part of the money right away, as a down payment."

Syd nodded. "And in case he doesn't agree, you might want to call Stan at the *Sun*. I'm sure his paper would be more than willing to make a donation."

Dot was already scribbling Stan's name on a piece of paper. "I'll do that. Thanks, Syd."

At 1:00 p.m., Jake left Syd's apartment and walked over to the nearby Tavern on the Square, an Irish pub on Locust Street that Ramirez had suggested he patronize while waiting for Victor to make his move. Sitting at the bar, he ordered a corned beef on rye and a Bud. He was sipping his beer and watching a March Madness basketball game on the TV hanging over the bar, when someone climbed onto the empty stool next to his and threw a folded copy of the *Philadelphia Daily Globe* on the counter.

"Five minutes in town and already you're in trouble," a familiar voice said.

Jake put his glass down and turned. All considering, the past fourteen years had been kind to Victor van Heusen. Except for the gray hair and a few more wrinkles around the eyes, he still looked like the fit, tough-as-nails man he had known during Desert Storm. Even in civilian garbs, there was an air of authority about him, a presence even the jaded bartender seemed to notice. Maybe it was his rigid stance, or the confident look in those steely blue eyes. Whatever it was, it commanded instant respect.

Jake allowed just enough surprise to show in his eyes before he spoke. "What the hell are *you* doing here?"

"Oh, I don't know. Call me sentimental. I read that jerk's article and I got pissed off."

"So you thought you'd look me up and comfort me?"

"Do you mind?"

Jake shrugged. "It's a free country."

"That's debatable." He looked around him, sizing up the small crowd. "I wasn't sure how you'd react if I came knocking at your door, so when I saw you walk in here, I followed you. I figured that meeting on neutral ground was a better bet."

Jake pretended to be shocked. "You've been watching me?"

"Don't make it sound like the crime of the century. I wanted to talk to you."

Jake took a bite of his sandwich and returned his attention to the game.

"Look." Victor hitched his stool a little closer. "I know you're pissed, and I don't blame you. But, Jesus, man, it's been fourteen years."

"Is that an apology?"

"Do you want an apology?"

"I want you to leave me alone."

When the bartender approached, Victor ordered a Miller Lite and waited until the beer had been poured before saying, "I'm sorry about your father."

Jake kept on ignoring him. Was he overdoing it? Should he show a little more interest? Ramirez had told him to follow his gut instincts, but so far, they hadn't told him a damn thing.

Glass in hand, Victor seemed to be following the action on the screen as well. "You think I've let you down," he said after a while.

Jake gave him a scathing look. "Are you under the delusion that you didn't?"

"I did what I did in order to survive. I just couldn't face twenty years in prison."

Jake watched Arizona State score a three-pointer. "But you thought nothing of letting one of your officers go down with you."

"You could have told the truth, Jake. Why didn't you?"

"Maybe because I cared about what happened to you. A lot more than you cared about what happened to me."

Victor was silent for a long time. When he spoke again, his voice was more subdued. "Don't you want to know how I'm doing?"

"Not particularly."

"I'll tell you anyway, because I think you'll appreciate it. I run a militia, one that is gaining momentum all over the country."

Jake turned around on his stool and hoped his shocked expression looked genuine enough to fool Victor. "You became a right-wing activist?"

"You sound surprised."

"I am. Militia is synonym with militant, isn't it?"

"Militia stands for freedom. I created it to protect the freedom and rights of all Americans."

"Last time I looked, my rights were being protected just fine."

"You better think again, Jake. This administration is run by a bunch of clowns, puppets who don't know the first thing about leadership. As a result, our allies have lost faith in us, our jobs have gone off shore and we are faced with a five-hundred-million-dollar deficit. It's clear that we need to restore the prosperity, honor and dignity this great country deserves."

Wow. Old Victor wasn't holding back any punches. "You have the right to believe what you want, but that kind of propaganda is wasted on me."

"Oh, come on. I know you, kid. Deep down, you're as bitter about how the army treated you as I am."

"Considering we lied, I'd say we both got what we deserved."

"We got *screwed,* Jake. Between you and me, we gave the army thirty years of exemplary service. And what did we get in return? A kick in the ass."

"You're right about one thing. I was pissed off at first, but not anymore. I have a good job, enough money to retire if I want to, and if I can mend fences with my father while I'm here, my happiness will be complete. So do me a favor, will you, considering you owe me one? Leave me the hell alone. I've got enough problems."

But Victor wouldn't give up. "That's why I'm here. I'm offering you a little distraction from those problems. Come to the camp for dinner. I'll have my cook prepare something special. I guarantee you, that alone is worth the trip."

"No thanks."

Figuring this was as good a time as any to make his move, Jake took a handful of bills from his jeans pocket and dropped them on the counter. Then, with a two-finger salute, he walked out.

He waited until he was inside his building before calling Ramirez. "Victor made contact," he said when the agent answered.

"How did it go?"

"Pretty much as you said, although he sounds a lot more dangerous than you've led me to believe."

"What makes you say that?"

"The way he talks about our government, the military. The man is carrying a huge grudge."

"I'll pass your thoughts along. Did he make plans to see you again?"

"He invited me to have dinner at his camp. I turned him down and walked out."

"Excellent. I suggest you make the tavern your regular watering hole from now on. And next time he invites you, take him up on it."

Twenty

As expected, Doug Avery's alibi had checked out. After several attempts, Detective Cranston had finally caught up with the witnesses and all three had confirmed Avery's story. The construction worker had been at Moe's Hole on the evening of March 6th and had remained there until closing time.

Unfortunately for him, however, while being detained, he had become enraged with his guard and had threatened to make oatmeal out of him unless he brought him a decent dinner.

Detective Cranston and Syd had agreed that keeping Avery behind bars was no longer a choice. It was a necessity.

Surprisingly, this time around, Victor van Heusen had not provided an attorney, making it necessary for the court to appoint a public defender.

On Tuesday morning, Syd sat in the courtroom,

patiently waiting for the twenty or so cases ahead of hers to be heard. At last, the bailiff called number twenty-seven on the docket—People vs. Avery. Syd watched Doug Avery being escorted into the courtroom. Hostile as usual, he threw her a look charged with venom before sitting beside his new attorney. Aware of her client's volatile temper, the woman looked nervous as well as inexperienced.

After introducing herself to the judge, in front of whom she had appeared several times, Syd stated her case, explaining that Doug Avery had proven that he was a menace to society, once by threatening Lilly Gilmore and the second time by nearly attacking a prison guard.

"The people respectfully request that Douglas Avery remain incarcerated until his trial on September 23rd."

"Can you provide proof that he threatened Ms. Gilmore?" the judge asked.

"Yes, Your Honor. Hank Vogel, a security guard at the *Philadelphia Sun,* has made a statement to that effect and is prepared to—"

Her cell phone, which she had forgotten to turn off prior to being called, chose that inopportune moment to ring. As she reached into her purse, Judge Archer leaned forward, clearly annoyed.

"Ms. Cooper, you know that all phones must be turned off before you enter the courtroom."

"I'm sorry, Your Honor." She glanced at the caller ID. Chief Yates. He knew she had court this morning. He wouldn't be calling her unless it was vitally important. "Your Honor. I need to take this."

"You *need* to go on with your case, Counselor."

"Your Honor." She took a shallow breath. "The call is from the Mullica Township chief of police."

The judge would have had to be from outer space not to know that Chief Yates was investigating the kidnapping of Lilly Gilmore. He waited a beat and did not glance at the defense counsel, who was trying to decide whether or not she should protest. "Make it brief," he said with a nod.

"Hurry up, Chief," Syd whispered into the phone. "I'm in court—"

"I know. I talked to Channel Three and they've agreed to interview Dorothy Branzini today at four, outside her home. Dot would like you to be there."

He could have left a message with Violet. There had to be more. "I can arrange that. Anything else."

"Bring Lilly's toothbrush with you."

Syd's stomach tightened. Toothbrushes were often used to determine DNA. "Why?"

"We found the van. There were traces of blood in the back seat."

Her mouth dry, Syd clicked off her phone.

"Ms. Cooper?" Judge Archer crossed his arms over his desk. "Are you all right? Do you need a minute?"

Syd shook her head. "I'm fine, Your Honor. And ready to proceed."

"Then do so."

Ten minutes later, having listened to both attorneys, Judge Archer made his ruling and revoked Avery's bail.

As a guard approached the defendant, Avery jumped up and turned toward the gallery. "You're not going to let them take me away, are you?" he screamed at someone in the back.

Syd followed his gaze and saw Victor van Heusen sitting in a back row. Arms crossed over his chest, he remained silent and stern-looking as he watched Avery.

The guard snapped handcuffs on Avery's wrists.

"General?" Then, as Avery realized that his commander wasn't going to acknowledge him, he went into an attack mode. "You son of a bitch," he hurled over his shoulder as two guards dragged him out of the courtroom. "I'll bury you, you hear? I'll bury you if it's the last thing I do."

Syd waited until he was gone before approaching van Heusen.

Smiling his usual affable smile, he greeted her with the utmost courtesy. "Ms. Cooper. It's good to see you again."

"What was that all about?" she asked.

"You mean Avery?" He shrugged. "That was just a case of sour grapes on his part. He called me yesterday to say he needed my attorney's services again. I told him that he had made one mistake too many and that I was washing my hands of him."

"I gathered that much. What I want to know is what he meant when he said he would bury you."

Another shrug. "I'm sure that's just a figure of speech, the expected reaction of a resentful man, nothing more." He glanced at his watch, then back at Syd. "Is that all, Ms. Cooper? I have a rather pressing engagement."

As much as she would have liked to question him further, she had no reason to detain him any longer. "Yes, that's all."

She watched him walk away, his steps so sure and precise he appeared to be marching. Had she been too quick in dismissing Avery *and* van Heusen in Lilly's kidnapping? Or was Avery's outburst totally unrelated?

The courtroom was filling up again. Her coat over her arm, Syd headed for the exit. If she couldn't get the answers she wanted from van Heusen, she would get them from Avery himself.

To her surprise, Detective Cranston was already at the jail. When he saw her, he walked over, looking grim. "Avery was badly beaten," he said as she pinned a visitor's badge to her jacket.

"Beaten? By whom? He just got here."

"Three cellmates claim that he went crazy after they brought him back from the courtroom, and attacked them."

"Where was the guard?"

"He was already gone."

"Did you question him?"

Cranston nodded. "He says Avery was just fine when he left him."

Syd thought about her conversation with van Heusen, how unfazed he had been by Avery's outburst. Arranging to have a prisoner beaten wouldn't be difficult, not for someone with van Heusen's connections. "Where is he?" she asked.

"They took him to the infirmary."

"I want to see him."

"You may not be able to talk to him. From what I understand he's pretty much out of it."

"I'll chance it."

He escorted her down a flight of stairs and a hallway.

"You can only stay a few minutes," a nurse told them as they entered the infirmary. "He's been heavily sedated."

Avery lay on a gurney, partitioned from other patients by a wraparound curtain. He looked bad. Both eyes were swollen shut. His bottom lip was split and still bleeding, and his chest had been wrapped in a tight bandage. He appeared to be sleeping.

"Mr. Avery?" Syd bent over him. "Doug? Can you hear me?"

One eyelid fluttered open.

"Did you start that fight, Doug?"

His hand moved to his stomach and rested there. "Go 'way."

"Doug, listen to me. I can help you. I can have you put in solitary where no one will be able to touch you. But you've got to help me out. Tell me the truth. Did van Heusen arrange for this beating?"

He looked at her and for a moment she thought he was going to cooperate. Her hopes were short-lived. "I did it," he said, speaking with difficulty. "I started the fight." He moistened his bloody lip. "I was pissed off. Started hitting."

She glanced at Cranston who stood on the other side of the gurney. He shook his head as if to say, "you're not going to get anything out of him."

She bent closer to Avery's ear. "What did you mean back in the courtroom when you told van Heusen that you'd bury him?"

He had closed his eyes.

Someone touched her shoulder. "You'll have to leave, Ms. Cooper. My patient needs rest."

She straightened up and turned to see a doctor standing behind her. She nodded to him before motioning to Cranston to follow her. "He's lying," she said, walking briskly down the narrow hallway. "He didn't start that fight. He's just too damned scared to say so."

"I'm inclined to agree, but that's not going to help you."

"I want a twenty-four-hour guard on him, and when he's released from the infirmary, make sure he's put in solitary. I'm not finished with him."

Twenty-One

From the jail, Syd hurried to Lilly's town house, took her toothbrush from the bathroom holder and dropped it into a plastic bag. She tried to tell herself that the bloodstains in the back of the van did not necessarily mean that the victim had suffered a mortal wound. Knowing Lilly, she had put up a fight and had gotten a little banged up in the process.

That thought kept Syd's morale from sinking to an all-time low as she sat in the back of a taxi for the ride across town.

Dot was already outside her town house, being prepped by one of the television producers. Members of her family were there as well. Her brother Joe, the star of the hit review *Divas in Drag,* had apparently rushed from an afternoon matinée with part of his stage makeup still on. Dot's sister Luciana was also here, along with her daughter Angie, the rebellious college student who fought for more causes than Syd could name. Even Roman, Luciana's son and a drag car racer, had come to offer his support. Not your everyday, average family for sure, but all were truly wonderful people, caring, generous and devoted to each other.

"Dot." Syd went to her, not sure if she knew about the van. "Sorry I'm late." She looked questioningly at Chief Yates, who stood nearby.

"It's okay, Syd." She felt Dot's hand squeeze hers. "It's not Lilly's blood."

The knot in Syd's stomach began to relax. "Then it's not the right van?" she asked the chief.

"Oh, it's the right van all right, right down to that soccer ball decal you described. The Somerset police in North Jersey recovered it. It was reported stolen several days ago and was found abandoned behind an old warehouse off Route 287 just this morning. They notified me immediately."

"And the blood?"

"The owner of the van is the mother of four boys. The blood came from a bloody knee her youngest son suffered during a basketball practice."

"Any fingerprints?"

"We're still working on that, but I don't expect we'll find anything useful. Those guys are too clever."

Uncle Joe walked over to where she stood. He was a short, stocky man with thick gray hair and a gravelly voice that had become his trademark.

"You look pale, honey," he said, looking at her through heavy eye makeup. "You want to sit down? I can find you a chair. Angie, go get Syd a chair."

"I'm fine, Joe, really. It's been a trying day, that's all."

"Mrs. Branzini?" The young producer smiled at Dot. "We're ready for you."

"Remember," the chief warned. "Don't mention the ransom note. You want the kidnappers to know that you're following their instructions to the letter."

Dot nodded, adjusting the lapel of her bright blue suit. Her relatives, all looking solemn, took their places behind her. The cameraman raised his hand, lowering one finger at a time and they were on.

A TV 3 reporter spoke into a mike. "Good afternoon," she said seriously. "We are talking to Mrs. Dorothy Branzini, the mother of kidnapping victim Lilly Gilmore." She turned to Dorothy. "Good afternoon, Mrs. Branzini."

"Good afternoon," Dot said a little stiffly.

"This must be a trying experience for you and your family. How are you coping so far?"

"I'm doing my best, but it's difficult. I thank God each day for the love and support of my family and this wonderful community. Several of my neighbors have volunteered to help Chief Yates look for Lilly. I'm so grateful."

"I believe that you want to say something to your daughter's abductors?"

"Yes." Behind her, Joe and Luciana each put a hand on Dot's shoulders.

"Please go ahead."

Dot looked directly into the camera and began. "This is much more than a statement," she said, her voice firm and clear. "It's an appeal to the men who kidnapped my daughter, a desperate plea for you to return Lilly safe and sound. I don't know why you took her, or what you intend to do with her. Whatever your reasons are, please think of the fear and pain you have brought to all those who love Lilly— me, her little daughter, who still doesn't know that her mother was kidnapped and wouldn't understand even if she knew. Her relatives, her friends, her co-workers. All are terribly worried, so I beg you, put an end to this agony and let Lilly return."

She attempted a smile, but couldn't quite pull it off. She handed the mike back to the reporter who had remained off camera.

"Thank you, Dorothy. We are all praying for Lilly's safe return."

"Thank you."

Joe and Luciana were already hugging Dorothy and there were a few misty eyes in the audience as well. Most of them were neighbors who had come in support of Dot.

"You think this will do any good?" Chief Yates asked Syd.

"Dot believes it will," she said skeptically. "And that's all that matters."

* * *

Violet looked up as Syd walked in. "Dot did great, Syd. She wasn't nervous at all."

"The good news may have helped."

"What good news?"

"The van used to kidnap Lilly was found abandoned in North Jersey with traces of blood in the back seat. It turned out to be a false alarm."

"Wrong van?"

"Wrong blood. The van belongs to the mother of four boys and the blood came from one of the boys' scraped knee."

"Are you relieved or disappointed?"

"Good question, Violet." Syd sat down across from the secretary's desk. "The truth is, I don't know. What I do know is that we're right back at square one."

Violet made a compassionate sound. "Why don't you call it a day?" she said. "You've been working much too hard for your first day back. Go home, honey. I'm sure Ron won't mind."

"You must have read my mind—that's exactly what I was thinking of doing. But first, I need your advice about something." She reached into the briefcase she had set on the floor and took out a small pad and a pencil. "I need you to help me plan a gourmet dinner for tomorrow night."

Violet's eyes brightened instantly. "Would that be a dinner for two, by any chance?"

"As a matter of fact, it is. I want to do something

for Jake in return for all the time he's been spending painting my apartment."

"That's a wonderful idea. You want me to cook the dinner?"

Syd laughed. "No, silly. I'd never ask you to do something like that. *I'm* going to cook it."

Violet's face fell. "You? But honey, you can barely boil water."

"Jake doesn't know that. In fact, he thinks I'm a great cook."

Violet burst into peels of laughter. "Where did he get an idea like that?"

Syd smoothed down her skirt. "I may have said something to that effect."

"Oh, you sly vixen, you, trying to get a man through his stomach."

Syd felt her cheeks color. "I'm not trying to *get* him, Violet. I told you I just want to repay him for all he's done."

"You could have bought him a gift certificate from Home Depot."

"Too impersonal."

"You like him. Why don't you say so? What's so wrong in admitting that you're smitten with the man?"

If this had been anyone other than Violet, Syd would have put an end to this conversation right now. "Because I'm not smitten. I'm just a little… He intrigues me, okay?"

"Has he made any moves toward you?"

"No!"

"Ah, and therein lies the attraction." She raised a hand to silence Syd, who was about to protest. "Don't deny it. I've been there." She leaned forward and whispered. "That's how George won me over—by playing hard to get."

"Playing hard to get isn't Jake's style. I think he's just…not interested."

"Oh, honey, I find that difficult to believe."

"The dinner?" Syd reminded her.

"The dinner. Okay." Violet tapped her chin. "Let's see. How fancy do you want this dinner to be?"

"Not too fancy. Jake is a down-to-earth kind of man. At the same time, it should be sophisticated enough for him to be impressed."

"French or Italian?"

"French. I was thinking maybe that dish you made the last time I ate at your house?"

"The cassoulet?" Violet shook her head. "Forget it. The beans burn too easily and we all know that you have a tendency to burn food. How about a stew? Men love stews. Of course, the French don't call it stew. They have names like *bœuf bourguignon* or veal Marengo, or *poulet chasseur.*"

Syd was writing furiously. "Spelling, please."

By the time she walked out of the building, Syd knew more about French stews than she'd ever wanted to know. She had a complete shopping list, recipes and a selection of wines to serve with each dish.

Now all she had to do was choose one and then cook the damn thing.

* * *

Behind the wheel of his rented Explorer, Jake coasted down Christopher Columbus Boulevard and scanned the waterfront area. He hardly recognized it from the days when he used to come here with his father and his older brother to look at the tall ships. A smart developer had turned the area into prime property by refurbishing several piers, adding luxury condominiums, nightclubs, restaurants and even a Dave & Buster's, an amusement establishment that boasted seventy-thousand square feet of food and fun under one roof.

After parking in D&B's garage, Jake walked down to the docks for a closer look at the impressive display of large boats—Silvertons, Sea Rays and Vikings. Several slips down, he stopped. In front of him was a Stolkraft 450 with a sign taped on the aft window— Available For Charters—555-6413. On its hull, the name *Three Naughty Nurses* was written in bold script letters. Entirely built in Australia, the Stolkraft was designed with a unique hull that provided great maneuverability and outstanding stability. This particular model featured a well-laid-out bridge that could easily sit eight, a roomy aft deck and a swim platform.

It was just the kind of boat his father had dreamed of sailing one day.

"Purty, ain't she?"

Jake turned to see a middle-aged man in a lumberman jacket standing beside him. Jake nodded and returned his attention to the boat.

"I work at the marina," the man said, nodding toward a one-story building behind them. "Owners put her back in the water a couple of days ago. If you're interested in chartering her, she's available. She comes equipped with a captain and a cook who doubles as a clean-up person."

"You said 'owners'?"

The man chuckled. "Three nurses from Hahnemann Hospital. They bought it as an investment and so far it's paying off. Last season, the boat was booked solid from April through November."

Jake glanced at the phone number again and memorized it. "Thanks for the info," he told the man.

"Sure thing. Don't wait too long, though. The Naughties are popular 'round here."

"I'll keep that in mind."

Twenty-Two

Two hours later, Jake called his father. As had been the case every day since that first ill-fated visit, Wendell let the machine pick up the call.

Jake cleared his throat. "Hi, Pop. Look, don't cut me off, okay? Hear me out. I've chartered a boat. Just for you and me. We can go anywhere you like, not right away, but maybe in a couple of weeks when the weather breaks. We can fish or just cruise, whatever we feel like doing. The boat comes with a staff—a captain and a cook who also cleans. Can you believe that? I told them to forget about the cook. We'll do our own cooking and cleaning. We always have."

He stopped, half-hoping his father, intrigued, would pick up the phone. Jake held back a sigh. "So what do you say, Pop? You feel like doing a little sailing down the coast? Maybe to the Chesapeake?" Still no answer. "Give me a call so we can decide when and where."

He left his cell phone number and waited another beat on the off-chance Wendell had a change of heart.

"Love you, Pop," he said and hung up.

His phone rang just as he was coming out of the Dave & Buster's garage. His hopes faded quickly, however, when he recognized Agent Ramirez's voice.

"May I speak to Nancy, please?" the agent said, using the code phrase they had agreed on.

"It's all right, Paul. I'm clear."

"Your apartment is now bugged," the agent announced as though this was an everyday occurrence. "The same man we spotted in the park the other morning went into your building shortly after you left, carrying a ladder, and installed a sophisticated listening device the size of a credit card. It's powerful enough to pick up conversation from anywhere in the apartment."

Jake didn't ask how the man, or Ramirez, had gotten into his apartment. He was dealing with pros, on both fronts. "Where did they put the bug?"

"On the ceiling fan. Oh, and your friendship with Sydney Cooper has not gone unnoticed."

"What makes you think that?"

"There's an identical device planted in her apartment."

"Oh, honey," Violet said on the other end of the line. "You should have started with something simple."

Syd switched the phone to her other ear and let her gaze sweep over her kitchen counter, where an array of food and utensils she never knew existed lay before her. Yes, why hadn't she stuck to something she could handle? Like mac and cheese. Or Campbell's mushroom soup over toast. But no, she had to impress her dinner guest and choose a complicated French recipe.

Violet had made the dish sound so easy. A little of this, a little of that, simmer, add salt and pepper, and voilà, veal Marengo. The recipe lay beside a bag of mushrooms, looking much more daunting now than it had a couple of hours ago.

"Maybe you still have time to order takeout?" Violet suggested.

"No, no takeouts. I told Jake I was going to surprise him with something special and I'm not backing down. The man has already painted two rooms and the hallway. I have to do something to show him my gratitude."

"Oh, honey." Violet's voice dropped down to a sexy whisper. "I'm sure you could think of something he'd enjoy much more than food."

"Do I look the type who would jump in bed with a complete stranger?"

"He's not a stranger if he's painting your apartment."

Syd picked up a shallot and turned it around in her hand. "This is going to be a disaster."

"You're not building a rocket, honey. Just a dish.

Now put me on the speaker phone and let's get started. Are you ready?"

"Not really."

"Have a glass of wine. It'll relax you."

Syd wasn't much of a drinker, especially on an empty stomach, but she had to agree that right now, a glass of wine sounded like an excellent idea. She picked up the bottle of Napa Valley sauvignon blanc Violet had recommended and filled up a glass. She took a sip, and another. It was cool, smooth and easy on the tongue, not like those dry, harsh wines Greg had preferred.

"Now I'm ready," she said, putting the glass down.

For the next half hour, Syd sautéed, chopped and stirred until all the ingredients were in the pot, simmering gently and oh, miracle of miracles, letting out a delicious aroma.

"By George, I've done it!" she exclaimed.

"I told you it was easy."

Syd covered the pot and picked up the phone again. "Thanks, Violet. You're a lifesaver."

"We'll make a Julia Child out of you yet. Now go get all sexied-up and have a good time."

Syd hung up and went to get ready. But when she glanced in her bedroom mirror, she let out a horrified laugh. The simple task of peeling and chopping onions had brought an abundance of tears, resulting in smeared mascara, raccoon-style. There was flour in her hair and a streak of tomato paste on her right cheek.

Thankfully she had two hours until Jake was due to arrive. Plenty of time to take a relaxing bath, shampoo her hair and make herself presentable.

Ten minutes later, she stepped into a steamy, fragrant bath, lay back and closed her eyes.

By the time she climbed out of the tub, she was all mellowed out and feeling wonderful. After drying herself, she padded to her bedroom closet to inspect its contents.

"Go get all sexied-up," Violet had told her.

But how? There wasn't a single garment in her entire wardrobe that qualified as sexy.

Standing naked in front of her closet, she flipped through its contents. Several suits in shades of black, brown and navy went from one side of the rod to the other, followed by skirts, slacks, an elegant black dress Greg had bought for her, and half-a-dozen blouses.

Hopeless. She may have looked great in the courtroom, but none of those outfits would dazzle a man.

Maybe she should keep the evening casual and greet him in a pair of sweats. Or…

Her hand stopped on a hanger. The dress had been the last one on the rod, pushed all the way to the back and forgotten. She took it out almost reverently, her eyes moving slowly along the light blue garment, a silky, shimmery little nothing she had bought six years ago for Lilly and Mike's first wedding anniversary bash.

She held it in front of her and looked in the mirror. It was as stunning now as it had been then. The question was, did it still fit? A diet of hot dogs on the run and nightly takeouts didn't exactly keep a girl's figure looking like Elle Macpherson's.

Not bothering to put on underwear, she slid into the dress, zipped it with more ease than she had expected, and looked at her reflection again.

"Wow."

The low scooped neck showed just enough cleavage to keep a man guessing, and the hem, which fell halfway to her thighs, showed off her legs, which weren't half-bad. To go with the dress, she had bought silver, high-heeled sandals that added four inches to her height. She dug them out from under a stack of boxes and put them on.

Now that was hot.

Too hot? As in too obvious?

"Well, it's either this," she said to her reflection, "Greg's sedate black dress or the sweats."

The blue dress won, hands down.

An hour later, her hair blown out in a soft, slightly mussed up style and her nails done, she spritzed herself with a cloud of Chanel No. 19 and was pinning on pearl studs when the bell rang.

After one last look in the mirror and a thumbs-up sign, she went to answer it.

Twenty-Three

"Hi." Jake held up the bottle of white burgundy. "I wasn't sure what you were making, so I played it safe and—"

The rest of his sentence caught in his throat. His mind no longer on the wine, he looked at the vision standing in front of him and felt his head go fuzzy. In those high heels, Syd's legs seemed to go on forever. And what legs. Slender, shapely, creamy white and bare. The rest of her was just as spectacular. The dress, a little number meant to raise a man's blood pressure to new heights, clung gently to rounded hips, a narrow waist and high, full breasts that swelled enticingly above the neckline.

Looking amused, Syd took the bottle from his hand. "You were saying?"

"I forgot."

"Hmm. I'll take that as a compliment." She

waved. "Come on in. We can have a glass of wine while I—" She stopped and sniffed the air. "Do you smell something burning?"

Before he could agree, she let out a shriek and ran toward the kitchen.

He followed her. She had taken the lid off a pot and was stirring frantically, looking totally distraught.

"I burned it! I burned the veal Marengo."

Jake cautiously approached the stove. There was no doubt about it. A distinctive scorched smell rose from the pot.

"It's ruined!" She was dangerously close to tears.

"Not necessarily. Do you have a potato?"

She gave him a blank look.

"To put in the pot," he explained. "The starch in the raw potato will absorb most of the burned taste."

She didn't look convinced. "Where did you hear that?"

"From an old Cajun man I know."

"Does it work?"

"I've burned my share of rice and beans in my time. Trust me, it works."

She opened a small wooden bin, took out a shriveled potato, and handed it to him. "I don't know how old it is."

"It will have to do." He took a knife from the counter top, quickly peeled the potato and dropped it into the pot.

Syd still didn't look convinced. "Now what?"

"We have a glass of wine and wait."

Familiar with the kitchen, now that he spent most of his time in Syd's apartment, Jake found a corkscrew and opened the bottle. While she watched, he filled the two long-stemmed glasses she had already set on the counter and handed her one. "To Mr. Marengo," he said, touching his glass to hers. "Whoever he is."

Syd took a sip. "Marengo wasn't a man. It's an Italian town where Napoléon defeated the Austrian army."

"And the town was famous for the dish you made?"

"Not until Napoléon's cook made it famous. After the battle, French food supplies were seriously depleted and the general sent his cook to look for provisions. He came back with chickens, vegetables, herbs and wine, all of which he had stolen from local farmers. The dish was later adapted to veal and became very popular."

"I'm impressed."

"Don't be. I just learned this today, from my friend Violet at the D.A.'s office."

"So this is your first try at veal Marengo?"

"This is my first try at anything beyond canned soup." She took a long sip of her wine, as though she needed an extra dose of courage. "I have a confession to make. I can't cook."

He was having difficulty keeping a straight face. "But you said—"

"I lied."

This time, he laughed. "Why?"

"I wanted to impress you. The truth is I live on takeouts and care packages from Dot Branzini. And the occasional can of soup."

He looked around him at the pot, now off the stove, and the array of utensils in the kitchen, some of which only a seasoned cook would know how to use.

She followed his gaze. "I bought all this today."

"And the dinner itself?"

"Violet walked me through each step of the recipe over the phone."

"You went to an awful lot of trouble."

"I wanted to do something special for you, to thank you for painting my apartment."

He gave her a long, appraising look that brought a flush to her cheeks. "You already have."

Half an hour later, the bottle of white wine finished and another one opened, they sat at a small round table Syd had set in front of the fireplace. The salad, already on their plate, was excellent and the potato trick had lived up to its reputation. While the fire crackled and Roberta Flack entertained them on the CD player, they ate and drank heartily. Syd talked about her day, which had been spent, for the most part, in the courtroom, and about Dot Branzini's moving televised speech.

Aware that Victor was most likely listening to every word, Jake quickly steered the conversation toward something harmless before she could divulge information the militiaman had no business knowing. Fortunately, Syd didn't notice and went along. She had drunk more than her share of the wine, he realized, and was beginning to feel the effect.

As if on cue, she started to refill her glass and spilled some of the wine in the process. "Oops." She laughed. "Can you tell that I'm not much of a drinker?"

"In that case, I'm ready for coffee, if you are."

She raised her index finger. "And dessert. I didn't make it, though. I bought it."

She refused his help and managed to get everything, including an old-fashioned deep dish apple pie, onto the coffee table in the living room. Even mildly intoxicated, she moved with a fluidity that reminded him of a slow, seductive dance, and her mouth, puckered in concentration as she cut two generous slices, was so appealing that if it hadn't been for the bug he knew was recording every word and every sound, he would have kissed her.

"At least let me help you with the dishes," he offered when they were finished.

"Absolutely not." She snuggled up close. "I like this song. Do you like this song?"

He looked down at her, at her head on his shoulder, and once again cursed Victor. "Very much."

"It's called 'Kissing Me Softly.'" Eyes closed, she started humming it, terribly off-key. She let out a girlish giggle. "I have another confession to make. Two, actually."

"If you keep this up, I may have to call a priest."

The remark seemed to strike her as incredibly funny. "The first confession," she said when she finally stopped laughing, "is that I'm a little tipsy."

"Fortunately, you don't have far to drive."

Another burst of laughter. "You're funny, Jake Sloan. Do you know that?"

"What's the second confession?"

"I can't sing."

"So let's see." He took on a serious expression. "You can't cook. You can't drink. You can't sing. And you obviously can't keep a secret. What *can* you do?"

"I can dance."

To prove it, she stood up, more or less steady on her feet, and pulled him up. She was really smashed. It must have snuck up on her all of a sudden, because she had seemed reasonably sober during dinner.

"Now it's my turn to fess up," he said. "I'm not much of a dancer."

"Yes, you are. I can tell you are."

She hooked two deliciously scented arms around his neck. She had kicked off her sandals and her head barely reached his neck. "All you have to do is move to the music and—"

Her head fell against his chest.

"Syd?"

No answer. She was sound asleep.

As her knees started to buckle, Jake scooped her off the floor. "To bed you go, young lady."

By the time he reached her bedroom, she was snoring softly. He walked over to the big brass bed, pulled down the white comforter and lay her down gently. He drew a raw, lusty breath as he unzipped her dress and removed it. Underneath she wore lacy, pale blue bikini panties and a matching bra. Mesmerized, he took in every inch of that smooth, pale skin. He was aching to touch her, to feel the weight of those gorgeous breasts in his hands, to kiss them, to kiss all of her until she woke up.

Damn you, Victor.

His pulse beating like a drum gone wild, he kissed her lightly on the forehead, brought the comforter over her body and quietly left the room.

Back in the kitchen, he put the dishes into the dishwasher, found a box of Cascade and filled the soap dispenser. Moments later, the place was spotless, the dishwasher humming softly and he had made a fresh pot of coffee, which he set to start brewing at six o'clock the following morning. Satisfied, he turned off the lights, leaving only a small table lamp on, and let himself out.

Twenty-Four

Syd was awakened by the clang and hiss of the garbage truck six floors below as it made its early morning rounds. Curled up on her right side, she opened one eye, then the other, trying to focus on a point on the white pine wardrobe.

The effort almost took her head off.

"Ohhh." She sat up slowly.

The pain in her head, and the churning in her stomach were distantly familiar. She hadn't felt this lousy since a sorority party at Temple had put her out of commission for an entire day.

In plain language, she had a hangover.

Hoping her eyeballs wouldn't fall out, she glanced down and saw that she was only wearing her bra and panties. The blue dress lay neatly over the back of the Queen Anne chair, although she couldn't remember putting it there. Or taking it off. Or getting into bed.

Bits and pieces of the previous evening slowly made their way through her foggy brain. *Jake*. She had invited him over for dinner and had proceeded on getting royally drunk. How did it happen? How could she have *allowed* it to happen? The question was fairly easy to answer. She had been a nervous wreck. Between the cooking, the burning and trying to be the perfect hostess, she had stressed herself to the limits.

And the wine had been the perfect antidote for her condition. Unfortunately, she'd had too much of a good thing.

The last thing she remembered was standing on unsteady feet and trying to get Jake to dance.

The rest was a blank. She must have passed out. She let out another groan. How humiliating. She would never be able to face Jake again.

Aspirin. She needed aspirin. No, this kind of pain called for Exedrin Extra Strength. And a cup of strong coffee for added caffeine. Nothing else would do. With any luck, by the time she had finished her first cup, the throbbing inside her head would have stopped and she'd be able to go for a run. The cold and the workout would clear her head.

Taking small, careful steps, she walked into the bathroom, eyes half-closed, and helped herself to two Exedrin from the bottle in the medicine cabinet. She filled a tumbler with tap water and downed the pills quickly.

Still in her bra and panties, she walked to the

kitchen where another surprise awaited her. Last night's mess had been cleared away, and— She sniffed the air. What was that she smelled? Coffee?

A glance in the direction of the automatic coffee-maker confirmed it. The carafe was filled with freshly brewed coffee.

"Bless you, Jake." She took a mug from the cupboard, filled it with the fragrant brew and took it to the living room. The mug held firmly between her hands, she sat down on the sofa, sipped slowly, then pressed her head back against the pillows and waited for the pain to recede.

Comfortable in her gray sweats, ski jacket and sturdy sneakers, Syd jogged gently, per her doctor's instructions, as she breathed in the crisp, invigorating morning air. Thanks to the Exedrin, her headache had reached a manageable level and she felt human again.

She cherished those few laps around Washington Park every morning. She loved the earthy smell of the damp ground, the invigorating air, the solitude.

"Good morning. How do you feel?"

A grinning Jake had fallen into step with her. *That* she had not expected. "Foolish," she said honestly.

"Don't. Actually, you were kind of cute."

"Getting drunk? Making a fool of myself? Passing out? You call that being cute?"

"You're being too hard on yourself."

She had to ask. "Did I make a pass at you?"

He laughed. "Several."

"I'm sorry."

"No need to apologize. For your information, you were very hard to resist."

She was tempted to ask why he had, but didn't. Making a fool of herself while drunk was one thing, but sober?

"Should you be running so soon after your injury?" he asked as she started on her third lap.

"The doctor gave me his stamp of approval—as long as I don't overdo it."

She saw him glancing around the deserted park. "And you're not afraid to be here alone at this early hour?"

"An old legend is protecting me." She increased her pace but he seemed to have no trouble keeping up.

"Legend?"

"You're not aware that Washington Park is haunted?"

"No."

"When Washington's troops began falling in large numbers, the square was used as a mass grave." She pointed at a row of markers on the park's south side. "Twenty years later, Philadelphia was nearly decimated by a yellow fever epidemic. The graves were dug again to accommodate thousands of bodies. To keep grave robbers at bay, a Quaker woman by the name of Leah began patrolling the square late at night. Her spirit still exists."

He seemed amused. "Don't tell me you've seen it."

"No, but others claim to have, including a Philadelphia police officer. If you can't believe one of Philly's finest, who can you believe?"

"And that's why you feel safe?"

"Exactly. Even the homeless stay away from the park at night—they're afraid of coming face-to-face with Leah's ghost. This place doesn't start filling up until about midmorning."

They jogged in silence, perfectly synchronized. They were about to start on a new lap when Jake glanced across the street. "Who's the clown with the fancy car and the mirrored glasses?"

Syd followed his gaze. Across the street, leaning against a bright red Porsche, his arms crossed against his chest, Greg Underwood was watching them. Syd groaned.

"Another friend's ex?" Jake asked.

"No. This ex is mine."

"Are we talking about Bozo?"

"In the flesh." She wiped her face with her sleeve. "This will only take a minute." Then, remembering the incident with Mike Gilmore, she added, "No interference, Jake. I mean it. I'll handle Greg my way."

Jake put both hands up to indicate he was staying out of this one. Syd left the path and jogged across the street. Even in Dockers and a parka, her ex-fiancé looked as though he had just come back from a fashion shoot. His blond hair was perfectly combed and as he removed his sunglasses, his eyes seemed bluer than ever.

When she was close enough, he detached himself from the Porsche. "Hello, Syd." He started to kiss her cheek, but she turned away a half second before his lips made contact.

"I see that you've recovered from your injuries."

"What do you want, Greg?"

"Who's the jock?"

"My new neighbor."

"Another rocker?"

"Jake is an oil driller. Are we finished with the interrogation, Counselor?"

"I'm sorry I didn't come sooner. I was in California when I heard you'd been shot." He seemed genuinely concerned. "Are you all right?"

"Fit as a fiddle."

"What were you doing at Dot's house in the middle of the night?"

"What I do and why is no longer any of your business, Greg."

"I didn't mean to be nosy. I'm sorry about Lilly, too. You must be devastated."

"She's not dead, Greg. We'll find her."

"Is there anything I can do?"

Now that was an odd question, considering that he was not a great fan of Lilly's. Her bluntness had been a constant bruise to his ego. "Why should you want to?"

"Because she's your friend. And since my father

YOUR PARTICIPATION IS REQUESTED!

Dear Reader,

Since you are a lover of fiction – we would like to get to know you!

Inside you will find a short Reader's Survey. Sharing your answers with us will help our editorial staff understand who you are and what activities you enjoy.

To thank you for your participation, we would like to send you 2 books and a gift – **ABSOLUTELY FREE!**

Enjoy your gifts with our appreciation,

Pam Powers

SEE INSIDE FOR READER'S SURVEY

What's Your Reading Pleasure...
ROMANCE? _OR_ SUSPENSE?

Do you prefer spine-tingling page turners OR heart-stirring stories about love and relationships? Tell us which books you enjoy – and you'll get **2 FREE "ROMANCE" BOOKS or 2 FREE "SUSPENSE" BOOKS with no obligation to purchase anything.**

Choose **"ROMANCE"** and get **2 FREE BOOKS** that will fuel your imagination with intensely moving stories about life, love and relationships.

Choose **"SUSPENSE"** and you'll get **2 FREE BOOKS** that will thrill you with a spine-tingling blend of suspense and mystery.

Whichever category you select, your 2 free books have a combined cover price of $11.98 or more in the U.S. and $13.98 or more in Canada.

And remember. . . just for accepting the Editor's Free Gift Offer, we'll send you 2 books and a gift, ABSOLUTELY FREE!

YOURS FREE! *We'll send you a fabulous surprise gift absolutely FREE, just for trying "Romance" or "Suspense"!*

® and TM are registered trademarks of Harlequin Enterprises Limited.

Visit us online at
www.FreeBooksandGift.com

Offer limited to one per household and not valid to current subscribers of MIRA, Romance, Suspense or "The Best of the Best." All orders subject to approval. Books received may vary. Credit or debit balances in a customer's account(s) may be offset by any other outstanding balance owed by or to the customer.

YOUR READER'S SURVEY
THANK YOU FREE GIFTS INCLUDE:

▶ 2 Romance OR 2 Suspense books

▶ A lovely surprise gift

PLEASE FILL IN THE CIRCLES COMPLETELY TO RESPOND

1) What type of fiction books do you enjoy reading? (Check all that apply)
- ○ Suspense/Thrillers
- ○ Action/Adventure
- ○ Modern-day Romances
- ○ Historical Romance
- ○ Humour
- ○ Science fiction

2) What attracted you most to the last fiction book you purchased on impulse?
- ○ The Title ○ The Cover ○ The Author ○ The Story

3) What is usually the greatest influencer when you <u>plan</u> to buy a book?
- ○ Advertising ○ Referral from a friend
- ○ Book Review ○ Like the author

4) Approximately how many fiction books do you read in a year?
- ○ 1 to 6 ○ 7 to 19 ○ 20 or more

5) How often do you access the internet?
- ○ Daily ○ Weekly ○ Monthly ○ Rarely or never

6) To which of the following age groups do you belong?
- ○ Under 18 ○ 18 to 34 ○ 35 to 64 ○ over 65

YES! I have completed the Reader's Survey. Please send me the 2 FREE books and gift for which I qualify. I understand that I am under no obligation to purchase any books, as explained on the back and on the opposite page.

Check one:

	ROMANCE
	193 MDL DVFW 393 MDL DVFY

	SUSPENSE
	192 MDL DVFV 392 MDL DVFX

FIRST NAME

LAST NAME

ADDRESS

APT.#

CITY

STATE/PROV.

ZIP/POSTAL CODE

The Reader Service — Here's How It Works:

Accepting your 2 free books and gift places you under no obligation to buy anything. You may keep the books and gift and return the shipping statement marked "cancel." If you do not cancel, about a month later we'll send you 3 additional books and bill you just $4.74 each in the U.S., or $5.24 each in Canada, plus 25¢ shipping & handling per book and applicable taxes if any.* That's the complete price and — compared to cover prices starting from $5.99 each in the U.S. and $6.99 each in Canada — it's quite a bargain! You may cancel at any time, but if you choose to continue, every month we'll send you 3 more books, which you may either purchase at the discount price or return to us and cancel your subscription.

*Terms and prices subject to change without notice. Sales tax applicable in N.Y. Canadian residents will be charged applicable provincial taxes and GST.

has an excellent rapport with the Philadelphia police—"

"Chief Yates, of the Mullica Township PD, is in charge of the case, but thanks for the offer." She started to jog in place. "Is that what you came to tell me?"

"Actually, I came to congratulate you."

"About what?"

"I heard about the conviction you won the other day." He smiled. "And the way you won it. That was brilliant, Syd. Risky but brilliant."

Was it her imagination or did she catch a speck of admiration in those discriminating blue eyes? "Thank you."

"My father was impressed." Impressing his father had always been a priority in Greg's life. "So was I. I'm proud of you, Syd."

Why was he talking in the present tense? As if they were still an item? "You never used to be. In fact, didn't you use to complain about my lack of ambition?"

He actually had the good grace to blush. "I was wrong."

"Yes, you were. I'm just as ambitious as the next guy. Just because I didn't join your father's firm—"

"I mean…" He looked around before continuing. "I was wrong to do what I did. The truth is, I miss you, Syd. More than you can imagine."

Before she could stop him, he had taken her hands in his. "Won't you forgive me? I swear I'll spend the rest of my life making sure you never regret it."

She yanked her hands away. "Greg, when I broke

up with you, I was serious. No forgiveness, no making up, no second chance."

"She meant nothing to me, Syd. I don't even know her name!"

"That's suppose to make me feel better?"

"What I'm saying is that you're the one I love. I can't imagine my life without you."

"You should have thought of that before you jumped in the sack with the blonde."

"I was stupid. I know it, my father knows it. Not a day goes by without him—"

"Your father put you up to this? He wants us to get back together?"

"No. I mean, yes, sure he wants us back together, but coming here was *my* idea. He doesn't even know I'm here. I've changed, Syd. I'm no longer under my father's thumb as I used to be. In fact…" He lowered his voice. "I plan on leaving the firm."

That was a surprise. "You're kidding. Does your father know?"

"Not yet."

"Why? What happened?"

He shrugged. "The same old thing. I don't want to work for my brother after my father retires. Matt and I never did get along, and this is the perfect opportunity for me to move on."

"Move on to where?"

"I can't discuss it yet. Let me just say that when you hear about it, it will blow your mind. And my father's," he added smugly.

She didn't know what to say other than to offer her congratulations. "I hope you'll be very happy."

"I want you to be a part of my new life, Syd. I want you to be a part of my success."

Syd let out an exasperated sigh. Where was all this whining coming from? "Greg, I don't know how to get through to you, so let me try to put it another way. I'm glad we broke up. And I'm relieved. Relieved that I didn't get to make the worst mistake of my life. Relieved that I didn't succumb to your father's pressure to join his firm. Relieved that I can finally be me again, me with all my flaws, my lack of ambition and what you once called my 'misplaced values.' Relieved that I no longer have to live in fear of offending you or one of your family members whenever I speak my mind."

Greg's delicate blush had turned a furious crimson. "Keep your voice down."

"I just want to make sure that you heard me. Loud and clear."

She saw him glance toward the park. When his mouth tightened, Syd followed his gaze. Jake was leaning against a tree, ankles crossed, watching them. As Greg looked his way, Jake touched his forehead with two fingers in a little salute, a gesture that seemed to incense the attorney.

"Are you sleeping with that jerk?" he asked harshly. "Is that why you're acting so out of character?"

"No, I'm not sleeping with him." Then because she couldn't resist, she added, "Yet."

His mouth twisted in distaste. "You're making a big mistake, Syd."

"You're the one who made the mistake, Greg. Live with it."

Feeling more or less vindicated, she turned away from him and jogged back to where Jake was waiting.

"Kiss me," she said, coming to stand in front of him.

"I beg your pardon?"

"Oh, for heaven's sake, am I speaking Chinese?" Before Jake had a chance to say another word, she pulled him to her and planted a passionate kiss on his mouth.

His response was instantaneous. Wrapping his arms around her waist, he pulled her to him and crushed his lips to hers.

More aroused than she had been in years, Syd closed her eyes and opened her mouth, shivering with pleasure as their tongues met.

When he finally released her, she dragged in a shaky breath.

"Was that to make Bozo jealous?" Jake asked. "Not that I'm complaining, mind you."

She met his amused gaze. "No. It was my own personal reward for closing the final chapter of a lousy relationship."

Needing no invitation this time, Jake took her in his arms again. "In that case, why don't we give your former beau an encore? Just in case he didn't get it."

Twenty-Five

With one eye on the TV screen and the other on the front door of Tavern on the Square, Jake sipped his beer. His mind kept wandering back to the heated kiss he and Syd had exchanged earlier. The lady, he thought without much surprise, was beginning to get under his skin.

That was something he hadn't experienced for a long time. Until now his life had been simple, orderly and had consisted of two major elements. Work and play. If playtime included an enjoyable woman, as it often did, all the better. Those brief relationships worked because none of the women expected more from him than he could give.

So what was it about Sydney Cooper that had him so hot and bothered? Sure she was beautiful, smart and fun to be with. But so were hundreds of other women, yet none had complicated his life the way this one was threatening to. He had even begun to consider the possibility of a long-distance relationship. Maybe he could buy the apartment on Washington Square he was renting and spend his R&Rs in Philly. Or Syd could fly down to Baton Rouge on weekends.

Or maybe she wasn't interested in any kind of relationship with him and his problems would be solved. Maybe.

A cold draft interrupted his thoughts and he glanced toward the door as a young couple entered the bar. He wondered if Victor had given up on him. He hadn't heard from his former commander since their last encounter and he was beginning to think that maybe he *had* overdone it.

At three-thirty, as North Carolina prepared to meet UCLA in the second round, Jake left his half-finished beer on the counter and went into the men's room to give Ramirez an update.

"Remind me again how all this waiting around is for the good of my country?" he asked when the agent answered.

"You won't have to wait much longer. Victor just entered."

When Jake returned to the busy bar, he found his glass gone and his stool occupied by a loudmouth demanding to be served.

Before he could ask the guy to split, the bartender pointed at a table in the back. "That gentleman over there said for you to join him."

Jake turned to see Victor sitting at a window table. He walked over to him, but remained standing. "You're beginning to be a pain in the ass, you know that?"

"Persistence is one of my many virtues."

"What do you want now?"

"Same thing as I did the last time I was here—to talk. Come on, don't be a poor sport." He gave the vacant chair a shove with his foot. "Sit down. Your beer is getting warm."

Jake held back a sigh of annoyance and sat down, wondering again if he was overdoing it. "Of all the bars in Philadelphia," he said on impulse, "you had to walk into mine."

At the famous, although slightly altered, phrase from the movie *Casablanca,* Victor chuckled. "Cute, but not very original, Captain."

Jake drained what was left of his beer. "I don't get out much."

"Then let's change that. Come to my camp. We'll have a little dinner, talk about old times, tour the compound. I'll even let you tell me what a louse I was in Iraq."

"Can I beat the shit out of you?"

Victor laughed. "If you're man enough to do it." He stood up. "Come on, Jake. I'm not asking you to join up, for God's sake. I just want to show you around, share my experiences with someone I know will appreciate all the efforts I put in this organization. Who knows, you might even have a suggestion or two on how to make it better."

"I doubt it. You were always the one with the vision."

Van Heusen seemed pleased by that remark. "You weren't too shabby yourself. The truth is, we made a damn good team, you and I."

"If I agree to go, will you leave me alone afterward?"

"Jesus Christ, man, when did you become such a hard ass?"

"Will you agree?" Jake repeated.

"You have my word as an officer and a gentleman."

At that remark, Jake tried not to laugh, and followed Victor out.

Lancaster County—or Pennsylvania Dutch Country as the locals called it—was one of those rare places on earth where the Amish and Mennonites had succeeded in maintaining a civilized, even workable relationship with their more modern neighbors, while retaining the values and traditions they had adhered to for centuries.

An hour's drive from Center City, the area was a land of rolling hills, windmills, covered bridges and horse-drawn carriages. The Amish and Mennonites who had settled in and around the Lancaster area were bound by their German backgrounds and a deep devotion to their church.

The thought that a military compound, even one devoid of tanks and heavy artillery, was in the proximity of such gentle people boggled the mind. But as Victor drove through the countryside, honking his horn and waving at the men, women and children working the fields, he understood why they had accepted this unlikely neighbor. The Amish were a private people, mindful of others' needs but respectful of their privacy. By remembering those basic rules, Victor had made it possible for both cultures to live in pleasant harmony.

Surprisingly honest, Victor told Jake about his initial fear of failing in his endeavor. Or of attracting the wrong people. "I wasn't looking for trigger-happy men with chips on their shoulders," he said. "I wanted intelligent, committed individuals who believed in *true* freedom as much as I did.

"Once I realized that my beliefs were catching on, I had to go one step farther. I wasn't satisfied communicating with the members through the Internet. I had to find a place where my men could meet and interact. That's when I found this place."

"It must have cost you a pretty penny."

"Everything my father left me when he died went into buying the land, putting up a few buildings and maintaining the camp. The annual membership fees help, along with generous donations from wealthy members."

As they passed another farm, a woman in a long, dark dress raised her hand in greeting. "You seem to have a good relationship with the locals."

"That wasn't always the case. They were resentful and suspicious at first. It wasn't until they realized we wouldn't be playing any war games, or indulging in wild drinking parties, that they began to accept us. Most of our food comes from those farms you saw. I also encourage my soldiers who live within driving distance to support them as well. As long as my men behave and don't cause any problems, we'll get along."

"But one of your men did cause a problem."

As Victor left the highway, he glanced at Jake. "You know about that?"

"The bartender at Tavern on the Square recognized you from a press conference you gave when Doug Avery was first arrested."

"I had great hopes for Doug, but he let me down. I had no choice but to revoke his membership."

"Because he was arrested again?"

"That's right. You know the saying 'Three strikes and you're out?' Well, with me, it's two strikes and you're out. No exceptions. Disruptive behavior and unlawful conduct is not what I look for in my men."

"How do you think it will all play out in court?" He tried to keep his tone casual.

Victor shrugged. "Hard to say. Avery's attorney, this time around, is a public defender. She'll be facing a tough opponent."

Eager to score points for honesty, Jake nodded. "You're talking about Sydney Cooper."

Victor did a fairly decent job of looking surprised. "You know her?"

"She lives across the hall from me."

"You don't say." Victor's tone turned playful. "So, how is she outside the courtroom? Stodgy? Sexy? Does she let loose at all?"

He *had* been listening. "She's definitely not stodgy," he replied. "But you're not going to get me to say any more than that."

"And you shouldn't. A gentleman never tells." He slowed down. "Here we are."

The first thing Jake noticed as they stopped at the front gate was the flag, which featured a pair of crossed bayonets over a yellow background. The guard, dressed in combat fatigues, snapped a salute and let them pass.

"How many men do you have living at the camp?" Jake asked.

"Fifteen. They hold a variety of professions—electricians, cooks, plumbers, computer operators. They keep the camp humming and earn as much as they would on the outside. The rest of the local membership comes to the camp two weekends a month for some healthy brainstorming."

More like brainwashing, Jake thought. "Did you keep in touch with anyone we knew?" he asked lightly.

There was only a slight hesitation before Victor answered. "No. What about you?"

Jake gave a shake of his head. "Nope. After I left Iraq, I wiped the slate clean." He looked around him. "I don't see any barracks. Where do those weekend warriors sleep?"

Victor laughed. "They're soldiers, Jake. They don't need barracks. They know that I'm on a budget and bring their own sleeping bags, their own food and do what soldiers do best—improvise."

"They bring any guns?"

"Certainly. The men are proud of their weapons, and there's no harm in bringing them along and showing them off. They also like to practice their marksmanship at the firing range, which is about two miles from here."

"You said earlier that you didn't engage in war games, but isn't that what a militia is all about? To train in the eventuality of a conflict?"

"Not necessarily."

"Then what's the point of it all?"

Victor's eyes narrowed. "You're pretty curious for someone who's not interested."

Jake gave a dispassionate shrug. "Sorry. I wasn't aware the subject was taboo."

An awkward silence fell between them. Victor was the first to break it. "It's not. And I'm the one who's sorry. I brought you here. You deserve an answer to your questions."

He stopped in front of a small building. "Right now, my main objective is to keep building my membership and to eventually join forces with militias from other states."

"And then what? Dismantle our military forces? Take over the Pentagon? Or the White House?" Jake put enough amusement in his voice to show that he wasn't serious.

"You've been reading too much government propaganda."

"Haven't you?"

"I keep up with the news. And I must say, I'm dismayed at the way we've been portrayed by the press. We're not savages. We don't relish the thought of dividing the country, and we certainly don't plan on using force and killing our countrymen. That's what the government wants you to believe, but it couldn't be farther from the truth. We are patriots. We believe in the constitution as it was written. And unlike the militia the FBI busted some years ago, we don't bury bomb components or heavy artillery on our grounds. And I didn't buy this land with the intention of using it as a detention facility."

"Did the government think you did?"

"The government thinks of all militia leaders as evildoers. They came here with warrants, arms and more than two dozen men. They thought they'd find a bunker, a large food supply, ammunition, white supremacist literature and God only knows what else. Do you know what they found? Zilch."

"What will you do after you've joined forces with other militias?"

Victor tiptoed around the question with a laugh. "That's still a long way off, Jake. I can't even think that far."

He cut off the engine. "Come on," he said as he opened the door. "Let's go in my office and have a drink. Then I'll give you the grand tour."

Twenty-Six

Considering that Victor was such an egomaniac, his office was a study in modesty. No larger than Jake's Washington Square living room, it managed to accommodate the essentials—a desk with a laptop, a printer, a bookcase, a couple of chairs and a small refrigerator.

"Do you still like martinis?" Victor asked.

"Only if they're very dry."

"Two very dry martinis coming up."

While he took what he needed from a small refrigerator, Jake let his gaze drift toward the laptop. If Victor was indeed the middleman for an illegal arms' ring, the names and phone numbers of his contacts would be in there. And like all classified documents, the list would be protected by a password—one that would change weekly, maybe even daily.

"Here you go." Victor handed Jake one of the glasses. "Here's to new beginnings."

After raising his glass in a toast, Jake walked over to an open bookcase on top of which stood the busts of some of the country's most famous generals. "I see that you still have your collection."

Victor came to join him. "I've added a couple since we last saw each other. Can you spot the newcomers?"

Jake looked at each one, recognizing the most notable—Eisenhower, MacArthur, Patton, Washington, Grant, Stonewall Jackson and a few Jake couldn't name. "Afraid not."

With the hand that held his glass, Victor pointed. "That one over there is General George Gordon Meade, who fought so bravely in the Battle of Gettysburg. And this one is General Robert E. Lee. Interesting man. He loved the Union, yet he was loyal to the state of Virginia when it seceded.

"All great soldiers," he continued. "Men who weren't afraid of making up their own rules whenever the need warranted it."

Whenever the need warranted it. Was he comparing himself to those generals? And to what he had done in Iraq? Did he, in his twisted mind, still believe that he had been right in defying orders and lying to his superiors?

Victor motioned for Jake to follow him. "Let me introduce you to my trusted aide."

That would be Philip Jenkins, the man Ramirez had told him about. He was making progress.

Victor led Jake through a door that connected his office to a smaller one. Seated in front of a computer was a handsome man in his mid- to late-thirties with short blond hair, a powerful physique and steady blue eyes. He, too, wore combat fatigues and snapped to attention when Victor entered.

"At ease, Sergeant. And meet that old friend I told you about, former army captain Jake Sloan. Jake, this is Sergeant Philip Jenkins. My right-hand man."

The man extended his hand. "Welcome to Camp Freedom, Mr. Sloan."

"Thank you, Sergeant." Jake sized him up. The handshake was firm and his smile wide, but Jake caught a flicker of dislike in those pale blue eyes. No, more than dislike. Mistrust.

"Jake and I fought in Desert Storm together," Victor continued. "He was one hell of a soldier, the kind you don't see much anymore. Isn't that right, Jake?"

Jenkins stood at ease, his hands behind his back. At Victor's words, however, the smile cooled a notch.

"Oh, I don't know, Victor," Jake said. "You don't seem to have fared so badly. From what you've told me, you seem to be surrounded with good men."

Victor watched him as Jake brought his glass to his mouth. "There's always room for one more."

Jake was wondering if that was an invitation when Jenkins said, "Will you be staying in the area long, Mr. Sloan?"

"I don't know yet."

Victor gave Jake a friendly slap on the shoulder.

"Let's hope he does." He put his glass down. "Come on. Time to go for that tour I promised you. Still know how to drive a Humvee, Captain?"

"Some things you never forget, Colonel."

Because Victor laughed, it was hard to guess whether or not he had picked up on Jake's double entendre.

Syd was unable to concentrate on the motion she had been trying to write for the past two hours. Giving up, at least for now, she pushed away from her laptop and went to pour herself a cup of coffee. The object of her distraction was painfully clear. The kiss. The kiss that *she* had initiated.

What had possessed her? Had she really intended to make Greg jealous? Show a wild, unpredictable side of her he'd never known? Or had she simply responded to some primal instinct and used Greg as an excuse to satisfy her craving?

She took a sip of the stale coffee. Now that was an interesting choice of word. Impulse might have been more appropriate, more…justifiable. But *craving?* Surely four weeks without a man wasn't long enough to make her do something so out of character. Before meeting Greg, she had been alone, and celibate, for an entire year. Had she gone bonkers at the sight of the handsome attorney? Had she paid attention to his physique the way she did with Jake? Found ways to be close to him, brush against him, *throw* herself at him? Of course not.

Girl in control. That's what she liked to call herself. No matter how tricky the situation, how complex the case, how handsome the man, Sydney Cooper could always be counted on to keep a cool head.

So what the hell had happened to her this morning?

She walked back to her desk. "Damned if I know," she murmured.

She was attempting to finish the motion when Detective Cranston called.

"Avery is back in his cell."

"Have you questioned him?"

"I tried. He won't give me the time of day. Maybe you'll have better luck."

"I doubt it, but I'm willing to try."

Avery looked only marginally better than he had the last time she'd seen him. His eyes were still swollen, his bottom lip had been stitched and it was obvious that he was still in pain, in spite of the medication the doctor had given him.

She knew his condition had improved, however, when he greeted her with one of his snide remarks. "Well, shit," he said. "Look who's paying me another social call. What's the matter, sweet cheeks, you didn't get a good enough look in the infirmary?"

While Cranston chose to remain standing, Syd pulled up a chair and brought it close to the cot where he had stretched out. "Do you know why I'm here, Doug?"

"You got the hots for me?"

"Besides that."

He tried to laugh but the effort was too much. "Nope."

"I was hoping you'd tell me why those three cell-mates beat you up."

"You know why. I hit them first." He shrugged. "Guess they wanted to teach me a lesson."

"You tried to take on three men?" She shook her head. "You're not that tough, Avery. Or that stupid."

He remained silent.

"Was that beating Victor van Heusen's way of sending you a warning?" she persisted. "And making sure you'd keep your mouth shut?"

"You're still as nuts as ever, lady."

Syd glanced at Cranston who shrugged.

"I can't protect you if you won't cooperate, Doug."

"If by cooperate, you mean tell you something that ain't true, then I can't help you, because I don't know anything."

"That's not the way it looked in the courtroom the other day. You seemed pretty upset with Victor van Heusen, then, and ready to say plenty."

Whatever anger he had felt toward van Heusen earlier seemed to have vanished. "I was just pissed off because he wouldn't spring for a decent attorney. I said the first thing that came into my head."

Syd looked at that battered face for a moment. They had done one hell of a job on him, physically and emotionally. Still, with the right approach, she might be able to win him over. "I could make your stay here a lot easier, Doug. Shorter, too. You tell me what you know about Victor van Heusen and if the information is useful, I'm prepared to offer you a deal."

"You mean you'd let me go? Free and clear?"

"No, but if you changed your plea to guilty instead of not guilty, and save the state the expense of a trial, I would recommend a much lighter sentence."

His laugh turned into a cough that brought tears of pain into his eyes. "Get out of here," he said, wrapping his arms around his midriff. "I have nothing to say to you."

Syd waited a few seconds to see if he would change his mind, then, when it was clear that he wouldn't, she nodded to Cranston and stood up.

"Let me know when he's ready to talk," was all she said when they walked out.

But deep down, she knew he wouldn't.

Twenty-Seven

Syd was only a block from her office when her cell phone rang. It was Dot, and this time she wasn't just upset. She was hysterical.

"A messenger just delivered a document from the court!" she cried. "Mike filed a motion."

"A motion for what?"

"Custody of Prudence! He's claiming we're holding her hostage," Dot continued. "That I am unfit to care for her and that in the absence or possible *death*… Can you believe he's saying that, Syd? That Lilly could be dead!"

"Finish reading the document, Dot."

Dot sniffed and took a moment to collect herself. "…Possible *death* of her mother, custody should revert back to him. Can he do that, Syd?" Her voice had turned shrill again. "Can the court reverse the judgment?"

Unfortunately, the answer was yes. Custody had been awarded to Lilly, not to her family, and certainly not to eight nuns, no matter how caring and well-intended they were.

"Not if I can help it," she said encouragingly.

"Is he right, Syd? Do you think those thugs killed my daughter?"

"No, I don't," Syd said with all the conviction she could muster. "Mike is just trying to increase his chances of getting custody, that's all."

"You've got to do something, Syd," she pleaded.

At this point, Syd had no idea what she could do, but she remained optimistic, for Dot's sake. "Let me think about it for a while, okay? If I come up with anything, I'll call you."

Thanks to some clever reshuffling of her schedule, Syd had kept the rest of the afternoon free of pressing matters and would be able to devote the time to Dot's problem. Her first step was to find out what Mike's chances of being awarded custody truly were, and for an answer to that question, there was no better person than Judge Ignatius Vargas.

The former juvenile and domestic court judge now spent most of his days in a downtown office, writing his memoirs. Syd was pleased to hear about his new endeavor. She had clerked for him while attending law school years ago, and had always felt that he was one of the most courageous and intriguing men she had ever met. His adventures, both in

Cuba and after he fled his native country, would make fascinating reading.

The moment she stepped into his office, he rose, clearly delighted to see her. "Sydney Cooper, what a pleasure."

He was a stocky man, with the burnished complexion of his Cuban ancestors, a full head of pewter-colored hair and a dark, intense gaze that had made more than one attorney uncomfortable. At the moment, however, he couldn't have been any friendlier.

"You look splendid," he said, taking both hands in hers. "I would never guess that you had been the victim of a recent shooting. How are you feeling?"

"Quite well, thank you. I wasn't sure you'd remember me."

"Not remember you? You were one of my brightest clerks. Never satisfied with a simple answer, if I recall."

"You're partly to blame for that, Judge. How many times did you tell me 'there are no simple answers'?"

"Not a very profound statement, I'm afraid."

"But true."

He pointed to a chair. "Please, sit down. Can I offer you something to drink?"

"No, thank you."

"I'm very proud of you, Sydney, and of all you have accomplished. I always thought you would go far."

"Thank you, Judge. I had good training."

"But you seem preoccupied. I assume that whatever is bothering you is the reason you came to see me?"

She nodded. "How much do you know about Lilly Gilmore's kidnapping?"

"As much as anyone else who reads the papers and listens to the news. She's a friend of yours, I understand."

"My best friend."

"Is there something I can do?"

"You could clarify something for me. Custody of Lilly's six-year-old daughter was awarded to her. Whenever Lilly is away, which is rarely, or when she has to work late, her mother takes care of Prudence. Dorothy Branzini has a close-knit family and they all adore Prudence. Now that Lilly has been kidnapped, her ex-husband has filed a motion with the court for custody of the child, claiming that Dorothy Branzini, at her 'advanced' age—she's only sixty-two, mind you—is unfit to care for a six-year-old."

"Custody is almost always awarded to the mother," Judge Vargas said, "so that's nothing unusual. But was there a specific reason the father didn't try to have at least partial custody?"

"I suspect there might be, but I'm not sure. Lilly never discussed the terms of her agreement with Mike. All I know is that he didn't fight her. Until now. He wants full custody of Prudence.

"Lilly has a will," she continued, "that gives legal guardianship of her daughter to her mother."

"But until proof of the contrary, we'll have to assume that Lilly is still alive."

"I realize that. I was hoping that Lilly's intention of having her mother act as guardian would be enough for a court of law not to change the original ruling. No matter how much Lilly loves her mother, she would never entrust her little girl to her if she didn't think she was fully capable of caring for her."

"Where is the child now?"

"Prior to being kidnapped, Lilly feared for Prudence's safety, so she put her in a secret location."

He raised a brow. "She's not with her grandmother?"

"No."

"I see." His expression was regretful. "You might as well prepare yourself, Sydney. In Pennsylvania, a parent has the right to contest placement of a child. Without evidence that Lilly's ex-husband is unfit to care for his daughter, I'm afraid the judge won't have any choice but to award him custody, at least until the mother returns."

Twenty-Eight

Mike's house, which he had bought soon after his divorce from Lilly, was a small but attractive row home in one of the nicest residential areas of Philadelphia. No doubt that detail would play well in court next week.

After much debating, Syd had decided to talk to Mike and appeal to something she wasn't sure existed—his sense of decency. A detective she didn't know had answered Mike's phone and told her he had come down with the flu and would be home for the next couple of days.

Lawndale Street was quiet at this time of day, making it easy to find a parking space. She was about to get out of her car when Mike's front door opened and a man with light brown hair and a yellow ski jacket came storming out. Judging from the scowl on his handsome face and the way he slammed the door behind him, Syd guessed he was in a lousy mood.

She watched him get into a dark blue Audi. As the car tore away from the curb, she memorized the license plate. Anyone upset with Mike Gilmore was worth knowing.

Mike answered at the first knock. He looked pale and tired, but managed to let out an irritated sigh when he saw her. "This isn't a good time, Syd."

"It wasn't a good time for me the other night, either, but you didn't let that stop you."

"What do you want?"

She hoped that being sick had mellowed him a little. "I want to talk to you about the petition you filed."

"You do realize that that's none of your business."

"I'm Prudence's godmother. Her well-being is very much my business."

"My legal dealings are with Dot, not you."

Okay, here goes nothing, she thought. "Mike, please, don't put that little girl through such an ordeal."

"What ordeal? I love her. I want her with me. Is that such a bad thing?"

"A judge will want to question her. She'll have to choose between her father and her grandmother. She's only six, Mike, and very confused right now. You'll only add to her anxieties."

"Vanessa and I will give her enough love and affection to make her forget any hardship she may have suffered."

"Vanessa doesn't love Prudence the way Dot does. Taking her away from what she considers her second home would be cruel and traumatic for her."

Mike laughed. "I love it when you grovel, Syd. Do it again."

Being sick hadn't improved him one bit. He was still the same miserable, vindictive jerk. "Withdraw the petition, Mike. For once in your life, think of someone else instead of yourself and do the right thing."

"You were fun there for a while, but now you're boring me." He opened the door and glanced outside. "You didn't bring your watchdog? In that case, I'd advise you to leave before I lose my temper."

"And what do you do when you lose your temper, Mike? Hit women?" She looked at him defiantly, daring him to do something stupid. "Maybe that's why Lilly left you? Because you were abusive?"

She saw his jaw tighten and braced herself for the blow, knowing it would be worth it if it helped her prove that he was a violent man and therefore unfit to care for his daughter.

Unfortunately, he had more self-control than she had given him credit for. "You're smart, Syd, I'll give you that." He leaned forward until she could see that nasty little gleam in his eyes. "But I'm smarter."

Violet's husband, who had been on the force at the time of Syd's humiliating downfall, was the only cop in Philly who still talked to her. Not only that, but he understood how a rookie could go through the academy's rigorous training, excel in the classroom and at the firing range, then inexplicably freeze when faced with a human target for the first time. He understood because it had happened to him, although not with the same tragic consequences.

But although she considered him a friend, she wasn't sure he would want to conspire against a former fellow officer. Whether they were retired or on active duty, cops stuck together. That was an unspoken rule, and God helped those who broke it. The only thing she had going for her, besides George's friendship, was his intense dislike for Mike Gilmore.

Luckily, she found him at home and, as always, happy to see her. Lean, fit and older than Violet by more than ten years, George Sorrensen bore his sixty-plus years well. Now that he was retired, he kept busy with his train collection, gardening and cooking delicious dishes from his native Sweden.

"Syd. How are you doing, kid?" He patted his side. "How's the wound?"

"Much better, thank you. May I come in?"

"Sure, but Violet isn't in yet."

"I know. You're the one I wanted to see."

He showed her into the couple's spacious living room with its contemporary teak furniture and thick white carpet. From the kitchen came a delicious aroma she couldn't identify. "What can I do for you, Syd?" he asked after they had sat down.

She took the slip of paper where she had jotted

down the blue Audi's license plates and slid it across the coffee table. "I need some information on the owner of this car—name, address, job and anything else you can find out about him."

"Is this connected to Lilly's kidnapping?"

"It could be, but I'm not sure. I saw him coming out of Mike Gilmore's house just a little while ago."

"What were you doing at Mike's house?"

She told him.

He was silent for a long time. After what seemed like an eternity, he nodded. "I should know something by tomorrow morning. Can I call you at the office?"

"Or on my cell." She gave him the number, thanked him and left, not wanting to take any more of his time.

Twenty-Nine

"I don't think your aide likes me," Jake said as he and Victor drove back toward the city later that night.

"Don't be insulted. Jenkins doesn't like anybody. He's an absolute bear, but he watches over me like a mother hen."

"How long has he been with you?"

"Five years. He had been in trouble with the law when I found him. I invited him to attend a meeting and before I knew it, he wanted to join."

"He's certainly devoted."

"And I appreciate it."

"Just don't put him in charge of PR."

Victor laughed. "He'll warm up to you. Give him time."

They had reached the light on Seventh Street. "You can drop me off right here," Jake said.

Victor did as requested and waited until Jake had

stepped out of the car before leaning over. "How about we get together for lunch sometime? Your treat."

Jake shrugged. "Sure. When?" Jake gave himself a mental kick for appearing too anxious.

Victor pursed his lips, seemed to give the question some thought, then said, "I'll let you know, okay?"

"Sure. You have my number."

Victor patted his pocket. "Right here."

"Thanks for dinner. You were right about your cook. Worth his weight in gold."

"I'll tell him you said that."

Jake watched him make a U-turn before starting across Walnut. He had barely reached the sidewalk when he stopped in his tracks.

Syd stood no more than five feet from him, her gaze on the disappearing vehicle.

Jake muttered under his breath, damming the lousy timing and hoping she hadn't recognized Victor. When she finally turned to face him, it was obvious from the expression on her face that she had.

"Hi." He raised a hand in greeting. "How was—"

She pointed down the street. "That was Victor van Heusen." It wasn't a question.

For the first time in years, Jake was at a loss for words.

"You two know each other?"

Jake nodded.

She walked over to him. Under the streetlight,

her expression was unreadable. "And you never said anything? All this time you let me go on about my suspicions regarding one of his men and you never gave a hint that you knew Victor van Heusen?"

"I didn't find it relevant."

"Relevant to what?" Her eyes, filled with dark suspicion, narrowed. "What's going on here, Jake? And don't insult me by saying nothing."

"Okay then, let's just say that it's not in your best interest to know what's going on."

She let out a dry laugh. "Oh, no, you don't. That kind of psychology is wasted on me. The fact is, I made a huge error in judgment. I discussed a case with a stranger, who, for reasons that now elude me, I trusted. Therefore, you don't get to worm your way out of an explanation with such a lame excuse. I'll decide what's in my best interest. I'm asking you again. What is your relationship with Victor van Heusen?"

There was no way out of this. Like it or not, he had to make a choice. He could fabricate a story and hope she'd buy it, which he seriously doubted. Or he could come clean and pray she wouldn't blow his cover.

He already knew which choice Ramirez expected him to make. The problem was, lying to Syd was no longer an option.

"I'm waiting, Jake."

He jammed his hands into his jacket pocket. "Victor was my commanding officer in Iraq during Desert Storm."

Syd waited a beat as she let that sink in. "And you kept in touch with him all this time?"

"No. I only recently found out he lived in Pennsylvania."

"How recently?" Like the experienced prosecutor that she was, she barely let him answer one question before firing another.

"Just before I left Louisiana."

"Then *he* is the reason you came back to Philadelphia, not your father."

"They are both the reason I came back."

"You're talking in riddles again."

He looked around him, saw that the snack bar on Locust was still open. He nodded toward it. "Why don't we get out of the cold and talk over a cup of hot chocolate?"

"I have a better idea. Let's go up to my apartment where I can tape your statement."

As she started toward the door, Jake grabbed her arm. "We can't do that."

"Why the hell not?"

"Because—" he took a deep breath "—your apartment is bugged."

Thirty

She stared at him for several seconds, her expression going from shock to disbelief before turning to anger. Anger may have been too tame a word. Jake could have sworn he heard her hiss as she tried to contain her fury.

"Did you say my apartment was bugged?" She didn't give him a chance to reply. "Who did it? Who planted the bug? You?"

"No, of course not."

"Then who?"

"Syd, listen to me. Don't look around, but there is a very strong possibility that we are being watched, if not by Victor, then by one of his men. So, let's go for some hot chocolate and, I promise, I'll tell you everything."

He saw her fight for control, first by inhaling deeply, then by releasing a long, slow breath. He couldn't help admire her poise and self-control as she resisted the impulse to look around her, and kept her gaze on him.

A couple of seconds went by, then, without a word, she walked past him and headed toward the coffee shop.

At this time of night, only a couple of tables were occupied, one by an elderly couple sharing a slice of carrot cake, the other by two teenage girls with rings in their noses, black turtlenecks and heavy black eye makeup. Large crosses hung around their neck. The Goth look was alive and well in Philadelphia.

Jake sat facing the door and gave the waitress an order for two mugs of the house's hot chocolate. When Syd shook her head at his suggestion of a pastry, the waitress left and Syd was on the warpath again.

Arms resting on the table, she leaned forward. "Are you aware that wiretapping is illegal? And that by knowing about it, and not divulging the information, you are, in fact, an accessory to the crime?"

"I do."

"Yet you let it happen."

"I had to. And by the way, my apartment is bugged, too."

She pulled back, looking confused. "Why?"

Seeing the waitress walk toward them, Jake waited until she had set the mugs down and walked away before answering.

He told her everything, from the time he had left the oil rig to the moment he was approached by Agent Ramirez, and eventually by Victor van Heusen.

Well-trained in the art of listening, Syd didn't interrupt him. Although she kept her expression blank, he was fairly certain that she believed him. How could she not? How could anyone invent such an outlandish tale?

The chocolate was scalding hot and she sipped it slowly while watching him. When he stopped talking, she put the mug down and stared into it for a moment.

"So," she said in a much calmer voice. "All that kindness on your part, making friends with me, helping me out. That was all an act? A way for you to find out what I knew about Victor van Heusen?"

"It wasn't an act. Yes, my moving across from you and getting to know you was planned. And yes, my initial willingness to help out was motivated by the task at hand, but all that changed once I got a chance to know you. And for the record, I hated deceiving you. A couple of days ago, I told Agent Ramirez that I wasn't going to do it anymore, that we would have to find the proof we needed some other way."

"Then why didn't you tell me the truth sooner?"

"Because the success of an operation of this type depends largely on the absolute secrecy that surrounds it."

"You sound like a fed."

"I guess I've been hanging around Ramirez too long."

"You said you were supposed to pump me for information. Yet, unless you gave me some sort of truth serum I'm not aware of, I don't recall you asking me for anything."

The front door opened to let in an elderly woman. She smiled at the girl behind the display case and ordered a blueberry muffin. After a quick glance in her direction, Jake dismissed her. Whoever was watching them and monitoring the recording devices was most likely one of Victor's men, not a little old lady.

"I couldn't," he said in reply to her question. "Deceiving you was hard enough. I wasn't going to compound the problem by exploiting you as well."

Her face softened and she was lost in her thoughts for a moment. "Can you really help the bureau prove that Victor van Heusen brokers illegal weapons?" she asked.

"I'm going to try. Today's visit to his camp was a step in the right direction, although I didn't play my part as well as I should have."

"What do you mean?"

"I may have made him a little suspicious with all my questions."

"Can you fix it?"

"Maybe. I'll have to talk to Ramirez. He's the brain behind the operation." He took a sip of the rich chocolate. "But *you* might be in a better position to help."

She looked surprised. "Me? How?"

"Since someone on the other side has more than likely witnessed our argument out in the park, I suggest we go to your apartment, or mine, and let them have an earful without letting on that we know. We can make up the conversation as we go. How imaginative are you?"

Her eyes filled with mischief. "You don't want to know."

Privacy was something Syd had cherished all her life. Even as a child, she liked nothing better than to hide in her room and spend hours there, in complete solitude. To know now that someone had invaded that privacy by entering her apartment, her *sanctum*, and installed a listening device, made her want to find the damn thing, rip it apart and throw van Heusen in jail.

But at the same time, Jake had appealed to something else close and dear to her heart. Her patriotism. Men, women and children, some of them Americans, were being killed every day because of the illegal weapons that were being brokered by men like Victor van Heusen. What Jake had told her hadn't come as a surprise. She knew what went on around the world on a daily basis. The prosecutor in her wanted every culprit to be brought to justice and properly punished. The more logical side of her knew that was impossible.

Therefore, she found it gratifying to know that she had a chance to catch one of those arms' dealers and make sure he would never be responsible for another death.

She tried not to be too upset at the thought of Jake betraying her trust. Betrayal was another pet peeve of hers, and because Greg's unfaithfulness was still so fresh on her mind, Jake's deception had hurt her badly. But she'd get over it. As for her opinion of him, it hadn't changed. He was still a good man, an honorable man, and she admired him for what he was doing, the risks he was taking to safeguard the lives of people he didn't even know.

Because she was aware that Victor van Heusen's device could pick up audio through walls, she waited until they were on the landing that separated her apartment from Jake's before speaking. "What I don't understand is why you didn't tell me sooner that you knew Victor van Heusen."

"Because that's a part of my life I'd rather not talk about."

"So what you're saying is that if I hadn't seen Victor drive away, you would have never told me?"

"Never is a long time." Once inside, he helped her with her raincoat and hung it on the foyer coatrack before doing the same with his leather jacket. "In time, once I knew you better, I would have probably told you."

"How do you feel about your old army buddy running a militia?" As she led the way into the kitchen, she saw him smile his approval at the way she was handling the conversation.

"A man is free to do whatever he wants."

"That's a cop-out answer. I want to know how you *really* feel." She reached into a cupboard and selected a bag of Kauai Koloa from Hawaii. It was a rich, aromatic coffee with chocolate tones—the perfect beverage for a cold winter night.

"All right then, I'll tell you. As a former army man who fought for his country, I find it hard to sympathize with anyone who would want to destroy our present system."

"Do I hear a but coming?"

"The but is that, as much as I hate to admit it, the man has a point."

"And that is?" She busied herself with the coffeemaker. She felt awkward, as though she was on a stage, playing to an audience. Actually, that's exactly what she was doing—playing to an audience of one.

"Citizen's rights in this country have been eroded. Nowadays, Big Brother is everywhere, watching, listening, forbidding you to do this, forbidding you to do that. People are being videotaped without their consent, cops shoot first and ask questions later and politicians have taken all the power away from the people."

"Wow." She laughed. "He did get to you, didn't he?"

"Not at all. You wanted an objective view of what Victor stands for and I gave it to you. That doesn't mean I'm ready to join his cause."

"Might you? Someday?"

Jake paused long enough to give van Heusen hope. "No."

Thirty-One

"**B**y the way," Jake said as he followed her into the living room. "You'll be glad to know that I took your advice."

"I wasn't aware I had given you advice."

"About chartering a boat?" He waited until she had sunk into the soft comfort of the sofa before sitting down beside her.

"You chartered a boat?"

"Call me crazy."

Although Syd was still conscious that their conversation was being recorded, she felt much more relaxed than she had been moments ago. "On the contrary, that's a wonderful idea. What did your father say?"

"He hasn't made up his mind yet." Jake gave a shake of his head. "The truth is, he hasn't called me back."

She understood his pain. Indifference was the worse kind of rejection, and when it came from a parent, the wound went even deeper. She wanted to reach out to Jake and comfort him, tell him to be patient, but after her silly behavior the other night, she thought it best to keep her hands to herself.

"Give him time," she said.

He gave a fatalistic shrug. "You and I might end up using that boat. How do you feel about deep-sea fishing?"

"The last time I was on the ocean, I was twelve and hopelessly sick."

The phone rang and she looked at Jake, who nodded and mouthed the word "careful."

It was Anthony. "I have that information you wanted," he said, sounding excited.

"I'm listening." She prayed that van Heusen's device wouldn't pick up Anthony's side of the conversation. Whether or not Jake's former CO had anything to do with Lilly's kidnapping, she had no intention of letting a stranger eavesdrop on classified information.

"The necklace was bought at Hansen's Jewelers on Samson Street on September thirtieth of last year. It was paid for in cash."

"How much?"

"Two thousand dollars. The person who bought it was a woman—middle-aged, nondescript. She told Bob Hansen's clerk that it was a birthday gift for a young woman whose birthstone was the opal."

A young woman. Lauren? The middle-aged buyer could have been her mother, although Syd had seen pictures of Carlie Fairbanks and she could hardly be described as nondescript.

"Is there a record of the sale?" Hopefully, the question was too vague to sound suspicious.

"Yes, but there is no personal information on it. None is required on a cash sale."

"Thank you. You've been very helpful." She was careful not to address Anthony by name. The less Victor knew about her friends, the safer they would be.

"I'm glad, darling. Kiss, kiss." The jeweler's voice turned coy. "And say hello to your friend for me."

She laughed. "You keep this up and I'll tell Brett to keep a leash on you."

She winked at Jake as she hung up. "That was my friend Antoinette. She owns a vintage clothing shop and has been trying to find me a dress for a benefit dinner I've been invited to next week."

"And did she find it?"

"She has one that was once worn by Jean Harlow. It's a little pricey, but it sounds great, just what I have been looking for."

"Do you need an escort to the dinner?"

She allowed her voice to turn playful. "Are you volunteering for the job?"

"Absolutely."

"Then you're on. You'll need a tux, though."

"For you, my sweet," he said, confirming that he

knew exactly who she had been talking to, "I'd agree to wear a suit of armor."

Syd was glad to see Chad in her office the following morning.

"I'm almost finished typing your motion," he said with his usual earnestness. "I hope you don't mind. I found the draft on your desk and figured you'd want a clean copy."

"Mind? Chad, you are an absolute godsend." She set her briefcase on her desk. "By the way, what do you know about semiprecious gems?"

"Not much. My girlfriend only likes diamonds."

Syd smiled. "Smart girl. Did you give her one yet?"

Chad kept right on typing. "On what you pay me?"

"Smart ass."

He hit the last key with a flourish. "What kind of semiprecious gem are we talking about?"

"Opals. Do me a favor, will you? After you're done with the motion, find out what birth month the opal represents and then see if you can find out what month Lauren Fairbanks was born."

"Can you wait?"

"No. I have a deposition at ten. Leave the information inside my desk drawer."

Syd was on her way to the office where the deposition was to take place when her cell phone rang. It was Violet's husband.

"The name of the man you're interested in is James Cabbot III of 12 Delancey Street," George Sorrensen said. "Six years ago, three narc detectives raided Club Apollo, a well-known nightspot in Society Hill they suspected was being used to deal drugs. More than a dozen people were arrested that night. Cabbot was there, snorting coke, but somehow he slipped through the cracks and wasn't busted along with the others."

"How come?"

"His daddy's the CEO of Cabbot Investments. He's got connections."

"Are you saying that those three cops were on the take?"

"I'm not saying that because I don't know. What I do know is that Cabbot should have been arrested and wasn't. Draw your own conclusions."

"Who made the bust?"

"Detective Ava Lamida, Detective Richard Steele and—you're going to love this—Detective Mike Gilmore. You didn't hear it from me, Syd."

"Of course not. Thank you, George."

Syd's thoughts raced ahead. Mike was a dirty cop. That's what Lilly had on him, and why he had been in no position to fight her on the custody issue. If it ever got out that he was on the take, his career in law enforcement was over.

But something kept nagging her. Lilly was one of the most honest persons on this planet. Syd had never known her to lie or to do anything even remotely unlawful, including withholding evidence, which was definitely illegal. Would she have made an exception in this case? Compromised her integrity?

Maybe, if that was the only way she could keep her daughter.

After the deposition, Syd returned to Mike's house, hoping she'd luck out again and find him home. She did.

"What's the matter, Syd?" He wasn't looking much better than he had the previous day, and was just as acerbic. "You have a death wish or something?"

She ignored the threat. It would be the last one he made for a long, long time. "Does the name James Cabbot III mean anything to you?"

The handsome features tightened. He tried to work out the sneer he had perfected, but some of the starch had left him and he couldn't pull it off. He looked at her for a few seconds, as though trying to evaluate how much she knew. "What if I do? What is it to you?"

"May I ask how you know him?"

"No, you may not, but I'll tell you anyway. He's an old acquaintance. Are you satisfied?"

"Not by a long shot. You see, I know exactly how the two of you got acquainted."

Mike moistened his lips and said nothing.

"You met him during a raid at Club Apollo six years ago. The place was being used by drug dealers, addicts and prostitutes. A dozen people were arrested that night, either for dealing or using. One who should have been arrested wasn't. You know who I'm talking about, don't you, Mike?"

"What are you getting at?"

"I'm trying to get you to level with me, but so far I'm doing all the talking." She shrugged. "That's fine. I don't mind. As I was saying, one of the users didn't get arrested. Why? Because the kid was loaded, or rather his rich daddy was loaded, and in the habit of paying cops who looked the other way whenever Junior did something naughty."

"That may be true but I never took a penny."

"You deny being one of the three cops who raided Appolo that night?"

"No. I deny taking money."

"How did the kid get away?"

His gaze shifted. "I don't know. Maybe he slipped out through a back door or climbed out a window. That's to be expected in a raid. Somebody screams 'Cops!' And those closest to an exit make a run for it."

"Did you ever see him after that?"

He blinked. "The kid? No. Why should I?"

"Then what was he doing at your house earlier? And don't say he wasn't because I saw him."

Although his complexion turned a shade paler, he managed to keep his composure. "How did you find out who he was?"

"I got a make on his license plate."

"Why? What business is it of yours who comes to my house?"

"None, except that your visitor looked pissed off and I got curious."

"Well, you wasted your time." His voice grew steadier. "There's nothing shady or sinister about James's visit. He was in the neighborhood and he decided to stop by and say hello."

"So why did you lie about it?"

"Because, like I said, who I see is none of your business."

"And like I said, James was very unhappy when he left here and that's reason enough for me to make it my business." She gave a light shrug. "Of course, if you'd rather I talked to James…"

It was an unbelievable sight. Looking as if all the air had been let out of him, Mike leaned against the wall and closed his eyes.

She almost felt sorry for him. "So I was right. You've been taking money from the Cabbots all along."

He opened his eyes. "What?"

"Cut the act, Mike. You're a dirty cop. That's what Lilly had on you all these years. That's why you didn't fight her for custody of Prudence. You couldn't afford to."

Mike gave a stubborn shake of his head. "I never took any money from James. Or from his father. The old man cut him off a long time ago."

"Then why was he here?"

Mike didn't answer.

"One way or another, I'm going to find out the truth. If not from you, then from James."

He took a shallow breath, as if trying to gather up his courage. "He was shaking me down. That's right," he added when she gave him a startled look. "James Cabbot is blackmailing *me*."

She didn't believe him. He was lying, still trying to weasel his way out of a tricky situation. "Why would he want to blackmail you?"

"Because I'm gay."

Thirty-Two

Syd couldn't do anything but stare at him. There were so many contradictions to that "confession," so many reasons for her not to believe him. Mike Gilmore was a man who had always personified machismo, arrogance and a sense of absolute power. And yet there he was, crushed and defeated.

"Since when?" she finally managed to ask.

"High school." He talked with his back still pressed to the wall. His gaze was fixed on a point behind Syd's shoulder. "I hid it well. I had to. All my friends were studs, guys I looked up to, played football and got drunk with."

"And Lilly? She didn't know?"

"Not at first. Then she began to suspect that I was cheating. One night she followed me and saw me with..." He still wouldn't look at her.

"With whom?"

"James."

Syd expelled a breath. It was all beginning to add up now. "Cabbot is gay."

"Yes. That's why his father disowned him."

Now she understood why Lilly hadn't been able to confide in her. She had been too embarrassed. "Why not just come out and tell the truth?" She thought of Anthony, so happy and outgoing. "Surely there are worse things in life than to admit that you're gay."

"Not in my job. I would have been shunned by the force."

"You could have told Lilly, instead of putting her through this farce of a marriage and hurting her the way you did."

"Lilly was good for my image. There were a couple of rumors about me already circulating around the department. My marriage to Lilly, and Prudence's birth a year later, dispelled those rumors."

"Your image." The moment of compassion she had experienced earlier vanished. He made her sick. "That's all you're worried about?"

"You got what you wanted, Syd. Now go away."

"Not just yet." Her mind flashed back to the farmhouse and the man who had shot her. "Did Lilly have pictures?"

"Pictures of what?"

"You and James."

He shook his head. "No, there are no pictures. She didn't need them. I've been giving money to James so he'd keep his mouth shut. All she had to do was up the ante and he would have told her everything she wanted to know. James loves money. And he doesn't care who knows he's gay. I do."

She could now officially scratch Mike off her list of suspects in the Erwinna shooting. With no hard proof to worry about, he'd had no reason to want to search Dot's house.

"Why was James so angry when he left your house?"

"He wanted more money and I told him I couldn't do it. I'm flat broke. I live from payday to payday as it is."

All the pieces were finally beginning to fall into place. "I think I get it now. You didn't file that petition for custody of Prudence because you love her and want to give her a stable home. Your daughter is your guarantee that Vanessa will marry you. Without her, there is no Vanessa, and without Vanessa and her money, you can't pay off your lover slash blackmailer. You were willing to disrupt a little girl's life and break the hearts of all those who love her just to save your hide. You are even more despicable than I imagined."

When he didn't answer, she walked over to where he stood. "Withdraw the motion, Mike. Today."

Syd waited to be back in her office before calling Dot. "You won't have to worry about Prudence," she said with a genuine lift in her voice. "Mike is withdrawing the petition."

She thought Dot would break down and cry. "Is it true? Are you sure?"

"Very sure. Prudence will stay where she is until Lilly returns."

"And…afterwards? Will he keep on pushing for shared custody?"

"I doubt it very much."

"Oh, Syd." She heard a soft sob. "I owe you so much."

"No, you don't. We're family, remember?"

Violet walked in just as Syd was hanging up. "Did you find the report Chad left for you?"

"Not yet." She opened her desk drawer and found two neatly typed pages. She held them up for Violet to see. "Thanks, Violet."

Everything Syd could possibly have wanted to know about opals was included in those two pages. The opal was the birthstone of people born in October. Unfortunately, Chad hadn't been able to find out Lauren's birth month. In fact, there was very little information on the teenager. Her family had kept her out of the limelight from the moment she was born. Then came the accident, and her face had been in all the papers along with her grade-point average at Sycamore High and her hopes of attending UCLA in the fall.

Chad had downloaded a color photograph which Syd studied. Lauren Fairbanks was a pretty girl, with long, straight blond hair, brown eyes and a shy look about her that didn't remind Syd of the sociable Mrs. Fairbanks or her charismatic, outgoing husband.

The big question now was if the necklace was Lauren's and Lilly had found it, possibly at the scene of the accident, why had she felt the need to hide it? What deep, dark secret did it hold?

Maybe Lauren herself would have the answers to those burning questions.

Four girls in blue jeans and pastel ski jackets walked out of Sycamore High, giggling as they threw sidelong glances at two handsome boys standing nearby.

Moments later, the group parted and Lauren Fairbanks walked toward her car, not the Mercedes Benz she had driven the night of the accident, but a spiffy red Mustang that looked as if it had just come out of the showroom.

Pointing a key at the car, she unlocked it, opened the driver's door and slid behind the wheel. Before she could turn on the ignition, Syd opened the passenger door and slid in beside her.

The girl let out a shriek and pulled back. "Who are you? What are you doing in my car?"

"Take it easy, Lauren. I'm not here to harm you." Syd spoke in what she hoped was a calm, reassuring voice. "My name is Sydney Cooper. I'm with the district attorney's office."

"What do you want with me?"

"I'd like you to answer a few questions about the accident you had earlier this month."

The girl was unable to hide her panic. "That case is closed."

"Lilly Gilmore didn't think so. You do know she was kidnapped, don't you? It's been in the news for the past week."

Recognition dawned in those fearful brown eyes. "Oh, my God, you're that woman who's been saying those terrible things about my dad."

"Is that what he told you?"

"He told me I didn't have to talk to you."

"Why is that? Do you have something to hide?"

"No! And neither has my dad! Just leave me alone."

"I'd love to do that, Lauren. In fact, I'd like nothing better than to see this whole mess go away. But I can't, not until I find my friend."

"I can't help you."

"I think you can," Syd said gently. "All you have to do is answer a couple of questions."

Lauren looked around her. Syd wasn't sure if she was thinking of calling out for help, or trying a quick getaway. "I don't know." She had calmed down somewhat. "What kind of questions?"

"The police report says that you were practicing your night driving." She looked around her at the plush leather seats, the fancy dash. "Congratulations, by the way. I take it you passed your test."

"Yes." She still looked suspicious.

"Are you a good driver?"

"Yes."

"And yet, you had that accident."

"It wasn't my fault," she said defensively.

"So I'm told. Tell me, Lauren, how fast were you going that you couldn't stop in time to avoid the collision?"

"I wasn't speeding, if that's what you're getting at."

"Would you say you were going the speed limit?"

"Yes."

"And what was that? Do you recall?"

The girl's cheeks turned red. "No, I don't."

"Then how can you say you were going at the speed limit?"

"Because at the time, I knew I was."

"Could your perception of speed have been altered?" Syd pressed.

"By what?"

"Alcohol?"

"No! Why would you say something like that?"

"Because according to the accident report, you ran into the bushes and were violently sick."

"I was scared, not drunk! I had just had a terrible accident. My first one ever."

Her voice trembled and Syd couldn't decide if it was from fear or outrage. She decided to push one more button. "Is that how you lost your necklace that night? When you were throwing up?"

"Necklace?" She frowned. "I didn't lose a necklace."

Syd's heart skipped a beat. She shrugged. "I thought I read that somewhere. I must be wrong."

"Will you leave now? My mom worries if I don't get home on time."

"Sure." Syd opened the door, started to get out, then as though she had just remembered something, she said, "What month were you born, Lauren?"

The question seemed to throw the girl off balance, but she answered it anyway. "March."

Thirty-Three

Syd was back in her office, trying to make up for lost time while waiting for Jake. He had called earlier to say he'd pick her up at seven and take her out to a restaurant he had been wanting to try.

She could do with a little pick-me-up. The excitement she had experienced when she'd found out that the necklace did not belong to Lauren Fairbanks had been short-lived. Yes, Lilly had found the necklace, most probably at the scene of the accident, but what did that prove? Anyone could have lost it there, except Ana Lee, or she would have reported it to the police. It could have been buried under the dirt for days, weeks, maybe months.

Chief Yates's call a little after six hadn't helped her mood. "I'm sorry," he had told her, aware that he would be disappointing her. "We couldn't get any decent fingerprints on the opal. They were too smudged to do any good."

A few minutes before seven, she shut down her laptop, slipped into her coat and went downstairs to wait for Jake. She found him chatting and laughing with the security guard as if they were two old buddies. They might as well have been. Justin was an ex-marine and as tough as they came.

"Comparing war stories, gentlemen?"

"Just making a friendly bet on tonight's game, Ms. Cooper. Would you care to make a wager?"

"And let you clean me out the way you did last year? No, thank you."

Justin was still laughing when Jake walked over to Syd and kissed her cheek. "Hi, beautiful. All set?"

"I am now." She meant it. The thought of spending the next couple of hours in Jake's company had lifted her spirits and would make her forget, at least for a while, that her best friend was still missing.

Syd and Jake sat at a window table at Palombe, Philadelphia's premier restaurant high above Rittenhouse Square. They had just finished their appetizers and as the plates were cleared away, Syd took a moment to look around her, at the elegant decor, the busy tuxedoed waiters, the lovely view of the square at night. The Fairbanks lived here, in a three-story town house that had been in the family for generations.

"How did you manage to get a reservation at this

late date?" she asked. "This is one of the hottest restaurants in Philadelphia. There's at least a three-week wait for a table."

"I guess it pays to have connections."

"Your FBI friend?"

"I have other friends."

"Then I'm very grateful to them. I was getting tired of going home and having to watch everything I do and say, knowing that Victor is out there, invading my privacy, spying on me." She gave him a half smile. "Unless…"

"Unless what?"

"Unless there is a tiny device hidden under the table."

"You can talk freely. The table is clear."

"You checked?"

"You can never be too careful."

"In that case…" She took a sip of her wine and put her glass back on the table. "I didn't get very good news from Chief Yates today."

"What did he have to say?"

"The lab couldn't get identifiable fingerprints on the opal."

"I'm sorry. Where do you go from here?"

"I'm not sure. I have one theory, but I can't prove it."

"Want to run it by me?"

She took a moment to answer his question, gently twirling her wineglass on the tablecloth. She had told him about her meeting with Mike Gilmore on the way to the restaurant, but hadn't yet mentioned her visit to Sycamore High, to him or to anyone else.

"I went to Lauren's school today."

"How come?"

"I wanted to talk to her."

"Wasn't that risky?"

"It could be if she tells her father."

"Did you find out anything?"

"She confirmed what Ana Lee told me about getting sick on the night of the accident, but when I asked her if she had lost a necklace, she looked surprised and said she hadn't."

"Do you believe her?"

"She had no reason to lie. Besides, her birth month isn't October. It's March."

Jake's eyes gleamed with wicked delight. "Are you suggesting that another woman was driving the senator's car? That one of the most admired men in the country *intentionally* deceived the police?"

"I'm not just suggesting it. The more I think about it, the more I'm convinced that another woman was involved. Why else would Lauren be so jumpy? So evasive?"

"But wouldn't the state trooper who answered the call realize that the woman behind the wheel was not the senator's daughter?"

"Not if she looked enough like Lauren to fool him *and* Ana Lee." Syd glanced around her before continuing. "Don't forget that it was dark, the girl was hysterical and the senator was anxious to take her home."

Jake leaned forward, arms on the table. "So what you're saying is that after his preliminary statement to the state trooper, the senator drove the woman back to her house, then he went home, woke up his daughter and asked her to lie for him?"

"I know it sounds outrageous, but yes, that's exactly what I'm saying."

"Where was Mrs. Fairbanks while all this was happening?"

"Out of town. She flew back home as soon as she heard that her daughter had been in an accident." She let out a small sigh. "I'm on the right track, Jake. I can feel it. The problem is I can't prove any of it."

"You could confront the senator with the necklace."

"What good would that do? He would simply deny ever having set eyes on it. And Lauren will back him up. It's their words against mine."

Their entrées had arrived—crispy duck in a cherry sauce for Jake, a roasted striped bass for her.

"Could it be that the necklace isn't as significant as you thought it was?" Jake offered as he cut into his duck.

"Then why did Lilly hide it? And why did she want me to find it?" She took a bite of her fish, which was excellent. "My only hope now rests in the chief's next move."

"What's that?"

"He's going to ask every TV station and every

area newspaper to show a picture of the necklace. Hopefully, someone will recognize it and come forward."

"If your theory is right, and Lilly did find out that Fairbanks was having an affair, the senator could become your prime suspect. Or is that too farfetched?"

"In this business, nothing is too far-fetched. Besides, the suspects aren't exactly beating down my door. Mike is off the list. So is Doug Avery, although he probably has information about your friend Victor that may help you, if not me." She told him about Avery's courtroom outburst and his subsequent beating.

Jake was immediately interested. "Did you question him?"

"I questioned both of them. Van Heusen claims to have no idea why Avery threatened him and Avery clammed up, even when I offered him a deal."

"Okay if I pass this information to Paul Ramirez?"

"Be my guest. It will be in all the papers by morning anyway."

"Ah, *mon ami*," a deep baritone voice said. "I see that you still like my food."

Startled, Syd looked up. André Garnier, Palombe's renowned executive chef, stood at their table, grinning down at Jake. He was a handsome man in his forties with white hair and compelling dark eyes. Under his snug white chef's coat, his stomach was as flat as a board.

Laughing, Jake stood up and the two men embraced, clapping each other on the back. "You old rascal," Jake said. "If you hadn't kept this place such a secret, I would have been back in Philadelphia long ago."

"Maybe if you were not hiding in the Louisiana bayou, I would have known where to find you."

His arm around the chef's shoulder, Jake turned back to Syd and made the introductions.

"Enchanté, mademoiselle." André shook her hand, bowing slightly. "I trust everything was to your liking?"

"To my liking?" Syd laughed at his understatement. "It was perfect. The best meal I've ever had. Thank you."

"You are very welcome." André turned to Jake. "And you, my friend, are a lucky man, although I am not sure you deserve this lovely lady."

A waiter raised a hand in a discreet signal and André excused himself. "Allow me to send something special for dessert," he said to Jake. "With my compliments. And do not leave Philadelphia without saying goodbye." After another bow to Syd, he was gone.

Syd was in awe. "You know Chef Garnier?"

"André was in the French army and part of the coalition during Desert Storm. He had been working as a cook in a Bordeaux restaurant when he was drafted."

"How did you meet?"

"During an R&R in Tel Aviv. When we returned to Iraq, he gave me several passes so my friends and I could eat at the French mess hall a couple of times of week. Needless to say, I was the most popular guy in the camp."

"Did you know he had become a famous chef?"

"Not until I read it in the current issue of *Philadelphia Magazine*."

"You are full of surprises, Jake Sloan."

He grinned. "And the evening is still young."

Unfortunately, although both would have loved ending the night with much more than a peck on the cheek, Victor was at his listening post. With a goodnight kiss, and the whispered promise to pick up where they left off one day soon, they parted.

Thirty-Four

"I think I screwed up," Jake told Ramirez when he spoke to the agent the following morning.

Paul was his usual unfazed self. "How so?"

"I may have made Victor suspicious by asking too many questions."

"Questions he couldn't answer?"

"No, he answered them. It's just a gut feeling I have."

"How did you leave it with him?"

"He suggested we have lunch sometime, but wasn't specific."

"Don't worry about it. He probably needs time to check you out a little more, make sure he can trust you. Don't call him, though. Let him make the first move."

"It could take a while."

"We have no choice but to wait until he's ready."

"I may have a better idea."

"Let's hear it."

"I have a friend I haven't seen in years. I'm pretty sure I can find out how to get in touch with him."

"Who is he?"

"A former army intelligence officer, one of the best. After his discharge, he was offered a job with a construction company in Saudi Arabia and ended up staying there. He's married to an Iranian woman. If anyone can find out what Victor has been up to, it's him."

"Why didn't you mention him before?"

"I didn't think of it."

"Can you trust him?"

"With my life."

"All right, then, go with it."

After three phone calls to Riyadh, Jake had finally learned that Ted Malvern had left Saudi Arabia three years ago and relocated to Middletown, Delaware, where he owned and operated a crop-dusting business.

The two men had met in flight school and had hit it off right away. Upon earning their wings, Jake as a helicopter pilot and Ted as a reconnaissance pilot, both men had been assigned to separate duties and lost touch with each other, as is often the case in the army. In 1990, shortly after Saddam Hussein invaded Kuwait, the two friends had found themselves stationed in Saudi Arabia—Jake as a DELTA Force officer, Ted as an intelligence officer.

Ted had stood by Jake during his legal troubles and hadn't believed for one moment that his friend was guilty of disobeying orders. He had made it clear to Victor that he blamed him for Jake's downfall, even if he couldn't prove it.

When Jake found his friend's number in the Delaware Yellow Pages and called him, Ted's wife of twenty-two years, Farah, answered the phone. Fond of Jake, she was delighted to hear from him, although she chastised him for vanishing from their lives the way he had. She told him that the crop-dusting business was a one-man operation, with Ted handling the marketing and the flying. He was out at the moment, but she would give him Jake's message. At her request for a phone number, Jake said he'd call back and promised to come down for a visit before leaving Philadelphia.

At seven o'clock that same evening, Jake went out to make the call. The dark sedan he had spotted earlier had been replaced by a green Pontiac Grand Prix, but the man behind the wheel was still one of Victor's types—big, tough-looking and busy reading a newspaper.

As he had before, Jake paid no attention to him, but headed to the tavern for a burger. He placed his order then went into the men's room to call Ted.

This time it was his old friend who answered. After the necessary banter, Ted brought him up to date on what had been happening in his life in the past fourteen years.

"I would have stayed in Saudi," he said, "but Farah was beginning to worry about the kids and their safety, so I left Algier Construction and came back here to be my own boss."

"Did you say kids? You have others, besides little Franky?"

Ted laughed. "I have two more and don't you dare let Frank hear you call him little Franky. He's sixteen now and almost as tall as I am. He wants to be a pilot."

"Like his old man."

"No, dummy. A *fighter* pilot, like Tom Cruise in *Top Gun*."

Jake laughed. "That's one tough act to follow. Tell me about the other two."

Jake could hear the pride in Ted's voice as he answered. "Sam is thirteen. He's the artistic one in the family. Takes after his mother. He plays the piano, acts. He's even written a short play for his drama class."

"And the third one?"

His voice softened. "My baby, Jaimie. She's nine and a handful."

"Then she must take after her father. You were always a rebel."

"Look who's talking." Then, in a sober tone, he asked, "What's up, old buddy? It's got to be serious for you to look me up after all those years."

"I should have kept in touch. I'm sorry, Ted."

"You had a lot on your plate when you left Iraq.

And I'm just as guilty, so let's not waste our time apologizing, okay?"

"Fair enough."

Jake told him about the reason for his call. Except for a low growl at the sound of van Heusen's name, Ted didn't interrupt.

"If there's anything I can do to help bring that son of a bitch down," Ted said earnestly, "I'll do it. Let me make a few calls. It could take a couple of days, but I'll get your answer."

"Syd!" Chad jumped up from his chair, almost knocking it over. "Where have you been?"

Syd glanced at her watch. "Why? I'm not late."

"The D.A. is in a foul mood. He wants to see you. Right now."

"What's his problem?" As if she didn't know.

"Beats me. Violet told me to steer clear, and that's what I've been doing."

She found Ron in his office, facing the door, his arms crossed over his chest. She knew that posture. He was out for blood. Hers.

"You wanted to see me?" she asked innocently.

The look he gave her could have stopped a runaway train. "Have your completely lost your mind?"

"What did I do?" The question bought her some time. To do what with it, she wasn't sure.

"Senator Fairbanks called me at home this morning. In fact, he got me out of bed. Would you like to hazard a guess what his call was about?"

"I'm not good at—"

"You!" he thundered. "He called about *you*. And your ambush—yes, that's the word he used, *ambush*—of his seventeen-year-old daughter."

"We just had a conversation—"

"You jumped in her car and scared the shit out of her!"

"She may have been a little nervous at first."

Ron came to stand less than a foot from her. "The girl had to be sedated when she got home, for Christ's sake. You call that being a little nervous? I'm lucky the Fairbanks aren't suing my ass. Hell, I'm lucky if I still have a job by the end of the day."

"She's lying about something, Ron. I was trying to find out what—"

"By using your credentials as an assistant district attorney? By making her believe that you represented this office in the investigation of Lilly Gilmore's kidnapping?"

"I never claimed to be representing this office. She just assumed—"

He put his hand up. "Stop right there. I'm not interested in your excuses. The bottom line is, lay off the senator. And his daughter. I know how badly you want to find your friend, but you're on the wrong track here, Syd. So back off. Is that understood?"

"How do you know that I'm on the wrong track? Because the senator told you so?"

"Sydney." He spoke in a deceptively calm voice. "If you don't back off, Alan Fairbanks is prepared to go to the mayor and demand both our resignations. I don't know about you, but I have no intention of standing in the unemployment line because one of my A.D.A.s decided to play tough."

"Isn't that what you taught me? To be tough? No matter how slim the odds?"

He sighed. "Look, Syd, I don't deny that you're a good attorney and that I'd hate to lose you, but I have my orders. Either you end the investigation of the senator and his daughter or you're fired."

The injustice of his ultimatum made Syd bristle. Couldn't Ron see that the reason he was being pressured was *because* the Fairbanks had something to hide? Or maybe he did see it, but as he said, he had his orders.

An unflappable optimist, however, she tried to come up with a workable compromise. Maybe she didn't have to end her investigation. Maybe all she needed was to let everyone *believe* that she was backing off. How hard could that be?

"Well?" Ron watched her.

She gave a curt nod. "All right. You win. From now on the Fairbanks are off my radar screen."

For a moment, Ron looked genuinely surprised, even disappointed, as though he hadn't expected her to give up so easily. Then, just as quickly, he nodded his approval. "Thank you."

She started to leave, then stopped when she saw him scratch his head. "There's one more thing."

"What?" she asked suspiciously.

"The senator wants you to apologize to his daughter."

"You've got to be kidding."

"You see me laughing?"

"Ron, that's ridiculous. I'm not in first grade."

"It's the only way he'll believe your intentions are genuine. Come on, don't look at me like that. It's just a little apology, not a death sentence."

No, but it was a classic case of power play. Feeling he had been wronged, the senator was flexing his influential muscles, making her look stupid. It was also a clear signal to anyone else who might be tempted to follow in her footsteps.

Resigned, she asked. "Where is this little shindig supposed to take place?"

"At the Fairbanks's home in Rittenhouse Square. Lauren has a half day today. She'll be home at one."

"I'll be there."

"Great. Oh, and Syd?"

One hand on the doorknob, she turned around.

"Make them believe you."

Thirty-Five

They looked like a welcoming committee, Syd thought as she was ushered into the luxurious living room of the Fairbanks's Rittenhouse Square home. The senator was there, with his George Clooney good looks and campaign smile. Standing beside him, his blond wife was the picture of elegance and good breeding. The senator's press secretary, Muriel Hathaway—aka The Barracuda—was also there, ready to rewrite the script the moment it went off-course.

Syd gave the woman a brief appraisal. Late forties, brown hair, stony face, a little matronly looking, although with a bit of effort she could have been attractive. As the senator's official spokesperson, she not only handled all matters that related to the press, but she had access to every aspect of his private life.

Including an affair?

Studying her a moment longer, Syd concluded that she could have been the woman who had purchased the necklace. She fit the jeweler's description to a *T*.

Lauren was the only person in the room unsophisticated enough to look nervous, although with the troops standing by and Syd on her best behavior, she certainly didn't have anything to worry about.

"It was good of you to come, Ms. Cooper." The senator shook her hand as though she was one of his loyal constituents.

"My pleasure." She wondered if he knew that being here was sheer torture.

Then, because they were all looking at her expectantly, she turned to Lauren. "I'm sorry if I frightened you yesterday," she said quietly. That much was true. "I should have known better than to approach you the way I did. My concern over my friend's kidnapping clouded my judgment."

Lauren glanced at her father, who gave a discreet nod.

"That's all right." The girl seemed to be having difficulty meeting Syd's gaze. "And I'm sorry about your friend. I hope you find her soon."

"Me too."

The perfect hostess, Mrs. Fairbanks pointed at a selection of sodas and mineral water, all elegantly presented on a silver tray. "Could I offer you something to drink, Ms. Cooper? We always try to get together for a few minutes when Lauren gets home from school. We would love to have you join us."

How civilized, Syd thought. And what a great photo opportunity for any paparazzi who might be lurking outside those Palladian windows.

"Thank you," Syd said, equally gracious. "Unfortunately, I can't stay. I have an autopsy to attend."

Mrs. Fairbanks made a face.

"Did you drive here?" the senator asked.

"I took a cab."

He turned to Muriel Hathaway. "Muriel, ask Connor to drive Ms. Cooper back to her office."

When Syd started to protest, he raised his hand. "Please. It's our pleasure."

And with that, he left, leaving Syd in the capable hands of his press secretary.

Back at the office, Syd had time to give a verbal report of her apology to Ron before rushing to the coroner's office for the autopsy of a local boxer, who had died under suspicious circumstances. By the time she returned, feeling a little queasy, she was looking forward to taking her mind off the gruesome sight by reading the file on Alan Fairbanks that Chad had prepared for her.

The man had had quite a year. Rising from semi-obscurity, he had entered the presidential race twelve months ago, much to the amazement of his more powerful colleagues. Not that the senator from Pennsylvania didn't have the credentials to become president. After eleven years in the senate, he had established himself as a strong supporter of the environment, had fought for campaign finance reform, health care for the elderly and a solid education for every child, rich or poor.

But although he had made himself heard on those issues over the years, he had never emerged as a true political power, much less as a man who could become the country's next commander-in-chief.

Then, just as his reelection to the state senate seemed in doubt in the year 2000, he had made an extraordinary comeback and was reelected with sixty-one percent of the vote.

That stellar victory was soon followed by appearances on programs such as *Meet the Press, Nightline* and *Face the Nation,* where he charmed audiences from coast to coast. The transformation from public servant to celebrity was meteoric. Suddenly, Americans began to see Alan Fairbanks not just as an elected official, but as a viable candidate in the next presidential elections.

On the day that he made the announcement that he was running, the news had made instant headlines. But while supporters for the charismatic senator grew, there were the usual objectors, some of whom tried to derail his chances by attacking his character.

His candor about a drunken brawl that had taken place in college when he was only nineteen had earned him the admiration of millions. "I was just a stupid kid doing a stupid thing," he had said in a televised interview. "I guess I was too embarrassed to bring it to light."

That's when the money started pouring in, allowing him to campaign heavily and buy more airtime than any other candidate. Rare was the day when you didn't see the face or hear the voice of Senator Alan Fairbanks.

His image as a devoted husband and a loving father was the stuff fairy tales were made of. The media followed him everywhere—to the Colorado ski slopes where he and his family vacationed every Christmas. To the Fairbanks's shore home in Ocean City, New Jersey, and outside their three-story town house in exclusive Rittenhouse Square, where they could occasionally catch a glimpse of Philadelphia's favorite son.

This past January, Fairbanks had won the Iowa caucuses, then went on to win not only the New Hampshire primary but the next eight primaries as well. To quote a friend of the family, "Nothing can stop him now."

And while his daughter's accident had caused a slight drop in the polls in the days that followed the crash, the setback was only temporary.

There was a knock on Syd's door just as she was finishing reading the report. It was Violet. "Ana Lee left a message on my voice mail while I was gone." She handed Syd a pink message slip. "She wants to talk to you. It's about Lauren Fairbanks's necklace."

Syd put the file down. "Did she say anything else?"

"No. She just asked if you could meet her at her

apartment at four." She pointed at the slip of paper. "I wrote down the address."

Syd glanced at her watch and saw that it was a little after three-thirty. She had just enough time to make it.

Thirty-Six

Ana Lee lived in the heart of Chinatown, in a four-story apartment building just a block east of the colorful forty-foot Chinese Friendship Gate, the largest gate of its kind outside of China.

She looked agitated when she opened the door but managed a smile of welcome. "Miss Cooper. Come in, please." She bowed slightly and led Syd to a small, tidy living room where the color red prevailed. On a low, ornate table, a teapot and two small cups were waiting.

"Please sit down. I make tea."

"Thank you, Mrs. Lee. That's very kind of you." Syd sat down in one of the two red-and-gold chairs and accepted a cup of tea—jasmine from the smell of it.

Ana sat directly across from her, still looking nervous. She took a sip of her tea before she spoke again. "Today, I see necklace on TV."

Syd held her cup tightly. "Have you seen it before today?"

"I see on senator's daughter on night of accident." She motioned at her own neck. "She wear open blouse. And I see necklace. Very pretty. Just like on TV today."

Syd put her cup down and searched frantically through her handbag. The photo she had taken with her disposable camera was still there, tucked in a zippered pocket. She took it out and showed it to Ana. "Are you talking about this necklace?"

Ana nodded vigorously. "Yes, yes. That one."

"The senator's daughter was wearing it? Are you sure?"

More emphatic nodding. "Very sure. I see it. Then, later, when she come back from bushes, necklace gone."

"What do you mean, gone?"

"You know…" She waved her hand in front of her throat. "Not around neck. Gone."

Syd was having difficulty containing her excitement. Ana's statement could be the proof she needed to confront the senator.

"Did you mention that to anyone? The police?"

Ana Lee looked slightly panicked. "No. I remember necklace now because I see on TV. Is necklace important? I do something wrong?"

"No, Mrs. Lee, you didn't do anything wrong. Far from it."

"What you do now?"

"I'm going to talk to the police and tell them that you recognized the necklace. That's why Chief Yates put the picture on TV and in the newspapers, so someone would recognize it and come forward, just as you did. You'll probably be asked to make another statement. Is that all right?"

She seemed relieved. "Yes, yes. I make statement. Okay."

As Syd walked back toward her office, she could barely keep her thoughts in order. The necklace did not belong to Lauren. It belonged to another woman, a woman who had been driving the car on the night of the accident. And now she had the witness to prove it.

"Got you," she said under her breath.

Standing on a ladder and listening to the lively sounds of Vivaldi's Mandolin Concerto on Syd's CD player, Jake was brushing a long stroke of white paint along the hallway molding when the cell phone he had hooked to his belt rang.

"May I speak to Nancy, please?" Paul Ramirez asked.

"You have the wrong number." Jake waited a minute or two after he had hung up before pretending to be looking for another can of white paint. "Now, where would she put it?" he mumbled to himself, knowing the listening device would pick up his voice, even at that level.

He went from room to room, cursed a little about

having to leave in the middle of his task. Then, jiggling his keys to signal he was leaving, he left the apartment and walked over to the hardware store two-and-a-half blocks away. Once there, he went into the aisle that displayed the various brands of paint and after making sure he hadn't been followed, he took out his cell phone and dialed.

"All right, Paul," he said when the agent answered. "I'm clear now. What's up?"

"I'm afraid I have bad news."

His first thought was for his father. "My dad?"

"No." There was a short pause. "It's Ted Malvern. He is dead."

Jake had to make a huge effort to hide his shock. "Dead? What are you talking about? How can Ted be dead? I spoke to him yesterday."

"I just got a call from the field office in Baltimore. Malvern's plane crashed about eight miles from his airfield last night. He was at the controls."

"Are you sure it's him?"

"I wouldn't have called you unless I had a positive ID."

Jake ran his hand through his hair. "Jesus, Paul. What happened?"

"The authorities and the FAA are investigating. They're not saying anything yet. I'll know more in a couple of hours."

"How did you find out?"

"When you told me about Malvern I called a field agent I know in Wilmington and had your friend checked out, just to make sure we could trust him. The agent heard about the accident and called me."

Accident. Jake had a difficult time accepting that. Ted had been a first-rate pilot, meticulous to a fault.

So what the hell had happened here? After three years in the crop-dusting business and thousands of hours in flying time, Ted had taken his plane out, at night, and crashed?

"This doesn't add up, Paul. I need to check it out."

"If you're thinking of going to Middletown, I would strongly advise against it. If Victor—"

"To hell with Victor. Let him think what he wants."

"Then let me do it. I'll be glad to make some calls."

"No. This is much too important to be handled by anyone but me. I'm going to Middletown. You know how to reach me."

After he'd hung up, he dialed Syd's cell phone. When only her voice mail answered, he told her that he had to leave town due to an emergency and didn't expect to be back for another three or four days. He would keep in touch.

Still numb from the news he'd just received, Jake moved stiffly, picking up what he needed from the shelf and taking it to the counter. He tried not to let his suspicions get the best of him. No matter how tempted he was to blame Victor, he would not make any assumptions until he had talked to Farah.

He had no idea how Victor, or whoever was listening to his comings and goings would interpret this sudden departure. What he could count on for certain was that his travels would be closely monitored, even more so if Victor turned out to be the one who had ordered Ted's death. If he was, then chances were Victor also knew who had sought Ted's help and why.

Pray I'm wrong, Victor, he thought as he walked out of the store. Or there will be hell to pay.

Thirty-Seven

"I don't understand, Jake." Farah took another tissue from the box on the coffee table and wiped her swollen red eyes.

She was still the same petite, attractive woman Jake had met twenty years ago, with only a hint of gray through that thick black hair. Born of an English mother and an Iranian father, and educated in London, she had been living in Saudi Arabia with her parents, both teachers, when she met Ted.

"Ted kept that plane in top flying condition," she continued. "He would have never gone up if there was something even remotely wrong with it."

Jake sat in the large, sunny living room of the Malverns' colonial home in Middletown. He had made the drive from Philly in less than an hour and had been relieved to find Farah alone. Her family, scattered all over the world, hadn't yet arrived and the children had been whisked away by their paternal grandparents, who lived in Maryland.

"Did he say why he was taking the plane up?" Jake asked.

She shook her head. "You know how he felt about flying. He never needed a reason to go up, especially at this time of year, when business is slow."

"You said he was expecting a couple of prospective clients?"

She blew her nose. "That's another thing. Why would he leave when he knew those two men were coming?"

"Could it be that they didn't show up?"

She shrugged. "That's possible. I never had a chance to find out."

"Did he tell you anything about them? Where they're from? How they heard about Ted?"

"All he knew was that they had bought a rather large farm a few miles from here and wanted to sign a contract with Ted for regular dusting."

"What's the name of the farm?"

"I don't know." She was watching him a little more intently now. "Ted didn't say."

"What time was his appointment?"

"Nine o'clock last night. That's why he left the house right after dinner. He wanted to take a look at his schedule for the spring."

"His appointment was at nine and his plane crashed at nine-thirty. Wouldn't he normally wait around longer than half an hour for what could have been a lucrative contract?"

Keen as ever, Farah observed him through tear-filled eyes. "What is it, Jake? What are you thinking?"

He hadn't meant to say quite as much. "Nothing." To avoid her gaze, too intense for his liking, he re-filled their coffee cups from a tray she had brought in earlier. "I'm afraid the shock of Ted's death did a number on my head." He wondered if his words sounded as lame to her as they did to him.

She took the offered cup. "He was so excited about your call, although I must say, he was a little mysterious about it. He said the two of you talked about old times, but I had the feeling he was holding back about something. Don't ask me why, but I even thought—" She shook her head. "No, that's silly. He would have told me."

"Told you what?"

"If he was in some kind of trouble."

Jake tried to take a sip of coffee, hoping it would relieve the dryness in his throat. It didn't.

"Jake? Am I right? Was Ted in some kind of trouble?"

"Not that I know of." God, he was lousy at this.

"Why won't you look at me?"

He put his cup down and looked up.

He wished he hadn't.

Farah's eyes, dry now, had gone flat. "You know something. Tell me what it is. I have a right to know, Jake!"

How? How could he tell her and not jeopardize the operation?

"Did it have anything to do with your call?" she persisted. "Or maybe he called you first? He needed you for something?"

"No, Farah." He put his cup down. "I'm the one who needed him."

He wasn't sure how long the silence lasted. Or how he managed to hold Farah's searching gaze. When she spoke again, he could barely hear her. "You needed him? To do what?"

"I can't tell you."

Her voice rose a notch. "Why not?"

"Because it's classified information."

"Classified?" She frowned. "As in intelligence work?"

"Sort of, except that this was a personal request."

He saw her expression change. Her eyes turned bright, almost feverish. She shook her head. "No, you can't be… Tell me that you're not responsible for what happened. Tell me I'm wrong to think that, Jake. I want to be wrong." She almost wailed those last few words.

"Farah—"

"Oh, God." She sprung out of her chair so fast, she almost sent the coffee service flying. She paid no attention to the tumbled cup. Standing in the middle of the living room, she covered her mouth with both hands and started shaking.

It took Jake a split second to be by her side. But

as he tried to hold her, she slapped his arms away with both hands. "Don't touch me!"

"Let me explain."

"It was you? *You* did this to him? Why?" Her eyes were dark with anger, her voice raw with despair. "Answer me, dammit! Or I swear I'll call the authorities."

"You can't do that."

"I damn well can and will."

Jake knew enough about human nature to believe she meant every word. Ramirez wouldn't like what he was about to do, but he had learned that often the most logical decisions were the least popular. "It's complicated."

"Seems simple enough to me," she said coldly. "You got my husband killed."

She was right. It *was* that simple. And nothing Jake could do or say would change that outcome. Or make his own guilt any less difficult to bear. "Sit down, Farah. Please."

She started to say something, then, as her body began to sway, she allowed him to lead her back to her chair.

He tried to be as direct as possible. To his surprise, she did not interrupt him, not even when he told her that he was the one who had thought of calling Ted. In fact, she was so still, with her hands primly folded on her lap and her eyes downcast, that she almost looked as though she had dozed off. Almost.

When he was finished, she raised her head. Her

expression hadn't changed. There was still anger there. And something else. Something that hit him like a wet rag in the face. Hatred.

"You bastard," she hissed at last. "Ted told you that we came back to the States because the situation in the Middle East had become too dangerous. He told you that he feared for the children, and you still asked him to do you a favor you *knew* could get him killed? What kind of friend are you?"

"I thought it was a safe enough request. Ted had some of the most reliable contacts in the area— men he trusted implicitly. In all those years he worked in intelligence, not a single one ever betrayed him."

"Times have changed, Jake. People have changed. You didn't think about that?"

"Not as much as I should have," he said, feeling miserable. Then in the same breath, he added, "I'm going to find out who did this, Farah, but I need your help."

He could tell by her bitter expression that helping him was the last thing she wanted to do. "Give me a couple of names. Or just one. Someone Ted trusted and kept in touch with in the Middle East. Someone who may have been in a position to give him the information I was looking for."

She took a while to answer. When she did, her voice was cold and flat. "Retired army lieutenant colonel Francis Longnecker. He now lives in Tallahassee, Florida. The other is an Englishman, Colin Wright. He was in British Intelligence before coming to work at Algier Construction with Ted. He is now an executive VP there."

"Do you have a phone number for them?"

Her back rigid, she walked over to a desk, took out a small book and flipped through it. She wrote down the numbers on a green Post-It. Walking back, she handed it to him. "You have what you want. Now get out of my house."

He didn't budge. "I don't blame you for hating me, Farah, but if you're thinking of going to the police, please don't. Hate me all you want, but don't jeopardize what the FBI is trying to do."

She remained silent.

"All I'm asking is that you think of all the innocent people who will be harmed if van Heusen and others like him are allowed to continue their dirty little business."

She gave him a stinging look. "You'll forgive me if I don't share your compassion, will you? I've just lost my husband. My three children have lost their father and I'll most likely lose the business." She let out a brittle laugh. "So spare me the melodrama. I've got all I can handle right here."

With trembling fingers, she picked up the fallen cup and set it back on the tray. "I believe you know the way out."

"Let me help you. You don't have to lose the business. We can go to the bank together and talk to—"

"No, thank you," she said flatly. "You've done enough harm as it is."

Thirty-Eight

Trying to speak in a coherent, concise manner, Syd stood in Ron's office on Friday morning and recounted her conversation with Ana Lee word for word. His initial anger when she had told him about her visit to the Asian woman soon turned to shock as she voiced the facts.

"I know you told me to stop my investigation," she said when she was finished. "But when Ana called and said she had information about the necklace, I couldn't stand back and do nothing."

Ron was pacing up and down, visibly shaken. "What exactly did you do?"

"Chief Yates is on his way."

"You're going to have the senator *arrested?*"

"That's not my call. Chief Yates wants to question him. Whether or not an arrest will be made is entirely up to the chief. Right now the scenario is pretty black-and-white, Ron. The senator and his daughter have been lying since day one. Lauren was not driving his car the night of the accident. Someone else was. And that makes Alan Fairbanks suspect number one in the kidnapping of Lilly Gilmore."

"You think Lilly knew about the other woman?"

"Yes, I do. She may even have confronted Fairbanks, although he denies ever meeting her. And if she did confront him, and he realized that the truth was about to come out, he could have been scared into taking the necessary action."

Ron stopped his pacing and came to stand in front of her. His expression had softened a little. "You realize that if that scenario of yours is correct, there's a strong possibility that Lilly is no longer alive."

That was the one thought she had tried to keep out of her mind. To hear Ron express that fear out loud now made it all the more real. "Yes," she said in a small voice. "I realize that."

"Where is the senator now?"

"Home. He's scheduled to leave for California in the morning, for the primary."

Violet, who had a mind like radar, gave a light knock and opened the door a crack. "Senator Fairbanks is on CNN."

Ron walked over to a shelf and turned on the TV. The loud chanting was the first thing they heard. "Fair-Banks. Fair-Banks. Fair-Banks." Banners with the words Fairbanks For President bobbed up and down. More than two hundred people, all holding small American flags, had assembled in front of the senator's town house for a special send-off.

At last, the senator appeared. Both arms raised in a sign of victory, he walked onto the makeshift stage. He was grinning from ear to ear.

"Thank you," he shouted above the roar of the crowd. His voice was hoarse from weeks of campaigning, but he could still be heard. "They said it couldn't be done. They said I wasn't tough enough, connected enough, experienced enough."

The crowd booed.

"But here we are!"

The crowd went wild. "Fair-Banks. Fair-Banks. Fair-Banks."

"Thanks for coming on this cold night. God bless you all." He punched the air with his fist. "California, here we come!"

A street band started playing "California, Here I Come." The senator waved at his adoring fans and walked back inside.

Ron turned off the TV set. There was a long silence before he finally said, "Go get him, Syd."

A light rain had begun to fall when the chief, accompanied by Deputy Brady, arrived at Syd's office a little after 2:00 p.m. From there the three of them drove to Rittenhouse Square in the chief's official car. Fortunately, the crowd that had been there earlier was gone. No one paid any attention to the car that parked in a "no parking" zone, or to the three people who walked into the building where the popular senator resided.

A maid in a plain black dress opened the door. From inside the town house came the sound of laughter, lively conversation and glasses clinking. The place was brightly lit and charged with electricity. Even the maid seemed excited.

Bits and pieces of conversation filtered into the foyer, words like "bury him," "won't know what hit him," and "somebody take a look at the current polls, please."

The maid started to say that the senator was busy, but Chief Yates raised a hand, no longer Mr. Nice Guy. "He's going to have to make time for this, Miss."

Looking flustered, she left the three of them in the large, elegant foyer with its expensive antiques and Aubusson rug. She was back moments later, followed by the senator.

His smile faded the moment he saw Syd.

Then his gaze swept over Yates and the deputy. Impressively, he remained calm. Years as a politician had taught him to face adversity with poise and decorum.

"Good afternoon, Chief Yates. I understand you have something to discuss with me? I can't imagine what it could be, but I hope it won't take long. I'm getting ready to—"

Without a word, the chief held up the plastic bag with the necklace inside.

The senator looked as if he was about to faint.

Behind him, Syd heard the tap of high heels on the black-and-white marble floor, then Carlie Fairbanks appeared, her hostess smile in place. "Alan? Our guests are wondering—"

Her gaze stopped on Syd. "What is she doing here? And who are these men?"

The chief lowered his arm and stepped forward. "I'm Police Chief Yates of the Mullica Township police department, ma'am. This is Deputy Brady and I believe you know Assistant District Attorney Sydney Cooper."

She looked at all three before looking down at the necklace in the chief's hand. "What is this all about?"

Syd addressed the senator, who hadn't said a word. "Would you care to tell her, Senator?"

"Tell me what, for God's sake?"

Once again, the chief raised the arm that held the plastic bag. "We were about to ask your husband if he had ever seen that necklace before, but perhaps you could answer the question."

"No, I haven't."

The chief raised a brow. "Senator?"

Having had time to pull himself together, Fairbanks shook his head. "No, I've never seen it."

"Careful what you say, Senator," Syd warned. "Mrs. Lee, whom I'm sure you remember, is prepared to swear, under oath, that she saw this necklace on the girl who was driving your car on the night of the accident."

"But that can't be," Carlie Fairbanks said. "That necklace definitely does not belong to my daughter."

"I never said it did."

Under the expert makeup, Mrs. Fairbanks's complexion turned ashen. She looked at her husband. "My God, Alan," she said in a whisper. "What have you done now?"

Now? Meaning that the good senator had cheated before?

The chief set the plastic bag with its compromising contents on a small round table beside him. "Why don't you tell us exactly what happened the night of the accident, Senator?"

"Aren't you a little out of your jurisdiction, Chief Yates?"

"Not at all. I'm investigating the kidnapping of Lilly Gilmore, and what happened on the night of the accident may be directly connected to that case."

"Why?" Carlie Fairbanks, although aware that something was terribly wrong, had not yet connected all the dots.

"Because your husband lied to the police, Mrs. Fairbanks. Your daughter was not driving your husband's car that night. She only claimed that she was."

"But of course she…" As the truth finally dawned on her, she shot her husband a horrified look. "Alan! Tell me that's not true."

Under the weight of her accusing stare, the senator's shoulders slumped. He no longer looked like the charismatic, confident man Syd had seen on the television screen earlier. In a matter of minutes he seemed to have aged ten years.

"Who does the necklace belong to, Alan?" Her voice had turned icy.

"To a friend of mine." The powerful timbre of his voice had been reduced to a mere whisper. "The accident…didn't happen exactly as I told you."

"Lauren wasn't driving?"

"No."

"Was she with you?"

Looking like a beaten man, Fairbanks shook his head.

Unmoved by this very public display of emotion, Mrs. Fairbanks skewered him with a murderous look. "One of your cheap girlfriends wrecked our car, and you had Lauren take the rap? You made her *lie* to the police? And to me? Claim to have done something she didn't do?"

"I didn't make her do anything. Once I explained to her—"

In the quiet room, the slap sounded like a gunshot.

Shocked and humiliated, the senator stumbled back, holding his cheek.

"You despicable bastard," Carlie said in a voice that seemed to need all her willpower not to explode. "You used your own daughter to cover up your dirty little secret. How could you do that to her? How low have you sunk?"

She was too wound up to give him time to answer.

"Who was it this time, Alan? An actress? A super-model? A campaign worker?"

"Brenda."

"Brenda?" She seemed to search her memory. When the name finally registered, her eyes grew wide with disbelief. "Not Brenda Cavanaugh. Not Lauren's best friend." Then, as Fairbanks's cheeks turned red, not from her slap but from embarrassment, she sank into the nearest chair. "Oh, dear God."

Syd understood her dismay. Although in Pennsylvania the age of consent was sixteen, the girl was still a minor and the charges would be severe.

At the moment, however, she was concerned with only one thing. "Where is Lilly?" she asked.

The senator shook his head. "I don't know. You seem to think that I had something to do with her kidnapping, but I didn't."

Syd pointed at the plastic bag on the table. "She found this necklace and she confronted you with it."

"No, she didn't! I never even met Lilly Gilmore. I learned about her kidnapping the same way everyone else did—from the news."

"You had to know that your girlfriend had lost the necklace."

"Yes, I did. We went there to look for it a few days later, but it never occurred to me that a reporter had already found it."

"I think it did, Senator. When Lilly began calling your office, requesting an interview, maybe even dropping a hint or two, you knew exactly what you were facing. You may not have kidnapped her yourself, but she was taken on your orders."

"Chief Yates." Mrs. Fairbanks, whose rage had lessened considerably, spoke in a low, controlled voice. "My husband may be many things, but he is not a kidnapper."

"With all due respect, ma'am, that's for me to determine."

"I realize that." She glanced nervously behind her. "The problem is, we have guests—"

The chief shrugged. "We could continue this questioning in my office, if that's what you'd rather do."

She and her husband exchanged glances. "Would you settle for our study?" she asked. "It's just down the hall."

Syd saw the chief hesitate, then, with a nod, he said, "Lead the way."

Thirty-Nine

After leaving Farah's house, Jake had spent the next two hours talking to real estate agents within a twenty-mile-radius, pretending to be looking for a farm to buy, one that was not too far from Middletown. Everywhere he went, the answer was the same. There were no farms for sale at the moment. The only one that had been on the market most recently was Ellis Farm on Route 13, but it had been sold about a year ago.

His suspicions had been right on the money. Ted's prospective clients had been phonies. The next step, one that would be much more difficult, was to find out their identity.

From his motel room, Jake took out the piece of paper where Farah had written the names and phone numbers of Ted's friends. Because he felt more comfortable speaking with a military man, he called

Longnecker first. A recorded message informed him that the retired colonel and his family were vacationing in Japan and wouldn't be back until the end of the month.

Without losing a beat, Jake checked his watch, saw that it was 7:00 p.m. in Saudi Arabia and dialed the number for Algier Construction.

He had to wait several minutes until Colin Wright could be located.

"Wright here," the man said in a strong British accent.

"Mr. Wright, my name is Jake Sloan. You don't know me, but I'm a friend of Ted Malvern."

"Really. How do you know Ted?"

There was a note of caution in the man's voice that Jake understood and appreciated. "He and I met in flight school years ago. We also served together in Desert Storm."

"Are you still in the army?"

"No, I got out in 1991 and became an oil driller. I work on a rig off the coast of Louisiana."

Wright laughed. "Ted likes to tell me that the American army has a way of preparing you for anything. I guess he's right." A slight pause. "Did Ted give you my name and number?"

"No, Farah did."

"Why Farah?"

Wright was definitely a cautious man, which was a relief. The last thing Jake wanted right now was to cause harm to anyone else. "I'm afraid I'm the bearer of bad news, Mr. Wright. Ted was killed in a plane crash last night."

There was a short intake of breath, then another silence. "What kind of plane crash?" His voice shook.

Jake told him the circumstances of Ted's death.

"What are the police saying?"

"Very little at the moment. They're still investigating."

"And you? You don't think the crash was accidental, do you? Or you wouldn't be calling me."

"I have my suspicions."

"Go on."

"The day before Ted died, he made some calls to the Middle East. I was hoping that one of them was to you."

There was a long silence Jake wasn't sure he should break. "We had a short conversation," Wright said at last.

"Were you able to help him?"

"Not directly. I gave him a couple of names of people I thought might."

"Could you share those names with me?"

"In view of what happened, I believe that would be very unwise of me. However, I could make a few discreet inquiries. I may be able to find out if anyone leaked out Ted's name."

"That would be very helpful." Jake told Colin where to reach him and hung up.

Jake had to wait until nightfall for Wright's call.

"One of the people Ted talked to," Wright said

gravely, "was a man by the name of Ali Sochoufi. That man is now dead. His house was destroyed by a bomb blast that killed him and his entire family."

"When did that happen?"

"Two days ago."

"Who ordered the hit?"

"The same man who ordered Ted's."

"A name would be very helpful."

"I would give it to you if I had it, but I don't. Sochoufi's death has made everyone here nervous and therefore closemouthed. If I were to make an educated guess, based on what I heard, I would say that the order came from someone in the U.S."

It was as close to Victor's name as he could get. "Thank you, Mr. Wright."

"Colin. And you're welcome. I hope you'll be careful."

Unable to get Syd on her cell phone the following morning, Jake left word with Violet that he should be back in Philly by midafternoon. Then he called Ramirez and brought him up to speed on what had happened in Middletown.

"I'm afraid I can't guarantee that Farah won't blow my cover," he said when Ramirez started making unhappy sounds. "She's angry, hurt and she wants her husband's killer caught. So do I."

The tone of his voice must have changed because Paul picked up on it right away. "Jake, listen to me.

I know what you're going through. You lost a good friend and you feel you're to blame."

"I *am* to blame." This was déjà-vu all over again and he hated it.

"If Ted had been in your situation, you don't think he would have come to you? And asked for your help?"

"He probably would have."

"He definitely would have. Because that's what friends do. Now that we've got that out of the way, give me your word that you won't go on some kind of holy mission to avenge Ted."

"I'm not stupid. And yes, I give you my word. I'll get the son of a bitch, but I'll do it the smart way." He could almost hear the sigh of relief at the other end of the line. "Before I let you go, though, I need you to do me a favor."

"What's that?"

"Find out who is holding the mortgage on Ted Malvern's business and get back to me ASAP."

It took Paul less than fifteen minutes to get back to Jake with the information. Ted had saved a lot of money during his years in Saudi Arabia and had put most of it in the business, leaving an outstanding mortgage of three-hundred-and-twenty thousand-dollars, held by the Heritage Bank of Middletown. The name of the vice president Ramirez had talked to was Al Washington. He would be in his office until noon.

Al Washington was a big, personable African-American with snow-white hair and a wide, welcoming smile. "How can I help you, Mr. Sloan?" he asked as he shook Jake's hand.

"I'm an old friend of Ted Malvern."

"So I understand." Washington's expression turned grave. "Ted was a fine man—a hard worker, a community leader and a great family man. We'll all miss him."

"I'm sure of that. Mr. Washington, I'll come right to the point. I'm here because I would like to pay off his business loan. I assume you can arrange that?"

After an initial look of surprise, the banker nodded. "Certainly, but that's a substantial sum, Mr. Sloan. Have you discussed this with Farah?"

"No."

"May I ask why?"

"I don't want her to know. She might regard the gesture as an act of charity and turn me down."

"I see."

"I was hoping you'd be able to make the necessary arrangements without Farah knowing?"

Washington was already clicking a few keys on his computer. "I can tell her that Ted bought mortgage insurance in the event that something happened to him. Actually, I had suggested that he do just that when he first came to me, but he was just starting off with the business and couldn't afford the premiums at the time."

Jake took a sheet of paper he had folded in four from his jacket pocket. "I've already talked to my bank in Baton Rouge. The information you'll need for the transaction is written here."

"Excellent."

A few minutes later, the electronic transfer between the two banks was complete. The rest was up to Al Washington, who assured Jake he'd do his best to pull the ruse off.

"I'll go and give Farah the good news in person," he said as Jake stood. "I'm sure she'll be greatly relieved."

Jake wished that paying off Ted's mortgage would have alleviated some of the guilt he felt, but it didn't. As he left Middletown, the part he had played, even indirectly, in his friend's death, still weighed heavily on his mind.

Forty

Outside the senator's town house, Syd had turned down the chief's offer of a ride home and chosen to walk instead. The rain had turned to a light snow that brought a damp chill to the air. Holding back a shiver, she jammed her hands into her raincoat pockets while going over the disappointing events of the last couple of hours.

In spite of all her hopes, the questioning of Alan Fairbanks had not brought the results she had expected. Anxious to prove that he had no reason to kidnap Lilly, the politician had waived his rights to an attorney and told the chief what had happened on the night of the accident.

He and Brenda Cavanaugh were returning from the senator's shore house where they went occasionally. Brenda, who loved to drive the Mercedes, was at the wheel when Ana Lee's car struck them. Aware that news of an affair with a minor would destroy his career, Fairbanks had come up with the idea of having Brenda impersonate his daughter.

The ruse couldn't have been easier. Both girls were attractive, with long blond hair parted in the middle, and were about the same height and weight. But although Brenda agreed to the pretense, the shock of the accident was too much for her. Moments after the impact, she became violently sick. That's when she had inadvertently pulled on her necklace, breaking the clasp. Too ill to worry about it at the time, she had shoved it in her pocket. Several days later, as she was about to take the necklace to a jeweler to be repaired, she noticed that it was missing. Certain she had dropped it at the scene of the accident, she and the senator went back to look for it, with no success.

Fairbanks wasn't overly concerned. Even if someone had found the necklace, they wouldn't be able to trace it to him. In the meantime, he had advised Brenda to keep a low profile and go about her business as usual.

While his wife stoically looked on, the senator admitted that the most difficult thing he'd ever had to do was to sit at his daughter's bedside that night and tell her about his affair with her best friend. The teenager had gone through a wide range of emotions—shock, anger, disappointment and disgust. But like Brenda, she had understood the terrible ramifications such a scandal would have on the entire family and had agreed to go along with the deception, even if it meant lying to her mother.

Although pressured by Chief Yates to change his story about Lilly, Fairbanks continued to deny knowing anything about the reporter's attempts to see him. "My staff receives dozens of phone calls from reporters every week," he said, looking from Yates to Syd with the same earnestness he used in his political speeches. "They select those they feel will do me the most good and pass them on to my press secretary. To my recollection, Lilly Gilmore's name never came up, but feel free to verify this with Muriel Hathaway."

The chief wrote down the name. "I intend to."

It was clear from his expression that he was unimpressed by the senator's so-called candor. But without proof of an implication in Lilly's kidnapping, as well as the apparent absence of a motive, he'd had no choice but turn the senator over to the Philadelphia authorities where he would face other charges.

Until the chief questioned Muriel Hathaway, there was nothing Syd could do except go home and wait for Jake who was due back from Delaware today. At Sixth Street, however, she changed her mind and turned on Pine Street, heading for Dot's town house two blocks away. Although Fairbanks would be able to keep the scandal from the press for a few more hours, the story would be out by morning and she didn't want Dot to hear the details from a television broadcast.

"Syd." Dot opened the door wide and stepped aside to let her in. "You're covered with snow." Her expression grew concerned. "And you look unhappy. What's the matter?"

"Make me a cup of tea and I'll tell you."

Syd followed Dot into the kitchen and while they waited for the water to boil, she brought the older woman up to date. Like many Philadelphians, Dot had been a strong supporter of the senator and was aghast to hear about his infidelity and the way he had used his daughter. But it was the possibility that he might be connected to Lilly's kidnapping that held her attention.

"Do you believe him?" she asked, searching Syd's face.

"No. Fairbanks has already proved that he is an accomplished liar. He's been cheating on his wife and pretending to be this great, wonderful family man for years. He didn't suddenly admit to having an affair because he was so eager to tell the truth. He did it because he had no choice. That's not the case with Lilly. There are no witnesses and no proof of foul play."

Dot put a tea bag in each cup and filled them with hot water. "Maybe that press secretary will turn out to be the proof we need."

"Chief Yates is planning to talk to her first thing tomorrow morning, but he's not holding his breath and neither am I. Muriel Hathaway has been with Fairbanks since he became senator twelve years ago, and she is a very ambitious woman. I suspect she'll lie for him if she has to."

Dot sat on the other side of the breakfast counter. "What about those two girls? Lauren and Brenda?"

"I doubt they know anything."

"Will they be charged for lying to the police?"

"That's a possibility, but considering their young age and the way they were manipulated, all they'll probably get is a stern lecture from a judge and a few months of community service."

"You started off with all those suspects, and now, what do you have?"

They were interrupted by the loud pounding on the front door.

"Dot, open up, quick!"

Dot and Syd rushed to the door. A woman Syd recognized as Dot's next-door neighbor stood on the front porch, her hair covered with snowflakes. She held a sheet of paper in her hand. "I just came to invite you for dinner, and I found this tucked inside your screen door."

Dot snatched the paper from the woman's hand, read it and handed it to Syd without a word.

Once again, letters had been cut out at random and pasted across the page. This time the message read: You have until midnight tonight to get the five-hundred-thousand dollars. Sydney Cooper will deliver the money at a location that will be disclosed later. Do not call the police, and stay close to your phone.

At exactly 10:00 p.m., you will be told where to deliver the ransom.

"Did you see anyone?" Syd asked the neighbor. "A car? Someone running from the house?"

The woman shook her head. "No." She lowered her voice. "Did you get all the money, Dot? The last time we talked you didn't—"

"Thank you, Donna," Dot said quickly, ushering the woman out. "And thank you for the dinner invitation, but not tonight though, okay?" As Donna nodded and murmured a quick goodbye, Dot closed the door and immediately turned to Syd.

"You're not delivering the money. Chief Yates can send one of his female deputies."

"We'll talk about that later. Right now I need to know if you have the half-million dollars."

"I told you I would have it, didn't I?"

"I know what you told me, but your neighbor—"

"Donna has a big mouth."

"You don't have the money." It wasn't a question.

"Not yet."

"Not yet! You only have a few hours left. What happened to the sale of the farmhouse?"

"It fell through."

"Oh, Dot, I'm sorry. How much do you have?"

"I took your suggestion and called Lilly's boss. The newspaper has contributed a hundred thousand dollars. With my hundred-and-twenty thousand, your fifteen and Joe and Luciana's sixty-five thousand, I have three-hundred thousand. The money is at Joe's. He put it in his safe. All I have to do is call him, any time of the day or night, and he'll bring it over."

"Dot, you are two-hundred-thousand dollars short! Do you think the kidnappers are going to give you a last-minute discount?"

"That's exactly what I'm counting on," she replied defiantly. "Who in their right mind would walk away from all that money."

"I don't think you realize how ruthless those people are, or how bold. Look at the way they kidnapped Lilly, right under the nose of an assistant district attorney. Believe me when I tell you that they will not settle for a partial payment. They don't have to. They hold all the cards."

"Then what do you propose I do? You said it yourself. We only have a few hours."

Syd walked over to her and wrapped a comforting arm around her shoulders. She had been mulling over an idea for a couple of days now and the time had come to put it into motion. "I may have an idea. I don't know how good it is, or if it will fly, but I'm going to give it a try."

Dot raised humid eyes at her. "Can you tell me what it is?"

"I'm going to ask Greg for the money."

The hopeful look in Dot's eyes faded instantly. "Your ex-fiancé? Oh, Syd, he'll never give it you. He hates Lilly."

"It's still worth a try. He's the only person I know

who can get his hands on that kind of cash with just one phone call."

She took her cell phone out of her pocket and dialed Greg's office. She hated to do it. After the way she had treated him at the park the other day, he had every reason to tell her to go to hell. But there was always the off-chance that he wouldn't. That's what she was counting on as she dialed the number.

"Good afternoon, Annie," she said when Greg's secretary answered. "This is Sydney Cooper. May I speak to Greg, please."

"He's not in today, Sydney. He went to the shore house to finish his closing arguments for the Gandolo trial."

A small setback, Syd thought, but not one she couldn't handle. "Thank you, Annie. I'll call him there."

"Don't bother. A salt truck hit a telephone pole. All the lines in Tuckerton and the surrounding areas are down."

"I can reach him on his cell, right?"

"His cell is right here," Annie said apologetically. "In his rush to leave, he forgot it."

The small setback had just turned into a major hurdle. "Thank you, Annie."

"What's wrong?" Dot asked when Syd hung up.

Syd glanced out the window. The snow had intensified and a thin white coat was already forming on the road. "He's at the shore," she said, already punching in the speed number for her office. "And the phone lines are down."

"Violet," she said, smiling encouragingly at Dot. "Something has come up. I won't be back at the office."

"Why? Where will you be?" Syd could almost see her looking worriedly out the window.

"I'm on my way to Greg's house in Tuckerton."

"Syd! You can't be serious. Take a look at what's going on outside."

"It's not that bad."

"But it will be. It's a southern storm," she said, sounding like a weather expert. "They're predicting more than a foot of snow by morning."

"By morning I'll be back home."

"Whatever you have to discuss with Greg—and I can't imagine what that would be," she added with a note of sarcasm in her voice, "can't you do it over the phone?"

"The phone lines are down."

"Then wait until tomorrow."

"I can't. Dot has just received a second ransom note. She has until midnight tonight to come up with the money and she is two hundred thousand dollars short."

"And you're going to ask Greg?" Violet sounded aghast.

"I have no choice. Time is running out."

"Your new beau won't like it."

"Jake is not my new beau. And anyway, this is strictly a business arrangement. A loan."

"And you don't think Greg is going to want something in return? You know, a little collateral? Like your hand in marriage, perhaps?"

Syd couldn't guarantee that wouldn't happen, but right now Greg's leverage was not something she wanted to dwell on. "I'll see you in the morning," she said. "Be careful out there." Before Violet could protest, Syd hung up.

She dropped her phone into her purse. "Would you mind giving me a lift to the garage where I keep my car?" she asked Dot. "It will save me a lot of time."

Dot was already standing. "Of course not. I'll get my keys."

Forty-One

A late winter storm had struck just as Jake left Middletown at noon on Friday, blanketing the entire East Coast and making driving conditions hazardous at best. From his hotel room last night, he had called Syd and told her about the unfortunate chain of events that had begun with his call to Ted and ended with his confrontation with Farah.

"I don't know Farah," she told him. "But I imagine she needs to deal with her grief as well as her anger. Once she's had a chance to put all you told her into perspective, she'll come around."

He doubted it, but talking to Syd had made his guilt a little easier to bear.

As he entered Philadelphia's city limits a little before two, he called Paul and told him what he had learned from Colin Wright.

"You should have consulted me before calling

Wright." The agent sounded angry. "What if Victor finds out?"

"I'm counting on him finding out. And before you tell me that the man's dangerous, let me remind you that I can take care of myself."

"Jake, listen to me." His tone had softened. "I checked with a couple of my superiors this morning, and we all agree. We want to bring you in."

The light on Sixth Street turned green and Jake eased back into traffic, his windshield wipers working double time to keep up with the snow. "What does that mean?"

"We want you in a safe place. Where van Heusen and his hounds won't find you."

"Let them find me. I'll be ready for them."

"No, you won't. Those people are fanatics. And unpredictable."

"Victor made it personal when he went after Ted. I'm going to finish this job, Paul. With or without you."

"Let's talk about that. How about we meet for a drink—"

He had reached Washington Square. Home, where the peace and quiet would help him sort out his thoughts. "Maybe some other time. I'll call you, okay?"

Jake rang Syd's doorbell, then, getting no answer, he unlocked his own door. They hadn't planned on meeting until dinnertime, but in view of the inclement weather, he decided to surprise her at the office and offer her a ride home. But first he had a little job to do—take that damn listening device down and destroy it. That should be a clear signal to Victor that the gig was up.

He had just closed his door when the hair on the back of his neck stood up.

He had experienced that feeling too many times during his counter-terrorism days not to recognize it.

Someone was in his apartment.

He listened for a sound, a movement, shallow breathing.

Nothing.

The old training came back in a flash. After making sure there was no one behind the front door, he started whistling an old show tune and went into the kitchen for a cold beer. Hopefully, the pretense would convince his unannounced guest that Jake believed he was alone.

Still whistling as though he didn't have a care in the world, he started toward the bedroom at the end of the hall.

Once there, he grabbed hold of the doorknob and slammed the door back. Hard.

He heard a muffled cry. The sound was immediately followed by another—a body hitting the wall.

Holding the beer bottle by the neck, he whacked it against the wall and jumped sideways, arms extended in combat position.

Jenkins, his mouth bloodied, had already scrambled to his feet. In his hand was a switchblade.

The younger man grinned as he started circling around Jake, both hands in front of him. There was a mean look in his eyes as the blade swished through the air. "Say your prayers, Sloan."

"What makes you think that a punk like you can take me on?"

"Oh, I can take you on, Sloan. Make no mistake about that."

The two men walked around in a slow, deadly circle, like two lions fighting for supremacy. The kid would be well trained, Jake thought, and quick; therefore, he had to be quicker.

Closer now, Jenkins swung his arm again. The blade came within inches of Jake's face. As the soldier's arm shot up again, Jake ducked, barely missing the blow. He gave a few jabs with the broken bottle, but Jenkins's head moved as if it were on a spring.

"Your boss sent you?" Jake taunted. "He didn't have the nerve to do the job himself?"

"The general doesn't dirty his hands on scum like you."

His arm shot up again. This time, the blade grazed Jake's sleeve, tearing into the insulated fabric. The sudden sting beneath told him Jenkins had cut through the skin as well.

The broken beer bottle was useless. Jenkins had obviously been in that kind of fight before and knew exactly how to keep his opponent at bay. Jake would have to consider another line of defense.

As he kept making feeble attempts with the bottle, he saw a possibility—the heavy lamp base on the end table.

"What's the matter, Sergeant?" Jake laughed, hoping to distract him. "You're breathing hard. Are you out of shape? Too much computer work and not enough physical training?" He made a *tsk-tsk* sound. "It shows."

"I'll show you how out of shape I—"

Jake didn't give him time to finish the sentence. He grabbed the base of the lamp with one hand and in one quick motion, threw it at Jenkins's head.

Although it was only a glancing blow, it was enough to send the younger man to his knees. Before he could recover, Jake hit him with an uppercut that made the kid's eyes roll. He fell back, out cold.

Working quickly, Jake yanked the cord that hung from the venetian blinds and tied him up, hands and feet. Then, for extra measure, he anchored him to the bed.

By the time he had secured the last knot, Victor's right-hand man was coming to.

"Welcome back," Jake said pleasantly. "You were saying?"

Jenkins just glared at him.

Jake crouched beside him. "You don't mind if I search you, do you, buddy? I'm the curious type."

Going through the sergeant's pockets, Jake found another switchblade. "You like knives, I see. Too bad you don't know how to use them."

A further search produced something else—an iPAQ small enough to fit in Jenkins's shirt pocket without as much as a bulge.

"Well, well. Look what we have here. And you left it on. How thoughtful of you."

Using the thin stylus attached to the iPAQ, Jake selected an icon and watched the color screen light up. The instrument was one of the latest handheld computers on the market and came with an impressive list of functions—e-mail, address book, Web access, word processor, MP3 player and much more.

"Give it back," Jenkins demanded. "That's personal property."

"Well, now, Jenkins, here is how *I* look at it." Jake remained in a crouching position so that the two men were eye to eye. "This is my apartment. You came in uninvited. In fact, you broke in, therefore everything in here is my property, including your belongings. Wouldn't you agree?"

Under Jenkins's hateful glare, Jake glanced down at the tiny piece of electronics. "What do you know?" He grinned. "You've got mail."

Forty-Two

Jake pressed the tip of the stylus on the envelope marked Victor. A message popped up on the screen.

"Where the hell are you?" Jake read. "Why aren't you answering your phone? I don't need to remind you that our plan is only hours away. We need to finalize it. Call me as soon as you receive this."

Jake looked at Jenkins. "What plan is Victor talking about?"

"Fuck you."

Operating exactly like a desktop computer, the iPAQ had the capabilities of storing lengthy reports. Jake pushed the program button. Three folders appeared on the screen. One was called "Training Exercise," the second "Recruiting Techniques," and the third "Depot."

He read the first two, found them of no interest and proceeded to the third. He knew he had hit the jackpot when he saw Jenkins's shoulders stiffen.

Jake started reading. "At 4:00 p.m. on Monday, March 17, three high-ranking army officers will be unveiling the Dwight D. Eisenhower Military Depot in South Philadelphia. On hand for the ceremonies will be Brigadier General Arthur E. Vetri, Major Randolph Fletcher and Lieutenant General Arlen Cunningham."

Jake didn't know the first two men, but he knew the third one very well. Based in Kuwait during Desert Storm and attached to the JAG office, Arlen Cunningham was the prosecutor who had fought the hardest to have Jake and Victor court martialed. Outvoted, he'd had to settle for a dishonorable discharge, but not until he had given both men a scathing and humiliating reprimand. He had been particularly hard on van Heusen.

Victor had hated that man with every fiber of his being.

Jake returned his attention to Jenkins, who was watching him. "What are you planning to do at the depot?"

Jenkins gave him an innocent look. "I have no idea."

"Then why did you store the information into your iPAQ?"

Jenkins shrugged. "I thought the general would get a kick out of it, that's all."

"Did he?"

"I don't know. I haven't had a chance to forward it to him."

"You're lying. Victor's e-mail proves it. He mentions a plan that will take place today, hours from now. The official inauguration of the military depot is at four o'clock. What are you planning?"

"Nothing!"

"Okay, let's see if I can find out without having to pull out your fingernails."

Jenkins gave a sarcastic laugh that sounded more nervous than anything else. Jake almost felt sorry for him. Total devotion to their commanders was a fairly common trait among militia men. Especially those like Jenkins, who had been rescued from a life of crime and misery and would have eventually ended up dead, if not for the man who had saved them. For these recruits, no task was too demanding, no mission too dangerous. They were in the militia for only one reason—to serve and obey their leader.

Suspecting the information he wanted was inside the computer but inaccessible to him, Jake decided that a call to the cavalry was in order. He took out his phone and called Ramirez. "I think you'd better come to my apartment," he said as Jenkins closed his eyes and hit the back of his head against the wall. "And bring backup. I've got Jenkins here, all trussed up like a turkey. Oh, and you may want to bring a computer expert, too. Someone who knows how to crack codes fast. I'll explain when you get here."

Ramirez and three other agents arrived in record time. Jake briefed them and showed them the iPAQ with Victor's e-mail and Jenkins's report.

"If there's anything else stored about the depot, I can't find it," he admitted.

"Barry!" Paul waved one of the agents over, a kid who didn't look a day over twenty-five. Paul made the introductions before telling Barry what he was looking for.

Barry took the instrument and moved to a corner of the room. He started pecking away with the stylus, his expression one of total concentration.

"Does he know what he's doing?" Jake asked Ramirez.

"Barry's one of the best computer hackers in the country. We recruited him right out of MIT last year. The kid is worth five times what we're paying him. He doesn't care about money, though. He just wants to be around computers all day long. The more challenging the task, the happier he is."

"You guys are interested in photographs?" Barry asked.

"Of the depot?"

"Don't know yet. All photos on file are protected by a password."

"We're interested."

"I'll need personal information on Jenkins—anything you have, from his mother's maiden name to the day he graduated from high school."

Paul made a call to the federal building for additional information and handed the phone to Barry so he could talk directly with the database programmer.

In another corner of the room, the other two

agents took turns interrogating Jenkins, who had been untied and cuffed. From the look on their faces, they weren't making much progress. His attention focused on Barry, Jenkins kept repeating his name, rank and serial number. Nothing else.

"Got it!" Looking pleased with himself, Barry held the PDA out to Paul. Jake peeked over his shoulder. On the screen was a color photograph of what appeared to be the outside of a one-story building. A sign stood in front of it, and read, The Dwight D. Eisenhower Military Depot.

"It's just a picture of the building." Paul sounded disappointed.

"There are about a dozen photos on file," Barry said. "Keep clicking. Maybe you'll find something."

Paul punched a key. Another picture appeared. This time the lens had focused on the rear of the building and a small parking lot. The next one showed the air-conditioning unit on the side of the building. The next three photographs were equally worthless.

"Dammit, this isn't getting us anywhere." Paul brought another image on the screen and was about to replace it with the next when Jake stopped him.

"Wait."

Paul looked at him. "It's the same shot as the others."

"I know, but the date at the bottom of the screen is different. All the previous pictures had a date of February 22nd. This one was taken on March 11th. Two days ago."

"So?"

"So something may have changed. Keep clicking."

The next picture showed an army vehicle parked at the rear of the building and two men in green fatigues unloading the truck. As the next picture was loaded, Jake grabbed hold of Paul's arm to keep it still. "That's the inside of the building."

"I can see that."

Jake saw a podium. Behind the podium was the flag of the United States, standing next to the U.S. Army flag.

On a pedestal and directly in front of the podium, was the bronze bust of the man after whom the building had been named.

General Dwight D. Eisenhower.

"Holy shit," Jake said under his breath.

It was the same bust Jake had seen in Victor's office less than a week ago.

Forty-Three

Moments after Jake had identified the bust, a team that included a bomb squad had been dispatched to the military depot in South Philly, and Jenkins was on his way to the federal building for further interrogation.

"Why don't you come back to the office with me?" Paul had suggested. "We'll wait for the outcome of the search together."

Jake had declined. He was growing increasingly worried about Syd, who wasn't answering her cell phone. He had tried her office, but the line was still busy. Hoping that whoever was there could tell him where Syd was, he pointed the Explorer toward Arch Street and within seconds, was on his way.

The security guard Jake had met during a previous visit was still on duty. He grinned as he handed Jake a pass. "Not quite the kind of weather you're used to in Baton Rouge, is it, Mr. Sloan?"

"Far from it, Justin, but it does brings back memories—school closings, sledding down the hill behind Joe Petrino's house, huge mugs of hot chocolate afterwards."

The guard gave a hearty laugh. "I hear you, bro."

Jake pinned the pass on his ski jacket. "Is Syd in, do you know?"

"Haven't seen her since they let everyone go at about three. Chad is in, though. Kid loves to work."

"Thanks, Justin."

Chad, whom Jake had also met earlier, was on the phone, which probably explained why Jake hadn't been able to get through. "Hello, Chad."

Chad hung up. "Hi, Mr. Sloan. Syd isn't here. I was just trying to get her on her cell phone again, but..." He shook his head.

"Do you know where she went?"

"I wish I did, because she'd love to hear about this."

Jake's followed his gaze to a stack of papers Chad had arranged neatly on Syd's desk. On the top sheet was a photograph of Senator Fairbanks. "Is that another report on the accident?"

Chad looked at him as if trying to decide how much to tell him. He must have appeared fairly trustworthy because suddenly, Chad turned into a chatterbox.

"It's got nothing to do with the accident," he said, talking excitedly. "A few days ago Syd asked me to find everything I could on the senator, so I went digging. I started noticing that large political donations were coming into his campaign fund from various companies."

"Nothing illegal about that, is there?"

"Not if the companies are legitimate."

"Are you saying they're not?"

"I didn't recognize the names, so I called my uncle who's a bankruptcy lawyer, and he did some digging for me. Six of the companies listed turned out to be dummies. They don't exist."

"Who set them up?"

"I don't know yet. My uncle is still checking."

"Fairbanks had to be in on this. You don't suddenly see your campaign funds skyrocket without getting curious."

"Curious about what?" a voice asked from the door.

Jake turned around to find a man standing in the doorway. He wore a tan raincoat, a matching vinyl hat and a wary expression. "Who are you?" Jake asked.

The man held up a badge. "Detective Cranston. Philly PD. And you?"

"Jake Sloan. I'm a friend of Sydney Cooper."

"Where's your boss?" Cranston asked Chad.

Chad shrugged. "I don't know. I was telling Mr. Sloan that I've been trying to locate her ever since..."

"Ever since what?"

Chad looked from Jake to the detective. "Ever since I found out that Senator Fairbanks was receiving campaign donations from dummy companies."

Cranston whistled. "That may be even better than my news."

"The only news that would top the list right now would be finding Lilly Gilmore."

"Then I'm close. Doug Avery finally decided that being in solitary doesn't necessarily guarantee complete safety. He's tired of looking over his shoulder and wants to talk."

"I thought his alibi was solid," Jake said.

"We're not talking about a confession. He has information and wants to pass it on—in exchange for a deal. That's why I'm here. I couldn't reach Syd on her cell so I came to pick her up."

Jake turned to Chad. "Are you sure she didn't tell anyone where she was going?"

"She was already gone when I got here. But Violet might know."

"Could you call her?"

Chad flipped through a Rolodex, found the number and dialed. Jake saw him heave a sigh of relief. "Violet, it's me, Chad. Jake Sloan and Detective Cranston are here. We're starting to worry about Syd. She doesn't answer—"

He handed the phone to Jake. "She wants to talk to you."

Jake took the receiver. "Hi, Violet. Do you have any idea where Syd is?"

"She drove to Greg Underwood's house in Tuckerton."

"She went to the shore? In this weather? What

was she thinking?" An emotion he recognized as jealousy, twisted deep inside his gut. "And what is she doing at Underwood's house?"

"I tried to talk her out of it, Jake. She wouldn't listen. Mrs. Branzini received a second ransom note, giving her until midnight to get the money together. She was more than two-hundred-thousand dollars short, so Syd went to ask Greg for the balance. He's the only person she knows who can get his hands on that kind of money quickly."

"Couldn't she have called him?"

"The lines were down because of the storm."

"Do you have his number?"

"Not with me, but tell Chad to look in Syd's Rolodex."

Jake pointed at the Rolodex and Chad's fingers got busy again. He found the card and waved it at Jake. "Got it, Violet. Thanks a million."

"I'm worried about her. No one should be driving in a storm like this. Call me the moment you locate her, Jake."

"I will."

Jake glanced at Underwood's number, picked up the phone on Syd's desk and dialed. "Damn." He slammed the receiver onto the cradle. "The lines are still down." He showed the Rolodex card to the detective. "Do you know how to get to that house?"

Cranston nodded. "Everybody within a hundred-mile radius knows where that house is. You can't miss it. It's huge, extravagant and painfully out of place in that setting."

"Maybe Syd is stuck in the snow?" Chad offered.

"Then why doesn't she call? Or answer her phone?"

"Because of where she is. You can't get a signal from the shore area with some phones unless you move around a lot."

Jake gave Cranston a tap on the shoulder. "Let's go."

The detective didn't stop to ask where they were going. He ran after Jake.

Forty-Four

Syd gripped the steering wheel a little tighter and leaned forward, trying to peer through the heavy falling snow. Violet was right. She had to be crazy to be driving in this weather. According to the car radio, the unexpected late winter storm had caught everyone by surprise and forecasters now predicted that as much as a foot of snow would have accumulated by morning.

Her predictions that she'd be back home by then seemed less and less certain.

So far, there had been no news of the scandal surrounding Senator Fairbanks. Maybe it was still too early. Or maybe the weather was all the news the stations could handle at the moment.

It had taken her almost two hours to reach Tuckerton and Great Bay Boulevard, which the locals called Seven Bridge Road. Except for a few brightly lit houses here and there to guide her along the way, Syd was alone.

As she passed Skinner's Marina, she reminded herself to start counting the bridges, although she could hardly miss the house, even in this storm. Contrary to what the name suggested, there were only five bridges on Great Bay Boulevard. Greg's house was located between bridge number four and bridge number five, overlooking a tidal creek and the Great Bay. Twelve years ago, after fierce negotiations with a stubborn seller, he had bought the old Northshore Marina from a local family and built a spectacular summer house that was later featured in *Architectural Digest.*

She and Greg had spent some great weekends in this area. Not fond of boats, she had been content to lie on the beach, reading and soaking up the rays while Greg sailed up and down the bay in his boat, *Mermaid III.*

At last, she saw the house in the distance, large, brilliantly lit, shining through the snow like a welcoming beacon.

At crawling speed, she maneuvered the car along the driveway, avoiding the drifts, and stopped close to the front door. The wind whipped at her face as she ran toward the house.

She rang the bell, then rang it again when no one answered.

"All right, all right," Greg shouted from inside. "I hear you." The door was flung open. "Syd!"

Judging from the way he was dressed—baggy pants, a gray sweatshirt and white socks, no shoes, he hadn't expected guests. Behind him, a bright fire roared in the big stone fireplace and the coffee table was heaped high with paperwork and an open laptop.

"Hi." Under his puzzled gaze, she felt suddenly foolish and self-conscious. "I know this must look odd, but I need to talk to you. It's important. And very urgent. I tried to call but the lines were down."

"They're back in service now, but don't just stand there. Come on in." He spread his arms out. "Here, let me have your coat."

He helped her out of her London Fog raincoat and, neat to a fault, shook it on the outside mat before hanging it on the antique coatrack. "How about some coffee? I just made a fresh pot."

"Thank you." She rubbed her cold hands together. "That sounds wonderful, although…"

"Although what?"

"I wasn't sure you'd want to see me."

"You mean because of the way you destroyed my ego the other day?"

She smiled. "Something like that."

"I must admit, I was hurt, even more so when I saw you kiss that…neighbor of yours. Unless it was meant to make me jealous, in which case—"

"It was my way of showing you that I had moved on."

"I see." He looked disappointed, but managed to

put on a happy face. He waved toward the fireplace. "Go get warmed up. I'll get you a cup."

She went to stand in front of the fire and let her gaze drift over the expensive butter-colored leather sofas, the forty-inch plasma TV on the wall, the custom-made cabinet that held state-of-the-art audio and video equipment. An impressive collection of DVDs occupied the two lower shelves.

He returned moments later with a large mug, filled with very black, very strong coffee, the kind she used to drink while studying for finals. She held the mug with both hands and took a sip.

"Do you recognize it?" he asked.

"Recognize what?"

"The coffee. It's that Arabica you like. You introduced me to it. Don't you remember?"

She didn't. The truth was, she had been trying to forget every detail of her relationship with Greg Underwood. "Of course I do," she lied. She took another sip. "I hope I didn't turn you into a coffee freak like me."

"You did."

"Oh, no."

He sat on the sofa next to her and gazed into her eyes, maybe a little too intimately. "It's good to see you, Syd, although I can't imagine what brings you here in this weather." She was about to tell him when he added, "I meant what I said the other day. I miss you. Everywhere I go, whatever I do, I think of you and all the good times we used to have."

"But it wasn't enough. Or you wouldn't have felt the need to have a fling."

"And that's all it was—a fling. A stupid mistake I swear I'll never make again."

Here he was again, talking in the present tense. Maybe Violet had been right about that, too. He was still intent on getting her back and could decide to put strings on her request. And then what would she do?

"Greg, we've been through all this already."

"I know. I thought that maybe, now that you've had time to…" He waited a beat and when she didn't answer, he nodded. "Okay, I won't pressure you anymore. It's clear that you didn't come here to listen to me beg for your forgiveness. So, why don't you tell me what's on your mind."

She took the first ransom note from her purse and handed it to him. As he read the words that had been pasted on the sheet, his head shot up. He looked stunned. "A ransom note? Lilly was kidnapped for *money?*"

"Why are you so surprised? Ninety percent of all kidnappings end up in a demand for money."

"But I thought…" He looked clearly troubled. "I mean, you were so sure that her kidnapping had something to do with either Senator Fairbanks or that militia man, I forgot his name."

"Doug Avery. It's not him. I'm still not sure about the senator, though." Since the news about Fairbanks's arrest hadn't been released yet, she didn't see the need to tell him about it.

"Are you going along with this?" He held up the note.

"I didn't want to at first, but I'm fast losing my options, Greg. Following those instructions now seems like the only way to get Lilly back."

"It could be a trick."

"I thought of that." Feeling a little more confident now, she handed him the second note. "This one came tonight. That's when I decided that paying the ransom may be the way to go."

He read it then quickly looked up. "They want *you* to deliver the money?"

"Yes."

"You're not considering it, are you?"

"I have no choice, Greg."

"You have lots of choices. One is to let the police handle it." His expression turned sour. "The other is to let that jock of yours dress up in drag and go in your place."

The thought of Jake trying to pass for a slender, five-foot-four woman made her smile. "I doubt that would fool anyone."

"I'm serious, Syd."

"I know you are, but you don't need to worry about me. Chief Yates will have the necessary backup."

"Have you talked to him about this?"

"I haven't had the chance. I came straight here, but I'm sure he will insist on backup."

"That's still too dangerous. Something could go

wrong. You could get shot again. Is that what you want?"

"No, of course not."

"Then why—"

"Greg, I truly appreciate your concern, but I didn't come here to discuss how the money will be delivered."

He gave a resigned nod. "All right, talk."

Syd gazed into her coffee. "Dot could only raise three hundred thousand dollars."

He looked at her for a moment, as if not quite comprehending what she had said. Or rather, what she had not said. Then, opening his mouth slightly, he gave another nod. "Oh, I get it now. You want *me* to come up with the rest of the money."

He didn't look angry, or upset, just sad, as though until this very moment he had hoped to still have a chance with her.

"I couldn't think of anyone else," she said truthfully.

"I guess not."

"It would only be a loan, Greg. I'm not asking you to—"

He waved the rest of her sentence away and she braced herself for the rejection. "We can talk about that later."

Her hopes soared. "Is that a yes? You'll give me the money?"

"Of course, I'll give you the money. You think I can sit here, look at that lost puppy expression in your eyes and not react? I'm not made of stone, Syd."

"Oh, Greg, thank you!" Without thinking, she threw her arms around his neck and kissed him loudly on the cheek. "Thank you, thank you, thank you."

"You do realize that another, less scrupulous man, would take full advantage of this situation and try to make some kind of deal with you."

"I'm grateful that you're not that kind of man."

"Tempting though it may be." He stood up. "I've got Jason Levy's phone number upstairs. I'll only be a minute."

Jason Levy was the owner of Metropolitan Bank in Philadelphia. He and Greg had been friends since college and whatever arrangements needed to be made, Jason would take care of them.

Greg hadn't been gone for more than a couple of minutes when the downstairs phone rang. Syd was about to call Greg when the answering machine picked up.

A voice she recognized instantly spoke angrily. "Greg, this is Victor. We have a situation here. We need to figure out some kind of damage control, and more important, how we can protect ourselves. Turn on your TV, any station, then call me."

Behind her, Syd heard footsteps. Mouth opened, she turned to see Greg standing halfway down the staircase. He was no longer smiling. His face had turned a couple of shades lighter and his mouth was tightly set.

He walked down the last few steps. "I'm sorry you had to hear that, Syd."

Forty-Five

Dumbfounded, Syd watched Greg open the drawer of a small bureau and take out a gun.

"Of course, this changes everything." There was a touch of regret in his voice.

It was a while until Syd could tear her eyes off the .357 Magnum and speak coherently. "You know Victor van Heusen?"

"I do."

"How?"

"Before I answer your question, I'd better see what's going on."

He was strangely calm, like a man with the advantage, which he had. With the hand that held the gun, he waved her back and positioned himself in such a way that an attempt on her part to run out of the house would be pointless. She would be dead before she reached the door. He picked up the remote control from the coffee table and pointed it at the TV.

A news anchor she didn't recognize looked directly into the camera. "…most amazing story," he was saying. "Charlene Bromski is standing by in front of Senator Fairbanks's home in Rittenhouse Square where the presidential candidate is about to make an unexpected announcement. Charlene? What's happening?"

A slim, dark-haired woman in a red wool coat stood in the snow, one finger on her earpiece. Behind her, the snow-covered square looked like a drawing right out of a Currier & Ives winter scene.

"Michael, this is completely surprising. We have just received word that Alan Fairbanks is about to announce that he is withdrawing from the presidential race."

Syd saw Greg's head snap back as though he had been hit.

"Do you know why?" the anchor asked.

"We keep getting conflicting reports. As you can see, dozens of reporters are assembled here, along with many of the senator's supporters. We are waiting for him to come out and either confirm or deny the rumor."

"Was he arrested, Charlene?"

"No. He was questioned by Chief Yates of the Mullica Township police department in South Jersey, then by the Philadelphia police before he was released on his own recognizance."

"What exactly was his business with the police?"

"It is believed that he lied about the accident that took place earlier this month, and that his daughter, seventeen-year-old Lauren Fairbanks, was not behind the wheel at the time of the accident."

"Who was?"

"Another young woman whose identity has not yet been disclosed."

His face ashen, Greg ran a hand through his hair. "Jesus," he muttered.

Why was he so upset? Syd wondered. He had never appeared to be a strong supporter of Senator Fairbanks. In fact, she couldn't remember him ever mentioning the politician one way or another.

"Where is the daughter now?" the anchor asked.

"In seclusion and under a doctor's care."

"And Mrs. Fairbanks?"

"At home, but definitely *not* standing by her man, Michael. We were told that she will be holding a news conference of her own sometime tomorrow."

"Can you confirm if Sydney Cooper of the district attorney's office is the person who exposed the senator?"

Greg's expression was one of complete incredulity as he gaped at Syd. "*You? You* are responsible for this?"

Syd didn't get a chance to answer. Charlene Bromski was doing it for her.

"Indeed, Michael, Sydney Cooper has once again made headlines and—"

The crowd grew louder. Charlene touched her earpiece again. "The senator is here now, Michael. Let's listen."

Syd watched as Fairbanks, looking pale, came to stand in front of the microphones. His wife and daughter were conspicuous by their absence. Only Muriel Hathaway and another member of his staff, possibly his attorney, stood directly behind him.

His face drawn, his voice subdued, he addressed the crowd that had gone strangely quiet. "Good evening." He cleared his throat. "Due to painful circumstances that will be made public shortly, I am no longer seeking the presidency."

As cries of shock rose from the assembled crowd, he raised his hand. "I take sole responsibility for what happened and apologize to the millions of supporters who placed their trust in me, and the dedicated volunteers who worked tirelessly on my behalf. I have let you down and for that I am deeply sorry. I will not be taking any questions." He inclined his head. "Thank you."

Back in the studio, the anchor could not hide his disbelief. "There you have it," he said. "In a short but emotional speech held outside his home in Rittenhouse Square, Senator Fairbanks has confirmed that he is withdrawing from the presidential campaign."

Someone handed him a sheet of paper and he read it quickly before saying, "We have just learned that Sydney Cooper, who was unofficially investigating Lilly Gilmore's kidnapping, stumbled on evidence implicating the senator and a young woman who may be underage. We still don't know how these events will affect the campaign, or who will now take over as the front-runner. Stay with us as we continue to follow these historical developments."

Greg muted the TV set. "You've been busy." He seemed lost, disoriented.

After nearly a minute, he picked up the phone and dialed. "Victor? It's me." His eyes remained on Syd as he spoke. "I just heard. What the hell happened?"

He listened for a long time, nodding occasionally.

"Has Fairbanks said anything?" he asked at last. "About us?"

Syd gave him a startled look. Victor and Greg were connected to Fairbanks? How?

There was another silence before Greg spoke again. "What about the ransom? Whose dumb idea was that? And why wasn't I told about it?"

Syd gripped the edge of the sofa. Victor had sent the ransom note? *He* had Lilly?

"I'll tell you how I found out!" Greg shouted. "Syd told me, Victor. That's right. She's here. She knows. She heard your message." He made an impatient gesture. "I'll explain later. Right now, we have to decide what to do with her."

She didn't like the sound of that.

Greg nodded. "I'll see you soon then. Don't worry. She's not going anywhere."

She looked at him for a moment, this man she had loved, had planned to marry. A man she had believed stood for decency and integrity. Of course, that belief had vanished the day she had found him in bed with another woman.

Greg hung up. "It's all over," he said, sounding like the voice of doom. "The dreams, the hopes, the vision. All gone. Because of you."

"What drea—"

"You ruined it all." His voice rose. "You and Lilly. The team from hell. You two bitches ruined my life!"

"What dream?"

"*My* dream. My one chance to get out from under my father's thumb. My one chance to show him that I was every bit as smart, as ambitious and as successful as my brother, that I could go places even *he* had never dreamed of reaching."

He had become agitated, waving the gun as he talked. Hoping to appease him, she spoke in a calm voice. "I don't know what you're talking about, Greg. I thought you were changing firms."

"Not firms, jobs. I was changing jobs. I was going to be the next deputy attorney general of Pennsylvania."

If he hadn't been so serious and the moment so charged with tension, she would have laughed. "You never showed any interest in becoming a public servant. You were always too preoccupied with money. And how to keep on making more."

"Maybe you didn't know me as well as you thought."

"You don't have the credentials to become deputy

attorney general. Or the expertise. Or the experience."

"I have the will, the drive, the passion." He took a shallow breath. "And the support of people who believe in me."

A new Greg was emerging right in front of her eyes. A stranger. "What people?"

"Powerful politicians." His smile was cynical. "Are you beginning to put it all together, Syd?"

"I'm afraid to."

"Then let me do it for you. Victor van Heusen has been financing Alan Fairbanks's campaign. He chose him years ago as the man who would someday become president. Victor molded him, indoctrinated him and hired a PR firm to fine-tune his image. Then he started financing his reelection for senator in 2000—a seat Fairbanks would have lost, if not for Victor."

So that was where all the money had come from. And why Fairbanks had risen to the top so quickly.

Alan Fairbanks and Victor van Heusen. The ramifications of such a partnership were terrifying. "How did you meet Victor?"

"At a gun rally he held during one of his recruiting campaigns. I liked what I saw, what Victor stood for, the dreams he had for the country. That same day, I joined his militia."

Of course. All the signs had been there—the gun collection, Greg's strong, almost fanatical support of the NRA, those violent movies he watched over and over. How could she have missed it? "What exactly do you do for him?"

"I'm his behind-the-scenes attorney," he said proudly. "I advise him."

"Do you also advise him on his criminal activities?"

"What are you talking about?"

"The man you admire so much is an arms' trafficker, Greg. A man who provides weapons to terrorists. A man responsible for the death of thousands of people."

"You're lying! Victor is an honorable man."

"He's a killer! Why do you think he's coming here, if not to kill me?"

"He is coming to take you into custody. After that, he'll decide your fate. Just as he will with Lilly."

Syd stiffened. "Then he has Lilly?"

He shrugged. "I assume he still does."

"Where is she?"

"In a cell at Camp Freedom, waiting to be tried by a military tribunal."

"*What?*"

"Lilly is an enemy of the state, Syd, and as such she will be tried and convicted. Or acquitted. That will depend on the jury."

My God, Syd thought, they were all crazy, pawns in the hands of a madman. Even Greg—smart, capable Greg—was totally brainwashed. Any effort on her part to make him see reason was hopeless. Still, she had to try.

"A jury chosen by van Heusen?" she asked. "Twelve gun-wielding rednecks? Men with no conscience? No morals? Men who live by only one credo—violence? Is that the brand of justice you stand for these days, Greg?"

"Shut up, all right? I need to think."

"Then let's think together. We always made a good team, you and I, didn't we?" She took a small step forward. "What I mean is, it doesn't have to be all over for you."

He gave her a blank look.

"As things stand now, you are facing years in prison. By coming back to Philadelphia with me and turning yourself in, you will greatly reduce the time you'll spend behind bars. The FBI has been trying to shut down van Heusen's arms-dealing operation for years. If you provide them with what they need to finish the job, they might even offer you some kind of immunity."

His eyes narrowed. "How do you know so much?"

"I have my sources."

"Well, your sources are wrong."

"You think so? Where do you think Victor gets those millions of dollars he poured into the senator's campaign? Or the kind of money he needs to run that camp of his?"

"From wealthy militia members."

"That's what he wants you to think. But the money really comes from arms-trafficking. And you, as his attorney, are in this up to your neck, Greg. Your only hope is to turn yourself in and tell us what you know. I know you're too smart not to see that."

"Turn myself in?" He let out a short laugh. "Do you think I'm stupid?"

"If you let van Heusen kill me, you'll be an accomplice to murder."

"No one will suspect me."

"People know I'm here. Violet, Dot, your secretary."

"I'll tell them you never made it. In this weather, it will be easy enough for them to think you got in some kind of accident. You could have missed a turn and driven straight into the bay. Happens all the time."

"They'll never believe it if they don't find the car."

"But they *will* find the car. Victor will make sure of that. It's you they won't find. They'll assume the current took you down, all the way to the ocean."

His confidence had returned. She'd had a small window of opportunity and she had lost it. Was it too late? Or did she still had a chance to get out of this mess alive?

Forty-Six

With Greg's threat echoing in her mind, Syd was now considering every option available to her. If she could get to her phone and press Jake's number, which she had on speed dial, he might be able to hear her as she talked to Greg and figure out where she was. Provided her cell phone would pick up a signal. She had been meaning to get a new one for months and hadn't had a chance to.

Trying to be as inconspicuous as possible, she inched her hand toward her purse.

Greg caught the movement. "Oh, no, you don't." Quick as lightning, he yanked the purse from her hand, found her phone and put it in his pocket. "Who were you going to call? Your oil driller?"

So much for that idea. Maybe it was time to try something a little more daring—like making a run for the front door. Unfortunately, at the moment, it seemed miles away.

"I'd save my energy if I were you, Syd. You're going to need it."

Pretending to be frightened, which wasn't much of a stretch, she placed both hands on her stomach. "Look, Greg. You know how I feel about guns. Couldn't you just…put it away? Or at least, not point it at me?"

Still holding her stomach, she started backing away from him. The problem was, she was also backing away from the door. Still, her ruse gave her time to think.

But think about what? What chances did she have against a .357 Magnum? A gun that could put a hole in her the size of an orange?

Greg smiled as if he had read her mind. "If you're thinking of making a run for the door, forget it. Unless you want to die before Victor gets here."

"You couldn't kill me. You're not a cold-blooded killer."

"I wouldn't bet on it if I were you. Men do strange things in desperate situations."

Maybe she could wrestle him for the gun. Her recent injury might slow her down a little, but she would have the element of surprise on her side.

The less intrepid part of her made itself heard. *Come on, Syd, don't be stupid. A Bond girl might get away with that scenario, but this isn't the movies. It's as real as it gets.*

Nor could she ignore the fact that the last time she had engaged in hand-to-hand combat was in third grade when Trish O'Grady had pushed her into a mud puddle.

"Even if you could bring yourself to kill me," she pressed on, "you wouldn't want to do it here. Think of all the evidence—blood, fingerprints."

"Victor and I would have plenty of time to get rid of it all."

Or she could try to put those self-defense lessons she had taken at Temple all those years ago to good use.

Another bad idea. She had probably forgotten every move she was ever taught. Or she would execute them so badly, she'd end up with that bullet in her stomach sooner than she thought.

Make him talk. Keep him distracted.

"Tell me something, Greg. Last week at the park and even in this very room, less than ten minutes ago, you claimed you still loved me and wanted to start a new life with me. Was that all an act?"

"No, I meant every word. Whether you know it or not, I have a great deal of respect for you, Syd. You're beautiful, smart, talented. I would have been thrilled to have you by my side as I climbed up the political ladder." He shrugged. "But that was before you heard that phone call."

"What if I told you that no one needs to know about that phone call? That it will remain between you and me."

Apparently the thought must have sounded as ridiculous to him as it did to her because he burst into laughter. "You? The defender of the underdog? The crusader for justice? Helping a criminal?" He shook his head. "You must think I'm stupid if you expect me to believe that."

Bad idea number two, which she had rejected earlier, returned, demanding to be heard. Did she dare? The only self-defense move she remembered fairly clearly was the kick, or rather a series of kicks she had executed well enough to draw praise from her very discriminating instructor.

But that was, what? Seventeen years ago?

"I mean it, Greg." She made her voice sound desperate, almost whiny. "I don't want to die. Let me go. Tell van Heusen that I got away."

"And look like a total incompetent? The general would love that. Just think, the man he was grooming for a cabinet post in Harrisburg outsmarted by a woman. Good try, Syd, but no. You're not going anywhere."

He took another lazy step toward her. This time she didn't take one back, but planted her two feet solidly on the hardwood floor, hoping he wouldn't notice. "In kicking techniques," her instructor had told her, "speed and precision are everything. Speed because you want to strike before your opponent does. Precision because if you miss, you won't get a second chance."

He had taught her the three most basic kicks. The

front kick, the round kick and the side kick. In her present situation, the *mae geri*, or front kick, was her best bet.

She gauged the distance that separated them. About four feet. She had to get closer. God, he was tall, almost as tall as Jake. She would have to bring her knee up high and tight if she wanted to go for his chin, or his solar plexus.

And pray she wouldn't miss.

"You look a little pale," Greg said. "You're not going to pass out on me, are you?"

Now! Do it now!

Mind and body went into action simultaneously. Her right knee jerked up and a microsecond later, her leg shot out, rigid as a board, her boot slamming into his face.

Greg's head snapped back and he let out an agonizing cry. The gun slipped out of his hand. Syd lunged for it, hoping she wouldn't have to use it.

Greg lay on the floor, harmless for now, holding his face and rolling from side to side. Panting and shaking at the same time, Syd grabbed her purse from the sofa, and ran for the door, yanking her coat from the rack on the way out.

Forty-Seven

The Ford was covered with snow. Syd didn't bother to open the trunk and search for a brush. She had to get out of here before Greg came after her.

With her bare hands, she wiped the powder off the windshield and side windows. Seconds later, she was behind the wheel. One turn of the ignition and the engine came to life. Relieved, she threw the gear shift into drive and pushed on the gas pedal.

The car didn't budge.

"Please, don't be stuck." She tried again. This time, she floored the pedal, but it was useless. Her rear tires spun helplessly into the accumulated snow. She was stuck.

She looked around her at the desolate landscape. She was at least a mile from the nearest house. Even if she made it there, it would most likely be shut down for the winter.

Her only recourse was to get back on Seven Bridge Road on foot and keep walking until she reached the village or an occupied house.

She let out a small cry. Greg stood in the doorway, his tall silhouette framed by the light behind him. He had taken the time to put on a heavy jacket, gloves and a hat. His right hand held a gun. Another Magnum? Or had he chosen something even more powerful from his vast collection?

She tumbled out of the car and took off. Her boots sank into the snow, slowing her down. *Run*, she thought. *Run fast. Imagine this is a race. You want to win it. You* have *to win it.*

She was breathing hard as the icy wind and snow pummeled her face, blinding her. She could no longer see Greg, but she could hear him behind her, hear his grunts as he tried to catch up with her.

Her legs kept pumping. She was cold. It was a wonder she was still moving.

In her coat pocket, she felt the weight of the Magnum and was reassured. If Greg gave any indication that he was going to shoot her, she would shoot him first. But what if she couldn't do it? What if she froze, just as she had on that terrible day when so much had depended on her?

She tried not to anticipate the worst as she plowed ahead. The fresh snow had covered her tire tracks, but she could make out the bridge up ahead, and beyond it, the road.

"Stop running, Syd! It's useless."

Her frozen fingers went to her pocket. She pulled out the Magnum, carefully. The last thing she wanted was to shoot herself. Wouldn't the Philly cops have a field day with that one.

Crack.

At the sound of the gunshot, she ducked and glanced behind her.

"That was just a warning shot, Syd! The next one will hurt."

She scrambled back to her feet. He didn't know she had the Magnum. Or if he did, he didn't care. Why should he? He had kept up his shooting skills with regular visits to the firing range. She hadn't.

She was looking around her for a place to hide when the sudden sound of an engine broke through the night. Up ahead, twin headlights shone brightly, illuminating the entire area. The SUV came to a stop and two men jumped out. She couldn't make them out but it didn't matter. They were the help she had prayed for.

"Drop the gun, Underwood!"

Cranston?

Syd peered through the falling snow. The two men were walking toward her. The one with the gun was definitely Detective Cranston, but the other...

Her heart jumped in her throat. Jake!

"Get down, Syd!" he shouted. "Flat on the ground!"

But it was too late. A steely arm had wrapped around her middle and pulled her up to her feet. The Magnum slipped out of her hand.

Greg didn't seem to have noticed. Holding her in front of him like a shield, he had more pressing matters to worry about. "*You* drop your gun!" he shouted. "Or she dies."

Both men came to a dead stop. "Underwood, listen to me. This is Detective Cranston of the Philadelphia police. Don't make it any worse for yourself, pal. Let Sydney go and we'll talk."

Greg's reaction was to jam the gun a little deeper into Syd's ribs. Wincing, she glanced down at the Magnum only a couple of feet from her, partially covered by snow. She prayed Greg wouldn't see it.

"Oh, God, Greg, I…I feel sick. I think…I'm going to throw up."

He made a disgusted sound, and pushed her away from him, without releasing her entirely. "Jesus, not on me, okay?"

Summoning every ounce of acting talent she may have had, Syd slid to her knees, heaving and retching, until her act was believable enough for him to let her go. Her hand crawled toward the Magnum, as she kept pretending to be throwing up. Once her fingers closed around the weapon, she pulled herself to her knees, then to her feet.

She spread out her legs and wrapped both hands around the grip. "Drop the gun, Greg."

His disgusted expression turned to one of bewilderment. In her peripheral vision, she caught sight of Jake moving away from Detective Cranston and fading into the darkness. She knew what he was doing. He was circling them, planning to attack Greg from behind.

Greg's gun was now trained on Cranston. There wouldn't be enough time for Jake to make his move. It was up to her.

"Don't make me shoot you, Greg." The pleading in her voice was sincere.

He laughed. "You're not going to shoot me. You don't have what it takes. I, on the other hand…"

Crack!

"Son of a bitch." The gun dropped out of Cranston's hand. He had been hit.

Jumbled memories shot in Syd's head. A crowded city street. Chaos all around. A crazed gunman. And she, standing alone, a .38 in her hand, unable to fire, unable to save her partner.

As Cranston went down for his gun, she saw Greg raise his again.

Syd took a deep breath, aimed and fired.

Forty-Eight

Forty-eight hours later

She wasn't as bad a shot as she thought.

Syd's bullet had hit Greg in the shoulder and splintered his clavicle. He was still in the hospital, recuperating while trying to negotiate a deal with the police. So far, neither he nor his father had been able to pressure the Atlantic County D.A. into considering a plea. Seeing an opportunity to make a name for himself, Fred Trinian had refused to compromise. This was his chance to shine and he wouldn't let anything, or anyone, stand in his way.

Victor van Heusen had been apprehended with all the fanfare afforded a real five-star general. Aware that the militiaman would be arriving in Tuckerton by helicopter, the FBI had waited for him to put his HueyCobra down on Greg's snow-covered lawn and had arrested him as he was stepping out.

Acting on information supplied by Doug Avery, a sixty-man team had stormed van Heusen's compound in Lancaster and rescued Lilly, who was weary but unharmed. All fifteen resident members were taken into custody. Well-trained, they, too, had stated only their names, ranks and serial numbers.

Not so with Victor. Fanatical to a fault, and proud of his beliefs, he had lashed out at the current administration, all branches of the armed forces and the world in general, all of which he still intended to change. Although the charges against him were serious enough to warrant the death penalty, a prominent attorney seeking fame had already offered his services and would be filing a motion stating that his client was not mentally competent to stand trial. The prosecution was building its own case, trying to prove otherwise.

Jenkins continued to deny any wrongdoings, even when Agent Ramirez told him that the tire impressions found in a wooded area adjacent to the Branzini's farmhouse matched the tire treads of his Jeep Cherokee.

The reason for Jenkins's trip to Erwinna was supplied by Lilly. Unlike Senator Fairbanks, Victor had immediately suspected Lilly of having found the necklace, an accusation she repeatedly denied. Uncertain, Victor had sent the sergeant in search of the incriminating evidence. When she didn't hear from him the following day, she assumed that Jenkins had come back empty-handed.

Thanks to Jake's quick thinking, a time bomb powerful enough to bring down the entire building, programmed to detonate at exactly four-thirty, had been found inside General Eisenhower's bust, and disarmed.

All three generals had expressed their desire to thank Jake personally and publicly, perhaps in a ceremony of some sort, but Jake had politely declined.

In a televised statement, an FBI spokesperson had also praised Jake's courage and patriotism and thanked him, on behalf of the fifty-three people who had been at the depot that afternoon, and whose lives he had saved.

Lilly had been taken to a local hospital, given a clean bill of health and discharged the following afternoon. Reunited with Prudence that same day, she had spent the entire night at her side, watching her sleep.

She had refused to talk about her ordeal as a prisoner until she was ready. What she *had* been willing to discuss, however, was her visit to the scene of the accident, which turned out to be quite different from Alan Fairbanks's version.

With the nose of a bloodhound, she had watched the story of Lauren Fairbanks's accident unfold on TV and noticed the girl's jumpy behavior. She had decided to conduct an investigation of her own, starting with a thorough inspection of the accident scene.

Finding the necklace wouldn't have meant much in itself. What had triggered the events that followed, was the fact that while she was in the woods, holding the evidence, she had come face-to-face with the senator and a young woman, a girl actually, searching for something.

Looking nervous, the senator had introduced his companion as his daughter and told Lilly they were looking for a school book Lauren had lost on the night of the accident. Lilly hadn't bought it. The girl the senator had called Lauren was definitely *not* his daughter. And Lilly was willing to bet her next paycheck they hadn't come looking for a school book.

Something about the way the senator had looked at Lilly just before he stepped into his car had sent a chill down her spine. Concerned that she had seen too much, she had taken Prudence to a secure location before driving to Syd's beach house where she hid the necklace. The postcard from Buck's County was extra insurance, in case something happened to her. The following day, she had called the senator's office, hoping to get his side of the story before she turned the necklace over to the police. When she received no reply, she decided to ask Syd for advice. That same night, she was kidnapped.

It wasn't until Fairbanks was told about Lilly's incriminating statement to the police that he reluctantly filled in the blanks. While he had been unaware at the time that Lilly had found the necklace, he knew she hadn't believed his story about

Brenda being his daughter. His fears were confirmed when Muriel informed him that Lilly Gilmore had called, wanting to discuss an urgent matter with him. He had immediately called his friend, Victor van Heusen, and asked him to deal with the nosy reporter.

Conspiracy of kidnapping was added to the senator's long list of felonies, and although he had pled not guilty, there was little doubt that he would spend the next several years not in the Oval Office, but in a federal prison.

More information would become available in the next several days as additional charges were filed.

It was now two o'clock on Wednesday afternoon. Jake was at the federal building where Victor van Heusen was being held and questioned. The militia leader had made only one request—to speak to Jake. Happy to confront the man he knew had killed Ted, Jake agreed.

Syd sat in Dot's living room, where once again the smell of good food and the chatter of happy conversation prevailed. Now that the snow had finally ended and the roads had been cleared, Joe and Luciana had taken Prudence to the playground to build a "giant snowman." Lilly was in the kitchen, where she and Dot were putting the finishing touches to a surprise.

"Just as long as it's not a brass band," Syd had warned.

Like Jake, she had shunned all publicity. Asked

to appear on several morning shows, she had declined. Ron had filled in for her, only too happy for the exposure now that the elections were getting near.

"Hey, what's taking so long out there?" Syd called out.

"Don't be so damn impatient." Lilly walked in, carrying a huge cake with far too many candles on it.

With her long blond hair freshly shampooed and hanging loose, her cheeks blushed and her lips glossed, she looked every bit as radiant as Syd remembered her.

She watched Lilly set the cake on the coffee table. "What's that?"

"I'll give you one clue. It's not an elephant. What do you think it is, silly? It's a birthday cake. You didn't think I'd forget your big day, did you? Or pass up a chance to remind you that you're three months older than I am? Thirty-five." Lilly whistled. "Wow, kiddo. Oops, I guess I can't call you that anymore. Not when you've reached middle age."

Syd took a small pillow, threatened to throw it at her but didn't. "Thanks, Lilly," she said quietly. "It's very sweet of you to have remembered."

Lilly hugged her. "It doesn't even begin to make up for all you've done."

"You would have done the same thing."

"True."

"So, when do I get to make my birthday wish?"

"When all the guests have arrived."

"Who's coming? Besides Jake and your family?"

"The Sorrensens, Ron and of course, Chad, whom I understand worships the ground you walk on. And I believe Jake is bringing Agent Ramirez." She stuck her finger into the chocolate icing and licked it. "Oh, and one other person."

"Who?"

She looked mysterious. "You'll see." The doorbell rang. "That should be him now. I asked him to come early."

Astonished, Syd watched as Detective Cranston walked in, a bouquet of flowers in his left hand. His right arm was in a sling and a heavy bandage was wrapped around his hand.

"Detective. What a pleasant surprise. I thought you were still in the hospital."

"They had to let me go. I was getting too cranky." Looking awkward, he handed her the flowers. "These are for you. Happy birthday."

"Thank you."

"Sit down, Detective," Lilly said. "We'll be cutting the cake soon." She walked away and left them alone.

"Who told you it was my birthday?" Syd asked.

"Lilly called the station and left word with one of the detectives, who put the information on the bulletin board."

Syd laughed. "That must have gone over in a big way."

"As a matter of fact—" Cranston reached inside his jacket pocket "—the guys in the squad room sent this." He handed her a large, square envelope.

Syd opened it. It was a birthday card, a humorous one with the cartoon of a woman, removing half the candles from her birthday cake and stuffing them in her pocket. She didn't read the card's verses, only what was handwritten. "Sometimes, even the smartest guys can be stupid. Sorry."

There were more than a dozen signatures, all names Syd recognized.

Syd's eyes misted. "That's very nice of them. Please thank them for me."

"I'm the one who thanks you. Without your quick intervention the other night, my wife and kids would probably be planning my funeral right about now."

"You came to my rescue, Detective, remember?"

Before the moment turned too mushy, Lilly walked in, carrying a cup of coffee which she handed to Cranston.

"Tell me, Detective," she said, sitting across from him. "Would you be willing to give me an exclusive account of what happened the other night?"

"Don't you already have Syd's story?"

"Yes, but I'd like to have yours as well. It would give my article more punch."

He smiled. "Call me and we'll make a date. Just keep in mind that I might be limited to how much I can tell you."

"I understand. Thank you, Detective."

Forty-Nine

"You let me down, old buddy."

Jake leaned against the wall, close enough for Victor to reach out through the bars if he had wanted to. He had asked to visit Victor inside his cell, but the guard had been adamant about his orders. Jake would have to remain outside the cell, with an armed guard nearby.

"My allegiance has always been to my country," Jake replied. "How could you have doubted that?"

"I wouldn't have if you hadn't set me up so well."

"You wouldn't have fallen into the trap if it hadn't been for your monumental ego." He looked different behind bars, not as subdued as Jake had expected him to be, but not as arrogant, either. "How did you get that bust inside the depot without raising suspicion?"

"By doing it in plain sight, as though we belonged

there." Victor laughed. "No one checked us. The event wasn't significant enough to warrant spending money on security. We didn't even get questioned. What could look more normal than two soldiers unloading props for the dedication?"

Jake remembered the photograph in Jenkins's iPAQ. Clever. And bold. "How do you sleep at night, Victor?"

"Very well, thank you."

"You have no remorse about the deaths you have caused? The fifty-three people who almost died yesterday because of your hatred for one man?"

"I didn't get where I am today by being soft."

"Look where being tough got you. Your camp has been raided. Your operation is permanently shut down and your men are in jail. As for the candidate you chose to be our next president, he is now awaiting trial for a number of charges that will keep him in prison for decades."

"You're enjoying this, aren't you? That's why you came, to see Victor van Heusen get his due."

"The sight has its rewards."

"I wouldn't count me out if I were you. In fact, you'd be smart to sleep with one eye open because I intend to beat this rap."

"You *are* delusional."

"Time will tell, as they say."

"Tell me something. How did you find out I was on to you?"

"Jenkins. You were right when you said he didn't like you. He didn't trust you either. That's why he decided to check you out. Did you know he was a computer genius?" He didn't wait for an answer. "He accessed your phone records and found out that you had made those calls to Delaware. Finding out to whom was easy. The *why* puzzled me. Until I heard from a friend in Riyadh."

Jake held his gaze for a moment, then voiced the question he'd been burning to ask. "How did you kill Ted?"

Victor looked smug. "Me? I wasn't even there."

"Stop playing games, Victor. We both know you ordered his murder."

"Correct me if I'm wrong, old buddy, but *you* are the one who asked Ted to spy for you. *You* are the one who signed his death warrant."

Jake grabbed the bars, but the guard was beside him in an instant. With a grip of steel, he took hold of Jake's arm and pulled him back. "Bad idea, sir."

"Yeah, you're right. Get me out of here. The stench of garbage has become unbearable."

As Jake approached his SUV, a few minutes later, a voice called out his name. He turned and, startled, watched Farah walk toward him.

"Agent Ramirez told me you were here." She looked up at the imposing building. "So he's in there? My husband's killer?"

"Yes."

He saw her fight off the tears. "They say he may get off—on an insanity plea."

"He won't."

She tore her eyes away from the building. Jake wanted to reach out to her, tell her all the things she hadn't let him tell her on the day of Ted's funeral, but wasn't sure where to start.

"That's not what I came to talk to you about." She looked up at him. "I know you paid off Ted's business loan."

He shook his head, ready to deny anything the banker may have let slip.

"I know," she continued. "Because Ted and I had discussed the possibility of buying mortgage insurance only last week. He said he was finally in a position to do so and should. You see, all the money we had saved for the past twenty years had gone into the business. We didn't have anything, except what we had earmarked for the children's education."

"You can't return the money," he said, worried that was the reason for her visit.

"I know. I came to thank you. And to apologize."

"Please don't do that."

"I have to. You were right." She looked far away, her eyes lost in the distance. "I needed time to think about all that happened, about your friendship with Ted, your devotion to one another even though you hadn't kept in touch. He hated Victor as much as you did, and he would have been upset if you had gone to anyone but him for help."

She returned her gaze to him. "He wouldn't be happy to hear that I was so unfair to you the other day. And quite frankly, I'm not happy about it either. I heard about what you did, how you stopped a disaster from happening. Because of you, Ted's killer is now behind bars and for that, I will be eternally grateful."

He didn't know what to say. Even if he had found the words, he couldn't have expressed them. The knot in his throat wouldn't let him.

"There's another reason I'm here. I'm not sure you'll agree, but I have to ask anyway."

He cleared his throat. "You can ask me anything, Farah."

"I need someone to take over the business. Someone I can trust. Someone I can completely rely on." She smiled. "Someone who can fly. I'm offering you a partnership," she said when he didn't answer. "Fifty fifty." She handed him a piece of paper. "I brought the books so you can see for yourself how well the business was doing. Ted had started giving flying lessons, partly for the extra income and partly because he wanted others to share his love of flying."

She was out of breath. He was speechless.

"Jake? You hate the idea, don't you? You can say so. I know you have a good paying job—"

"I don't hate the idea. In fact, I like it very much."

"You do?"

"Are you sure that's what you want?"

"Oh, I'm sure, Jake. I've thought of nothing else for the last forty-eight hours. You wouldn't mind leaving your job? Or relocating?"

"No. Actually, I've been toying with the idea of moving back in this area."

"You'd still be an hour from Philadelphia."

"Not a problem."

"Oh." She looked pleasantly surprised. "I didn't think it would be so easy."

"We can argue a little if it'll make you feel better."

That got a small laugh out of her. "No."

"In that case, I guess we're partners." He put out his hand. "Should we shake on it?"

They shook hands, then hugged and even shed a couple of tears. "Where is your car?" he asked when they finally let go of each other.

She pointed at a dark blue SUV parked behind his.

"Follow me," he said, taking her arm and escorting her to her truck. "I'd like to introduce you to someone you'll be seeing a lot of from now on."

Fifty

Two weeks later

Syd stood on the deck of *Three Naughty Nurses*, prepared to fight off the nausea she knew would come. She had felt sorry for Jake, who still hadn't heard from his father, and had agreed to pump herself full of Dramamine and go on a short sail with him, just up and down the coast.

These past two weeks had been the most exciting time of her life. It had begun at Dot's house during her birthday celebration. Requesting everyone's attention, Jake had announced that he was quitting his job on the oil rig and moving to Middletown to take over Ted's crop-dusting business. Then he had introduced his new partner, Farah Malvern, who had stood shyly aside while he talked.

"Middletown is only an hour's commute away,"

he had told Syd with an excitement that matched her own. "That might sound like a lot to some people, but when you're in love—"

"Love?"

"Love?" the Branzinis had repeated in unison. "You're in love with our Sydney?"

"You're in love with me?"

"Yes, I'm in love with you! Don't you know that? You're supposed to be so smart."

"You never said anything."

"I'm saying it now!"

She hadn't been able to put a word in edgewise after that. Everybody had started to talk at the same time. Joe had gone down to the cellar and returned with a bottle of champagne. He had made a toast, to Jake and Syd, congratulating them and slapping Jake on the back as if they had just become engaged.

She and Jake had made love that night, crazy, passionate love that had left her exhausted, happy and, by morning, ready for more.

The only shadow was Wendell Sloan's stubborn silence. At Syd's urging, Jake had made one more call, to let his father know that he'd be sailing out on April third. "The weather is perfect," she had heard him say to an empty line. "Call me so we can discuss where we want to go."

And so here she was, excited at the thought of sharing one of Jake's passions with him. At the same time, she was sad because she knew that until the very last moment, he had hoped his father would show up.

She heard Jake come up the steps from the cabin below. He wrapped an arm around her waist. "Ready to cast off, Captain?"

"You're not really going to let me pilot this boat, are you?"

"I'm going to teach you. That will take your mind off your sea sickness."

"You mean I don't have to take a Dramamine?"

He laughed. "Take it anyway."

She grabbed his arm. "Jake?"

He looked at her. "What? Are you getting sick already? We're still docked."

"No." She swallowed. "I mean, look over there."

He followed her gaze. She felt him go very still.

Coming down the pier was an older man. He wore blue pants, a navy windbreaker and blue boat shoes that looked suspiciously new. In one hand he carried a suitcase, in the other a tackle box.

"Son of a bitch," Jake murmured. "He came."

Syd felt tears roll down her cheeks. "Go to him, Jake."

"You'll stay, right?"

She shook her head. "No. This time is just for the two of you." She smiled at him through her tears. "I'll be here when you get back." She gave him a little shove. "Go to him. Hurry."

She jumped off the boat and watched Jake run toward his father. They embraced and held on to each other for a long time.

Syd quietly walked away. Once inside the marina,

she turned around. Jake and his father were walking toward the Stolkraft. Jake had his arms around the older man's shoulders. He was grinning like a kid on Christmas morning.

"I love you too, Jake," Syd murmured.

KILLER BODY

"...a real page-turner. Hill gets the reader's
attention with a contemporary issue
(Is slim the only way to be?),
intriguing characters, and clever plotting."
—*Publishers Weekly*

**A remarkable novel by
the author of *Intern***

Bonnie
Hearn Hill

Julie Larimore, spokesperson for Killer Body Weight
Loss, is missing. And now the search is on for the
new ultimate ideal woman.... Three desperate
women try for the position—but in a world where
beauty is the ultimate sales tool and honesty the
rarest commodity of all, these women are about
to learn what Julie Larimore learned the hard way:
Some people would die for a killer body.

*Available the first week of January 2005
wherever paperbacks are sold!*

MIRA®

**A remarkable novel
by the bestselling author of *Kiss River***

DIANE
CHAMBERLAIN

Annie O'Neill's daughters weren't prepared for her tragic
death—or the shocking truths they'd find about their mother.
As the secrets of the O'Neill family are brought to light,
Her Mother's Shadow explores how the dark corners of the
past can be illuminated by the hope that honesty brings.

HER MOTHER'S
SHADOW

"Chamberlain adeptly unfolds layers...while gently
preaching a message of trust and forgiveness. Complex,
credible characterization..."—*Publishers Weekly*

*Available the first week of January 2005
wherever paperbacks are sold!*

If you enjoyed what you just read,
then we've got an offer you can't resist!

Take 2 bestselling novels FREE!
Plus get a FREE surprise gift!

Clip this page and mail it to MIRA®

IN U.S.A.
3010 Walden Ave.
P.O. Box 1867
Buffalo, N.Y. 14240-1867

IN CANADA
P.O. Box 609
Fort Erie, Ontario
L2A 5X3

YES! Please send me 2 free MIRA® novels and my free surprise gift. After receiving them, if I don't wish to receive anymore, I can return the shipping statement marked cancel. If I don't cancel, I will receive 4 brand-new novels every month, before they're available in stores! In the U.S.A., bill me at the bargain price of $4.99 plus 25¢ shipping and handling per book and applicable sales tax, if any*. In Canada, bill me at the bargain price of $5.49 plus 25¢ shipping and handling per book and applicable taxes**. That's the complete price and a savings of over 20% off the cover prices—what a great deal! I understand that accepting the 2 free books and gift places me under no obligation ever to buy any books. I can always return a shipment and cancel at any time. Even if I never buy another The Best of the Best™ book, the 2 free books and gift are mine to keep forever.

185 MDN DZ7J
385 MDN DZ7K

Name	(PLEASE PRINT)	
Address	Apt.#	
City	State/Prov.	Zip/Postal Code

*Not valid to current The Best of the Best™, Mira®,
suspense and romance subscribers.*

Want to try two free books from another series?
Call 1-800-873-8635 or visit www.morefreebooks.com.

* Terms and prices subject to change without notice. Sales tax applicable in N.Y.
** Canadian residents will be charged applicable provincial taxes and GST.
All orders subject to approval. Offer limited to one per household.
® and ™are registered trademarks owned and used by the trademark owner or its licensee.

BOB04R   ©2004 Harlequin Enterprises Limited

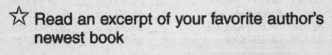

CHRISTIANE HEGGAN

32005	SCENT OF A KILLER	___ $6.50 U.S.	___ $7.99 CAN.
66870	MOMENT OF TRUTH	___ $6.50 U.S.	___ $7.99 CAN.
66783	BLIND FAITH	___ $6.50 U.S.	___ $7.99 CAN.
66648	DEADLY INTENT	___ $6.50 U.S.	___ $7.99 CAN.
66577	ENEMY WITHIN	___ $5.99 U.S.	___ $6.99 CAN.
66536	TRUST NO ONE	___ $5.99 U.S.	___ $6.99 CAN.
66466	DECEPTION	___ $5.99 U.S.	___ $6.99 CAN.

(limited quantities available)

TOTAL AMOUNT	$_____
POSTAGE & HANDLING	$_____
($1.00 for one book; 50¢ for each additional)	
APPLICABLE TAXES*	$_____
TOTAL PAYABLE	$_____
(check or money order—please do not send cash)	

To order, complete this form and send it, along with a check or money order for the total above, payable to MIRA Books, to: **In the U.S.:** 3010 Walden Avenue, P.O. Box 9077, Buffalo, NY 14269-9077; **In Canada:** P.O. Box 636, Fort Erie, Ontario, L2A 5X3.

Name:_____

Address:_____ City:_____

State/Prov.:_____ Zip/Postal Code:_____

Account Number (if applicable):_____

075 CSAS

*New York residents remit applicable sales taxes.
  Canadian residents remit applicable GST and provincial taxes.

MIRA®